SKYSHIP ACADEMY

SKYSHIP ACADEMY

Strikeforce

NICK JAMES

flux
®
Woodbury, Minnesota

First Edition
First Printing, 2013

Book design by Steffani Sawyer
Cover design by Kevin R. Brown
Cover illustration © Aaron Goodman Studio Inc.
Cover images:
  © iStockphoto.com/18006045/Johan Swanepoel
  © iStockphoto.com/8574407/Jacom Stephens
  © Shutterstock.com/16308559/Luminis

Flux, an imprint of Llewellyn Worldwide Ltd.

Library of Congress Cataloging-in-Publication Data
James, Nick
  Skyship Academy : strikeforce / Nick James. — First edition.
    pages cm. — (Skyship Academy ; #3)
  Summary: As the alien Authority attacks Earth using a terrible new weapon that sends Skyship soldiers, the Surface government, and an army of Drifters into turmoil, Cassius Stevenson and his brother Jessie Fisher hold the planet's fate in their hands.
  ISBN 978-0-7387-3637-2
  [1. Science fiction.] I. Title. II. Title: Strikeforce.
  PZ7.J154195Sld 2013
  [Fic]—dc23
                            2013020950

Flux
Llewellyn Worldwide Ltd.
2143 Wooddale Drive
Woodbury, MN 55125-2989
www.fluxnow.com

Printed in the United States of America

1

My fingers burn. The bricks are hotter than I remembered—some supernatural heat that seems to seep out from deep inside. You could fry up dinner on these things. In fact, I bet if you were to crack an egg and watch the insides spill down the side of this building, the yolk would cook before it hit the ground.

But I am not an egg. Right now, I'm not sure if that's a good or bad thing.

Cassius glowers down at me, the tips of his boots pressed into my knuckles. My fingers tense on the ledge, gripping onto that impossibly scalding brick with every last drop of energy I've got. I already know it won't be enough. I've been here before, time and time again. Only one time was real, and it hadn't ended well.

Syracuse, New York.

Fringe Town.

I know this is a dream. I know if I concentrate hard enough I can control it. I could rip away the scenery and replace it with whatever I want. It doesn't make it feel any less dangerous.

I take a cautious glance below me. I see my feet first,

dangling into thin air. I let them hang loose. Beyond that, twelve stories down, is the cracked pavement of the Fringe roadway. Utterly still. Hotter than a griddle.

"Please!" I hear my voice choke on the word, but I don't feel my mouth open or close. I'm going through the motions. It's like I'm part of a movie. It's playing out all around me.

Cassius smiles. His dark bangs are perfectly combed, unnaturally tidy for the wasteland below us. I notice his navy Unified Party sport coat, the silver badge against his chest. He looks more adult than me, somehow, even though we're both fifteen.

This is the old Cassius. Perfectly confident. Dutiful to a fault. A real killing machine. I don't see any of myself in him. It's impossible to dig past the façade and uncover the truth. He's my brother. My brother who's trying to kill me.

He sneers. "Where is the Pearl?"

I open my mouth to speak, but end up with silence. It doesn't matter anymore. The Pearl Wars are over. The old rivalries between the Unified Party and Skyship Community seem like child's play. We have new problems. Red Pearls. Invasion. A looming extermination at the hands of an otherworldly power.

I'm done with this. I'm *past* it. But my brain keeps wanting me to revisit this moment. Night after night I'm brought back to our first meeting, forced to endure Cassius's cocky smile until I release my hold on the brick ledge and let myself fall. It's exhausting, but I've learned not to fear it.

I don't have the patience for this.

I begin to wriggle free from his heel. He barely tries to fight back.

The world lights up around us.

This is different.

At first, it's like a sunset. The sky goes dark, then red like someone's poked a vein and let loose torrents of blood. The air grows thicker until it pushes up on me, like my feet are supported by invisible hands. I'm reminded of the Scarlet Bombings, all those years ago when the Authority first attacked us. Clouds of crimson. Death, all around, and a dismantling of the country's biggest metropolitan centers. We'd been naïve, thinking that the bombings were of human origin.

The syrupy atmosphere heats up. The frying pan bricks are nothing compared to this. I must be on fire.

I look up at Cassius. Flames dance around him. They engulf his legs and crawl up his body, eating away at his flesh until all I can see is his silhouette through the smoke. Before I can do anything, the fire streams down at me. I hardly feel it course its way into my body. I'm completely numb.

The sky drips red. The building begins to crumble under my fingers and I know this isn't like the other times. It used to be, I'd wake with a start right about now and the nightmare would be over. Easy escape from my raging subconscious. Now, I'm not sure there'd be any street to hit if I let go.

A laugh pierces the atmosphere. It comes from a distance, off in the sky somewhere, but feels so close that it could have started right inside my ears.

Cassius is nothing but a charred corpse on the roof. Bones break and blow away as dark ashes, sucked up by the red cloud of energy circulating around us. Without his boot, there's nothing keeping me upright. The bricks pulverize in violent explosions around me. I fall, engulfed in flames.

The laughter follows me down. It's not human.

I wonder: If I keep on falling without an end, will I ever wake up?

And then comes the real question. It's not one I want to consider, but it's there just the same, nagging at me:

Do I even want to?

2

"This is not acceptable."

Madame reclines at the foot of the gleaming metal table. It's unnecessarily long, just as the room around us is unnecessarily big. This is a place made for armies. We're twenty-seven strong on our best days—a tight collection of my closest friends and a handful of alien Drifters from the Resistance. Only Madame, Cassius, and I are in the war room now.

This bunker is our temporary home, and has been for just over a week. Northeast Nevada—a secret Unified Party stronghold a quarter of a mile below the ground.

I glance across the table at Cassius, who chews on the remaining end of a stale nutria bar. Madame's gaze remains fixed on us. She's intense. Hiding underground without the luxuries of the Surface hasn't stopped her from dressing well, or keeping her dark hair expertly pinned at all moments. But it's all a façade, and it's crumbling day by day.

I find it difficult to meet her eyes, even for a second. Could be because she's tried to kidnap me on more than one occasion. But even now that she's pledged to fight on our side, she's still mass intimidating. It's like Captain Alkine times a hundred.

It's the next morning, after my dream. Turns out I did wake from it, albeit in a pool of sweat. That was three A.M. I haven't slept since. It's with the continued threat of yawns that I listen to Madame rattle on.

"Communication is down all throughout the country." She glares at Cassius like it's his fault that the Unified Party is crumbling. "Even lines that should be secure are fractured and crisscrossed. I make an attempt to contact the office of the President and end up at the Department of Agriculture. And even then there's nobody present to take my call. It's maddening."

Cassius takes the last bite of his bar. "We don't know exactly what's happened on the Surface. Everything's screwed up. Even if Pearl Power's still functioning, the infrastructure is bound to be damaged."

I bite my lip. I don't have much to add. Watching the two of them talk, I can imagine the conversations they used to have, back when I considered Cassius my enemy. From what he's told me, he's always been a gold-star student, capable of discussing military strategy and politics the same way most of us discuss our favorite program on TV. That's not me. I act on instinct, or to be even more accurate, I *re*act. I'm getting better, but none of this war-planning stuff is my element.

Madame rubs her eyes. She looks more human now, under these subterranean lights without all the makeup she used to wear. I can see wrinkles. But beyond that, I see fear. A lack of control. I don't even know her that well, but I can tell that being down here is killing her. She's not the only one. The longer we stay, the more distant the Surface seems. A person could lose touch with reality down here. Physically, we may be safe. Mentally? The jury's out.

"I've been up all hours," Madame continues. "I haven't gotten more than a few bursts of sleep here and there. I fear that they've dismantled communications. I'm sure the President is hiding underground like we are, but that doesn't do us any good if we can't reach him."

Cassius stretches. "Does it even matter? What good will the President do anyway?"

"We're not doing this alone, Cassius. Regardless of how far you and Jesse have come, you're in no position to topple an army. We need allies. We need the power of the Unified Party."

I glance at the ceiling. It's pristine, just like the rest of the bunker. I'm not sure this place has ever been touched. If there are explosions going off on the Surface—if cities are falling—we'd never know it. We're cut off completely. Sound, vision, smell. It's all a mystery to us.

"We don't know how many of them there are." My voice catches in my throat. I shouldn't be nervous, not after all we've been through already. "In the Authority, I mean."

Cassius meets my eyes. "We all saw the red Pearls falling from the sky like a meteor shower. There were hundreds. Thousands, maybe. And that was just the beginning.

Before Skyship Altair sank, when Theo held me prisoner, he made it sound like once the Authority started coming, they'd never stop."

I pull my bare wrist toward my waist. There used to be a bracelet fused to my skin. I still haven't gotten used to the way my arm feels without it. Turns out that the bracelet, along with Cassius's, was the only thing keeping our enemies at bay. Theo Rayne—the psychotic young prince in the Authority's crazed dynasty—had removed them, thus breaking the barrier that had previously kept red Pearls from falling to Earth. These crimson Pearls don't need my power to break them. They hit the ground, burst open, and attack.

"Theo was always one for dramatics," Madame says. "I wouldn't necessarily take him at his word."

Cassius grits his teeth. "But we know the Surface is under attack. We need a plan."

I nod. Last night, our Drifter scouts—Talan and Sem—returned from their latest venture to the Surface. Our bunker is too far from a Chosen City to see much, but with the benefit of a good pair of specs, they witnessed enough.

Billows of smoke in the distance. An explosion, rumbling through the Nevada Desert from god knows where. A fleet of Unified Party Cruisers flying low, with speed reserved only for battle. Glimpses. That's all, but they paint a pretty lousy picture.

And the longer we stay down here in hiding, the worse it'll be when we go back up.

Madame slams her fist on the table. "I don't know what to do. I simply don't."

Cassius's eyes slit. "Feels terrible, doesn't it?"

"You're relishing this," she replies. "Do you consider this my punishment, for all I've done to you?"

"I think it's punishment for all of us," he mutters. "No need to be selfish. Oh wait." He smiles. "Selfish is all you know how—"

"You should let me go." I grip the edge of the table and lean my chair back. "I'm the Pearlbreaker. I should be *doing* something."

"No." Madame frowns. "You don't sacrifice your queen to attack an army of pawns."

My brows furrow. "Wait, did you just call me a—"

"Chess, Fisher," Cassius interrupts. "She's talking about *chess*. Calm down."

"Look," I say, "after what happened back at the Academy ... being stuck in there like a prisoner ... I'm not listening to any adults anymore, no matter who they are." The words escape my lips before I realize who I'm talking to. Madame's shoulders tense. I don't think she expected something like that from me. I'm not sure if anybody, kid or adult, has challenged her and gotten away with it.

I swallow. I could say more if I wanted, but that was ballsy enough. We may be safe from the Drifters in this bunker, but I'm certainly not safe from her. Only a few days ago, she'd been hunting me down. Even if we're allies, it doesn't mean I trust her.

"The Drifters are getting restless," Cassius says. "And remember what Theo told us. Matigo is already here. He's gearing up."

A shiver runs down my spine. Matigo's the Authority's king, as well as Theo's father. I haven't had the misfortune of meeting him yet, but I know it's inevitable. And given that his own son died bringing red Pearls to Earth, I can't imagine the guy's too pleased with us.

Only a short while ago, Cassius and I had been given a glimpse of Matigo's throne room on our home world of Haven—a peek at his plans via catalogued memories from the Resistance. He'd sent Theo as a herald, but he'd long since arrived on Earth himself. He's hiding. He could be anywhere.

Madame rubs her temple. "Perhaps this will all be taken care of before you have to."

"Don't bet on it." Cassius pushes back his chair and stands. "If there's nothing else—"

"There's nothing." Madame closes her eyes as if she's trying to fend off a headache. "Absolutely nothing at all."

"Forty-eight hours," he continues. "That's how much longer I can stay down here. We're going to have to fight eventually. Stalling just drains our spirits."

I glance up at him. "Where are you going?"

"Around," he answers, and it's enough. I've learned not to follow him unless he asks. It doesn't usually end up well.

Of course, that doesn't mean that I wanna be stuck here with Madame either.

I stand.

She chuckles. "You both can't wait to get away from me. I suppose it's natural, after the game we've played."

Cassius freezes. I can see him working it out in his head—to engage in verbal sparring with her or not. In the end, he can't help it.

"*Game*," he repeats. "You've got a pretty screwed up vision of the world, don't you?"

"The world is obviously more screwed up than either you or I could have guessed, Cassius. I'm trying to help you. A little respect would—"

"I'm done." He turns and leaves.

Madame's lips purse. "Hotheaded," she says to herself. "Always has been."

I stare at her, wondering if she's making a joke or she's seriously upset. There's no way she can expect us to be all friendly after everything she's done. If it weren't for her connections with the Unified Party, we wouldn't even be listening to her.

She meets my eyes. "Talk some sense into him, please. I'm tired. This is emotionally draining."

I shake my head and move from my seat. "Nobody believes a word you say. You know that, right?"

Before she can respond, I head for the door, keeping my face forward.

If this is the help we have, how are we supposed to fight an entire war? We're screwed.

3

Cassius keyed in the six-digit code and stepped back to allow the door to slide open before him. His hand trembled at his side. He made sure to steady it before moving into the room.

It was one of the bunker's larger living areas, outfitted with two dozen beds positioned up and down each side like an army barrack. A long gray rug ran down the middle, the only attempt to make the place look inviting.

It was also the home of their Drifter allies, at least the few that they'd managed to find before heading underground. The Drifters preferred to be housed together like this, separate from the humans. Cassius supposed that if he was on an unfamiliar planet in the midst of a war, he'd want to be amongst similar types as well. And although he still didn't feel it, stepping inside this room was doing exactly that.

He tried to force Madame's words from his head. Even looking at her infuriated him. There was a time, years ago, where her face had been the one he'd longed for most. He'd called her "Mother," even if she hadn't one hundred percent acknowledged it herself. But ever since she'd started lying to him, then *hunting* him, he couldn't use the word anymore.

He scanned the room. Some of the Drifters crouched on the beds. Others stood in groups, whispering in a language he didn't have any hope of understanding. They all looked human enough, of varying ages and heights, but even if he couldn't easily say why, there was something off about them. The residual glow from the Pearl energy had long since faded from their bodies. Instead, regardless of age, their skin was a pale, babylike complexion. Any wrinkles that were present were surface deep at best. No pockmarks or pimples. The sight of it reminded Cassius of the first time he'd burst into flames. It was as if the voyage from Haven to Earth had seared their bodies of any imperfections.

Angels.

The thought had occurred to him more than once before. In a strange way, they almost looked heaven sent.

Every last one of them turned to stare the moment he stepped through the door.

They were sensitive like that. Good hearing. It made sneaking up on them difficult, not that he'd ever want to try something like that.

He raised a hand. "Hello."

They stared at him in silence for a moment. Then Talan—one of the more advanced English speakers they'd freed from a Pearl more than a week ago—moved forward to meet him.

"Cassius." The Drifter said his name in a way that made

Cassius feel like he'd snuck up on something illicit, that these aliens were planning something he shouldn't be privy to. "Greetings, my friend."

He glanced up at the Drifter's eyes. Talan's pupils were a dull green. He still held the faintest amount of Pearl energy he'd come to Earth with, though it was buried deep inside.

"We're flatlining," Cassius said. "It's always the same when too many people talk at once. Nothing gets done."

Talan nodded. "Have you come to discuss Haven?"

"No," Cassius responded. This wasn't the first time he or Fisher had been in to see the Drifters. After all, their information was invaluable. Though they hadn't been able to reveal anything new regarding the Authority's plans for conquering Earth, just hearing about his home planet was like a drug to Cassius. The more he knew, the more real it felt. Simple things like the planet's geography and seasons made the abstract seem so much more real in his mind. "I just... I needed to get away for a moment." He bit his lip. "She'd look for me in my room. She doesn't like coming here."

Talan nodded. "Your Earth mother."

"She's not—" He stopped himself. "She doesn't have anything to do with me. Not anymore."

"I see." Talan stepped back to take a seat at the edge of a cot. "Well, you're very welcome in our chamber, though you'll notice there are not many distractions. We've been discussing the war at hand, as I'm sure you'd expect. As you say, the longer we're hidden down here, the greater chance Matigo has of taking over without our resistance."

Cassius leaned against the wall. "Where do you think he is?"

"Anywhere," Talan responded. The other Drifters looked on in reverent silence. "He arrived before any of us, just as the war on Haven was beginning to disintegrate. He's been on Earth for more than a year now…that much is sure. Beyond that, he could be hiding anywhere. Close. Far. It's inconsequential, really. If the rumors are true, he's powerful enough to be anywhere he wants to be in no time at all."

"Meaning he could attack us down here? I mean, if he really wanted to?"

"I suppose," Talan said. "But it seems to me that Matigo…that the Authority as a whole is waiting for something. There is nothing rash about his plan. He's hidden this long. It doesn't appear that he's opposed to waiting longer."

"For me," Cassius replied. "And Fisher. Right? He's waiting for us."

"You are the key to our Resistance. That's all we know. I wish there was more. Your parents would know."

Cassius ground his fist against the wall. "Well, my parents aren't here right now." He paused. "Besides, you're wrong."

"About what?"

"I'm not the Key," he muttered. "I'm the Catalyst, remember? The reaction. The excess to Fisher's power."

Talan stood, shaking his head. "You're mistaken, Cassius. You're every bit as important as your brother, if not more so."

"And how do you know that?"

"The Key cannot exist without the Catalyst," Talan continued. "Together, the two of you are stronger than anything Matigo could imagine."

Cassius tried hard not to chuckle at the words. He pictured the times he and Fisher had fought together, the mistakes and messes they'd made.

"We're lucky to be alive," he said. "Let alone *strong*. The best thing we've done is bring down an entire Skyship ... brought in the whole of the Authority to conquer the planet. You know what ... maybe we just need to stay out of the entire thing. Let the Chosens and the Skyships fight it out. I mean, what have we done so far that's worth celebrating?"

Talan frowned, then moved forward to grip Cassius's shoulder. "Wait and see, my friend. Wait and see. You may think you're a small part in the grand scheme of things, but my companions here ... we've bet our entire existence on you and your brother. Wait. Your hour will come, and you will not disappoint."

Cassius brushed free from the Drifter's grip, meeting his eyes for a moment more before turning and heading for the door, his heart heavy with a looming sense of dread.

"I can't be here," he muttered. "I can't be in any room down here." He craned his neck, closing his eyes. "It used to be so simple, you know? Before all of this. When I knew who I could trust and what ... what I'm supposed to do."

Talan's voice came from behind him, but the Drifter made no attempt to approach. "There are no easy answers,

I'm afraid. Trust in yourself. You'll do what's right. You'll know it when the time comes. It's like a second skin, the destiny you wear. You're not used to it. It's new. But it fits you completely—inside and out. You are a champion, Cassius Stevenson. Never forget that."

4

That first night in the bunker, sleep had come so easy. It helped that I'd been running around from city to city without any shut-eye. Right now, I wouldn't mind a bit of exhaustion. Insomnia is ten times worse.

It's not so different from back at the Academy, except down here the corridors are impossibly dark, lit only by tiny circle-shaped nightlights every few yards. No moonlight streaming in to give a sense of perspective. Together, the hallways form a large rectangle, branching off here and there but offering little in the way of escape. Basically, there's nowhere to go but your room if you want to be alone.

Avery Wicksen sits across from me on the opposite side of the corridor, back against the wall, knees up. I'm against the other, slumped into a shape that can't be good for my posture. My chin's pressed into my chest, knees just far enough apart to frame her face. We bounce a rubber ball back and forth—an oddly lo-fi relic Skandar found in the bunker's pitiful rec room. Disregarding everything that's happening above us, it's just like old times. We're out of our rooms, sneaking around when we should be sleeping.

Except neither one of us really has the energy to do much sneaking. It's mostly sitting.

"I had that dream again last night." My voice rebounds against the silent walls, though I try to keep it at a whisper.

Avery bounces the ball once more before cupping it in her hand. She brushes her straw-colored hair over her ear, eyes narrowing. "Falling off the building?"

"It gets worse the longer we're down here." I yawn. My body wants to conk out. It's my mind that won't let me.

"Do you think it means something?"

"I don't know." The truth is, I've learned never to discount my dreams, especially if they repeat over and over. "The fire was stronger this time. It came down at me, got inside me."

"Cassius's fire?"

"I think so." I catch the ball. "He's getting antsy."

"We all are."

"Yeah, but I think it's worse for him. He's not a sitter, or a waiter. And I think I'm starting to feel the same. I mean, I know we're safe down here, but it doesn't feel right."

She yawns. "Do you ever wonder what Captain Alkine's up to?"

"I'm sure Skyship's still hunkered down in Siberia. They'd have seen the red Pearls by now." I pause. "Hopefully they're safe."

Avery sighs. "It's the not knowing, isn't it? That's the worst."

"I think I liked it better when we were running around on the Surface."

"I had the same feeling when Madame brought me back to the Lodge," she says. "Hooked up to her devices, not knowing whether you were in danger or not. It's killer." She meets my eyes, biting her lip. "But you know, maybe the darkness isn't all bad. We could make the most of it."

My brows rise. There was a time, not too long ago, where the mere idea of Avery coming on to me would have sent my head reeling. In my mind, it would have been impossible, something I could only dream about.

Now, down here in the darkness, she's what I could safely—maybe—call my girlfriend. And with everything that's going on, I can't even enjoy it.

"I don't—"

Something in the distance stops me. I tilt my head to make sure that I'm not imagining it. If I hadn't walked down these corridors countless times in the past few days, it would be impossible to tell how long they stretched. Dark is dark, no matter how far it reaches. Pools of black surround us on either side.

Except for the tiny red light.

It hangs some distance to my right before disappearing around the corner. It's too small to be a Pearl. More like the blinker on a com-pad.

I turn back to Avery, whispering, "Did you see that?"

She shakes her head.

On instinct alone, I pull myself from the ground and ball my fists.

"Whoa." Avery stands. "Calm down. What did you see?"

I stare into the darkness. "You know of anything down here that would make a red light? Communicators? Weapons?"

"It's late," she says. "I wouldn't trust my own eyes. Maybe you should—"

"Do you still have that flashlight?" I hold out a hand.

She hesitates before reaching into her pocket and placing a palm-sized light in my hand.

I flip it on. Full power, by mistake. It casts the hallway in a glaring blanket of white light. I dial it down before stepping forward. "Just give me a second. It's probably nothing."

Avery glances behind her. "I used to be the one getting *you* in trouble."

We tiptoe all the way to the corner. I freeze. Avery bumps into me, then grabs my shoulder to steady herself.

"Footsteps," she whispers. We both hear them. Light, but not far away. "I guess we're not the only insomniacs around here."

I block the flashlight's beam before shutting it off. Taking a deep breath, I peer around the corner.

I see it immediately.

One red light bobs ever so slightly several yards away. Try as I might, I can't make out any other details. The footsteps have disappeared. The red doesn't seem to reflect on any of the walls. It's not strong enough.

"Skandar?" I keep my voice at a whisper. "Eva?"

The tiny light freezes before shifting to the right. I watch as a second light parts from the first, moving slowly apart. I step back in horror as I realize that what I'm looking at is looking back at me as well.

These aren't lights at all. They're a pair of eyes.

Before I can do anything, the creature floats off the ground and careens toward me. The flashlight hits the ground as a cold hand slams against my throat, knocking me off my feet and pushing me back through the air.

"Jesse!" Avery's voice fades as I'm propelled farther down the hallway.

Fighting for breath, I reach up to my throat and pry at the fingers, not daring to look up at the red pupils that blaze mere feet from my face.

I break the creature's grip and fall to the ground. The back of my head thuds on the floor, sending a dizzying shockwave through my body. I try to ignore it, fighting through the pain as I climb to my feet.

I take a shaky step forward as the creature lands behind me and spins around. Avery's flashlight clicks on again in front of us, forcing my eyes shut. I hear a gasp, but can't tell if it's from the creature or her.

I lift my hand to shield my eyes and feel the creature's fingers tighten around the back of my skull. I cry out. The thing doesn't care. It shoves me forward, too fast and forceful for me to react. I can't catch myself. My face plants hard into the ground.

The corridor spins. Avery's voice pops in and out of my consciousness.

"Stop!" she yells. The beam flickers off, then on again.

Something grabs my ankle and yanks upward. My left leg twists unnaturally, like it's about to be pulled from my body. I grit my teeth and claw at the ground. Blood starts to pool under my face.

Avery screams. "Put him down!"

I hear footsteps. My body inches across the floor.

"He's killing him!"

A second voice joins the fray, but everything's spinning and throbbing and blacking out. I can barely focus.

An incredible heat streams over my head, like someone's just brought the full brunt of the Fringes inside the bunker. The corridor lights up. I feel my leg drop to the ground. Something shrieks behind me, otherworldly. Inhuman.

Before I can react, hands reach around my wrists and pull me forward. I flip onto my back to see Cassius and Avery looking down at me.

"Are you alright?" Cassius meets my eyes.

I nod, then glance over at his fist. It's still sparking.

Fire eats away at the corridor. Soon, the crackle of the flames overtakes the screaming. The bunker falls silent. The creature is dead. If not for Cassius, I would have been, too.

5

The charred body of the enemy Drifter lies before us, placed unceremoniously in the middle of the wide circular table like a sick centerpiece. Nine of us stand around the perimeter of the bunker's tiny war room, staring in at the corpse with a mix of revulsion and curiosity.

The creature is human enough, but even past the darkened patches of flesh, it's easy to tell that it's different. It's not the same kind of "different" as our allied Drifters, either. This is something new.

Its arms are bulky like a body builder's, with strange ribbed indentations from the shoulders to the elbows. I can't tell if they're functional or simply decorative. Its mouth, from what I can see, is wider than any human's. Its eyes are pure gray, dulled of their red glow from last night. It wears a dark tunic and trousers covered in colorless body armor, though much of the clothing has been ripped from its burnt flesh.

Sem, one of the friendly Drifters, stands at the head of the table. "This is an Authority foot soldier." His thin eyebrows sink as he glances down. "Not every soldier will draw attention to himself. Some will look no different than you or I. This man has clearly been ... augmented."

Cassius rubs his chin. "How did he get in?"

"It appears this base is not as secure as you thought." Sem frowns.

"It's unheard of." Madame crosses her arms as she flashes the soldier's body a look of disgust. "If nothing else, Unified Party bunkers are secure. I wouldn't have suggested we come here if—"

"Nobody's blaming you," Cassius shoots back.

Avery stands beside me. Her hand moves from my back up to my shoulder. "How are you feeling?" she whispers.

I shrug. Better than I look, probably. A black eye and a thumb-sized scrape across my cheek won't exactly inspire the king of leadership I'm going for. The truth is, the mental effects are much worse than the physical ones. I keep replaying the confrontation in my head—what I could have done differently, how I could have reacted better. The Drifter had taken me by surprise, and I was careless enough to walk right toward it.

But the real question that's been nagging me doesn't have anything to do with my own reaction. Had the soldier attacked on instinct or had he intentionally targeted me? The way things have been going, I can't be sure of anything anymore.

Eva Rodriguez clears her throat. She stands next to Skandar Harris on the left side of the body. They've both been in this with me since the beginning. Fellow Skyship trainees, and now fellow Resistance fighters. Eva's made for this kind of thing—a soldier through and through, and definitely more physically imposing than I am. I know that Skandar would like to think he's equally up to the task, but he's so impulsive. I'm worried that he'll do something stupid and get himself hurt.

The two of them have been chummier than usual these past few days. I don't know if it's the isolation of the bunker or something else, but I've never seen them cling to each other like this before. Maybe they just don't know what their place is in all of this. Cassius and I are Haven-born. So are the Drifters. Eva, Skandar, Avery, and Madame got pulled into this.

"Bottom line," Eva starts, "is that it isn't safe in here anymore. That's what everybody's thinking, right?"

"Right now I'm thinking about *him*." Skandar rustles his messy brown hair, motioning to the soldier. "*This* is the kind of thing we're up against? We don't stand a chance!"

Sem glances at his fellow Drifters, one on either side of him, before addressing us. "The crimson in their eyes is the giveaway, but we won't always be engaging them in darkness. In the light, especially sunlight, it will be impossible to distinguish the enemy without getting close. Without seeing the reds of their eyes."

Cassius clenches a fist. "He didn't like my fire, that's for sure."

"Odd," Sem responds. "As a former resident of Haven, he should be accustomed to the heat."

"I went in full blast. I don't think anyone's accustomed to *that* sort of heat."

Avery nods. "I was lucky enough to jump back in time. Even then, I felt the flames. Jesse was right under them."

"I'm fine," I say.

"But you shouldn't be," Madame counters. "You should have caught fire. We should be dealing with third-degree burns right now."

I glare at her. "Gee, thanks."

"I channeled it well," Cassius says. "The flames hit what I meant them to hit, and nothing more."

I glance at him, wondering if he's telling the truth. He doesn't look back.

"If they're gonna start creeping down here," I start, "I think I'd rather be on the Surface. At least then I'd know to expect danger and be ready for it. They wouldn't have a chance to corner us. We could find weapons ... allies ... "

Avery's hand drops to her side. "Are we ready for that?"

Cassius scoffs. "Will we ever be?"

"You don't win wars by hiding," Eva adds. "Fisher's right. We need to get to the Surface."

Avery cringes at the word. "But what do we do once we get there? We can't just abandon shelter without a plan."

Madame rests her hands on her hips, staring at the floor. "I give up. I can't seem to contact the President, and without him I have no line to the Unified Party. If we travel to the Surface, the Unified Party needs to know what we know. We have the means to defeat this enemy, but not the leadership to see it through."

I take a deep breath. "No. The Unified Party's gotten us into enough trouble already. What we need is the Skyship Community."

Eva nods. "In an invasion, you attack from higher ground. The Skyships are our biggest weapon. Head up to the Tribunal if you want the government involved. At least we know where they are."

"I can't go to the Tribunal," I mutter.

"Why not?"

"I'm the Pearlbreaker. Standing around and talking isn't my thing, and it isn't gonna help. I need to get out there and free more Drifters. We'll have a better chance that way."

Sem nods. "Jesse is correct. The more friendly Drifters on the ground, the better. Haven's natives are the backbone of this war. We don't need the government to fight. We need the Resistance."

"There's a framework," Madame starts. "There is order to war."

Cassius leans his hands on the edge of the table. "Why not do both? Split into two groups?"

Madame shakes her head. "I'm not sure it's wise to separate ourselves."

"I'm not sure it's wise to stay *together*," Cassius counters.

It's silent for a moment as each of us ponders what tactic is in our best interest.

In the end, it's decided that there will be a pair of

forces: one to head up to Skyship Atlas and speak to the Tribunal, and one to help me break Pearls, releasing as many allies as I can manage in a short timeframe.

It's decided that my support team will be Avery, Skandar, and a couple of our Drifter friends. A small group, but at least I trust them.

Meanwhile, Cassius and Madame need a loyal Shipper to get them past clearances, so Eva's heading up to Skyship Atlas with them.

It all gets thrown down in what seems like no time. I think everyone's just eager to get out of this bunker, especially now that we know it's not safe. I certainly am, but that doesn't mean that the idea of traveling back to the Surface doesn't bring anxiety. Everything bad that's happened to me has happened up there. I don't see that changing.

Our mission code name: Strikeforce. Get our respective jobs done and rendezvous as soon as we can.

We have communicators. And Unified Party cruisers. It should be manageable, but the thing is, we've got very little idea of what's going on above us. There are a thousand unseen variables—possibility after possibility for something to go wrong.

Still, it gets us out of the bunker, so I'm not going to argue. For now.

Two groups.

Avery clutches my arm. "We're sticking together, Fisher."

I nod. "There's no way I'm letting Madame close to you, especially when I'm not around."

She chuckles. "Well, aren't you just the big hero?"

"We'll see," I respond, staring forward at the wall. "We'll see."

———

I head for Cassius as soon as the meeting breaks. He walks through the door into the outside hallway. I follow him.

"What do you want, Fisher?" He marches forward without looking at me.

I match his pace. "You're sure this is a good idea? I mean, if you hadn't have been there last night, I would be dead right now."

"You can take care of yourself," he replies. "Besides, you'll have Wicksen and Harris. Plus the Drifters."

"I just want to make sure..."

He stops and turns. "We're targets. You realize that, don't you? Matigo's hunting us. Hell, the entire Authority's hunting us. If we stay together, we're a bigger target." He starts walking again.

"I get it. I get the logic. I guess it's just... you guys have a clear plan. A destination. All I do is go up there and break Pearls?"

"Not just Pearls," he replies. "Find a storage center. Break as many as you can."

"Where?"

"A Chosen City. Portland, maybe, since you've been there before. Trust me, the Unified Party's got way more

Pearls in storage than the Skyshippers, and the west coast hubs are particularly well-stocked."

I follow him around a corner. "How do you know that the Unified Party is better stocked than the Skyship Community?"

"How do you think?" He shakes his head. "How do I know anything about Skyship?"

I swallow. "Madame."

"It used to kill me how naïve you guys were," he says. "Floating up there like we weren't watching your every little move. I guess we were all naïve, though." He stops outside his makeshift room. "Suit up, Fisher. We leave in an hour."

He shuts the door and leaves me standing in the hallway. I close my eyes for a moment and am instantly brought back to my dream two nights ago. I see him bursting into flames, and not coming back from it. I hear the laugh, echoing in my mind.

We have to do this. There's no choosing. But that doesn't mean it isn't gonna end badly.

6

The row of Unified Party cruisers sits at the far end of the transport bay, five in total. The one we came down in is parked at an awkward diagonal in the opposite corner. The five unused models gleam and sparkle with the reflection of the overhead lights. The one in the corner is too scratched and dirt-caked to reflect anything. Sort of like us.

Skandar stands to the right of me, Eva to the left. For a moment, it seems like we're back in the docking bay of Skyship Academy.

I tap my foot on the ground, mostly to break the all-encompassing silence of the bay. "It's gonna be weird doing this without you, Eva."

She crosses her arms. "Don't be silly. You've got Harris. Unless you don't want him."

Skandar frowns. "Of course he wants me. I'm every bit as good in battle as you are."

"You keep telling yourself that."

My mind runs through the conversation I had with Cassius. Portland. Last time I was in the city, Cassius had been hunting me down. Avery and I had crash landed, right through the Bio-Net. This time, we'll have to break in from the ground. No small feat.

Footsteps sound behind us. I don't need to turn and look to know who's waiting.

Avery walks up and massages my shoulder. I watch Madame stride in front of us, thrilled to take command even though nobody's officially appointed her. She can do the talking if she wants. I'm not gonna argue.

She stops and pivots, hands on hips. Her mouth's curved in a deep frown. Cassius and the Drifters fill in on either side of us, creating a semicircle. I close my eyes for a moment, hoping to feel any residual Pearl energy from the Drifters' bodies, but they're drained of it, which means if we get into a scrap on the Surface, they'll be as much help as a human.

Madame takes a deep breath. "You all have your com-pads. They will be our only link until we rendezvous again. If anything goes wrong." She pauses and stares at me. "*Any-thing*, we all need to know of it as soon as possible. Don't be a maverick. We're here because we want ... *need* ... to help each other. Even if we don't like one another, we're in this together, and all the stronger for it."

She clasps her hands behind her back. "We'll take the pair of cruisers in the center. Avery, I'm confident you remember how to operate Unified Party transportation. I know it's been some time."

Avery's eyes slit. "Don't worry about me."

"I'm not," Madame responds pointedly. Then, her

expression softens and for a moment it looks as if she's going to walk over and give us a hug. Lucky for everyone, she stands her ground and releases a sigh instead. "Good luck."

I nod. "You too." And it's not even completely disingenuous.

"Cassius?" She motions him to her side. He glances back at me before joining her. I watch them all disappear into the cruiser. Eva's last. She turns and gives me a slight nod and a worried smile, but says nothing.

There aren't any long-winded goodbyes. Nobody down here is really the type. It's better that way. It keeps our focus. Besides, goodbyes give the sense that we're not going to see each other again for a long time.

"C'mon, Jesse." Avery's voice snaps me out of my thoughts.

I swallow, then turn to take one last look at the bunker before boarding our cruiser.

Once inside, we take our seats. Skandar stays in the back cabin with the two Drifters while Avery and I man the cockpit.

I watch Cassius's ship take off first, hovering up toward the ceiling of the bunker, which peels open with slick silence. Soon we've got a chimney of sorts to guide us up to the Surface.

Avery brings our cruiser safely underneath theirs, providing enough distance to keep any of the residual effects of their thrusters at bay. I watch as the sight of the bunker outside my window is replaced with dark earth. Soon we're pushing up through the narrow, claustrophobic tunnel.

Then, the sky.

As hazy and troubled as it is, it's still a relief to see. I've been living under low ceilings for too long. The vast expanse of the Surface stretches all around us—an unending blanket of barren brown. In a way, it feels liberating.

That liberation is short-lived.

As I watch Cassius's cruiser pull away to the left, I spot a red Pearl in the distance. It hurtles toward us, falling faster than any normal Pearl I've seen. And I know that, despite all of my powers over green ones, I can't stop it. When it comes to red Pearls, the Authority's in charge.

Avery tilts us from the Pearl's path, just as it rockets past our port side. I feel intense warmth in my gut that only begins to fade once the Pearl is far enough away from us.

"They're still coming down," I mutter.

Avery straightens us out, not saying a word. We continue to speed from the bunker door, which has now closed and blended in with the desert surroundings below.

I take a look at the Surface ground. It's quiet and still. That much is unchanged. This far from a Chosen City, there's not much that the Authority could destroy. Of course, that doesn't mean that they won't still be nearby. Waiting.

An explosion sounds in the distance, somewhere off to my right. I glance out the window to see a shuttle—I can't tell if it's Skyship or Unified Party—come bursting through a thin layer of clouds. It's little more than a speck from here, but it hurtles to the ground in a clear diagonal path, too fast for landing.

Seconds later, I watch the shuttle collide with the ground in a second explosion. I don't see a parachute. Worse yet, I've got no idea what brought it down. The skies seem quiet.

The cockpit door slides open, revealing Skandar.

"Whoa!" He runs up to the console. "Did you just see that?"

"The skies aren't safe," I reply. "I didn't think there'd be so many of them, so close."

Avery flips a switch on the ceiling. "I wish this thing had some cloaking."

I grit my teeth. I've crashed before. It can't happen again. "Just get us to Portland. The faster we can be on the ground, the better."

"Roger that," she says. "Out of the frying pan, and into the—"

"Don't." I close my eyes and take a deep breath. "I'd rather not think about fire. I'm sure there'll be enough time for that later."

7

The Rodriguez girl insisted on staying in the cruiser's cockpit, much to Cassius's annoyance. The two of them had always butted heads, ever since he'd nearly shot her in the Fringe Town of Syracuse. Of all of Fisher's friends, she was the only one with the military knowledge to challenge him. In a way, it made them perfect allies in this particular mission. Not a whole lot of shared history between them, no feelings of loyalty or honor beyond those of fellow soldiers.

But as much as she annoyed him, at least it kept him from being alone with Madame. Even though current events were forcing her to think beyond herself, Cassius knew that Madame always had backup plans. She'd double-crossed him before— done anything and everything to suit her needs. Could he really trust her now?

He looked out the window, scanning the horizon. Fisher's cruiser had long since disappeared into the distance, heading west. Cassius spotted a stream of smoke, far off in the distance. It most likely came from a Chosen City. He prayed that the Unified Party had enough resources to fend off the Authority. More than that, he hoped that Fisher would be okay in Portland.

After all, the Chosens had to be one of the invaders' first targets. Beyond the Skyships above, they were the centers of the country's population. Destroy all fifty Chosen Cities and America wouldn't be worth saving.

He glanced forward. They were approaching one of the cities now.

"This would be Boulder," Madame stated, then scooted forward to peer out the window. "My god."

Cassius did the same. Before them lay a dark city, half fallen. The Bio-Net surrounding the perimeter harbored noticeable gaps—chinks in the city's armor. The sky began to thicken, choked with smoke from the multiple fires blazing below. Bolts of red energy darted around the city's edge like fireflies. Authority foot soldiers, no doubt. There were no shuttles or cruisers present.

Cassius imagined what it would be like to have been in the city when it was first attacked. The Bio-Nets themselves were outfitted with cannons to shoot down any unauthorized Skyship vessels, but the rate and speed that the red Pearls had fallen would have made them impervious to cannon fire. He'd been in Chosen Cities when normal, green Pearls had dropped. He'd seen the destruction that just one could create. Multiply that by a hundred, and add the relentless enemy invaders who lived inside the crimson Pearls, and you had a real problem.

Cassius kept forward, transfixed at the sight. "Should we stop?"

"No," Madame said. "We can't get involved with every mess we see. Not now."

"There are people dying down there." Eva's choked voice came from behind them. "The government's not equipped to deal with—"

"I'm sure there are, my dear," Madame interrupted. "People die every day. Sometimes the bravest thing you can do is know when it's not your time to fight."

Cassius felt the cruiser speed up and gain altitude, bringing them farther from the city. He sat back, teeth grinding.

"Anxious, Cassius?" Madame's voice cut the silence.

"How can I not be?"

"Calm yourself," she replied. "Think of Skyship Atlas. The Tribunal." Her voice quieted. "At least that's an enemy we can understand."

"You know," Eva started, "if you keep thinking of Skyship as the enemy, we're not going to accomplish anything."

Madame's brow rose as she glanced at Eva from the rearview mirror. "None of us will be welcome onboard Atlas, even a Shipper like you. Not after all we've done. If I had any concrete destination on the Surface, you can bet that's where I'd be heading."

Eva met her eyes. "They won't recognize me. I'm not important to them ... not in the big scheme of things."

"You were on Skyship Altair when Matigo's son sunk it. You're friends with Fisher. That makes you important."

The console beeped. Cassius moved to the radar and

instantly spotted activity. He turned to Madame. "Something's following us."

She cursed. "I thought I brought us far enough above the city..."

Cassius returned to the radar. "There's three of them. Too small to be cruisers."

Before he could continue, a flash of red zipped past his windshield, so fast that it was like a slice of light through the sky. Another ripped across the left window, then a third directly above them.

"What the hell?" Madame brought the cruiser in a steep upward incline almost immediately.

Cassius flew back into his seat, gripping the side paneling to keep from falling out. "Don't panic. Want me to drive?"

"I'm fully capable—" She was interrupted as the three crimson lights surged forward on them. And for a split second Cassius could see exactly what they were. Authority foot soldiers. *Flying* Authority foot soldiers.

Cassius reached over to flip the emergency steering, then pulled open a nearby hatch to reveal a second wheel— the co-pilot's override.

Madame pounded her fist against the console. "Damnit, Cassius. I can do this!"

Instead of arguing, he took control and brought them in a spiraling climb, past clouds up into Skyship territory. He knew he was a better pilot than Madame, despite her bravado. She'd been on the Surface too long, coddled by the Unified Party's amenities.

Still, his breakneck climb wasn't enough. The soldiers matched their speed, clamping onto the cruiser's underbelly. Hitching a ride.

They must have seen the cruiser over Boulder and decided to attack. Madame had been foolish for flying so low in the first place. This was exactly why they were headed to Atlas rather than a Chosen City. Still, the fact that these things could fly made everything more dangerous.

A pounding came from below them as the soldiers climbed up the underbelly of the cruiser, seconds from tearing through the metal and working their way inside.

He had to lose them.

"If you puke," he started, "don't puke on me."

With that, he brought the cruiser into a dizzying series of loops, whipping the ship back and forth in violent bursts, hoping to knock the foot soldiers off.

And he did. With a screech, he felt the weight drop from the cruiser. He couldn't tell where the creatures ended up, but he knew they'd come right back, angrier than before.

"I'm using a boost," he announced, though he didn't expect any argument.

Before the soldiers could come back, he reached up and turned the dial to full power. With a series of flips and clicks, the system's emergency boost kicked in, counting down from five. It would use much of their power up, but they needed to get away if they were to survive. He didn't want to crash land on the Surface, especially with the soldiers nearby.

He straightened out the cruiser before the countdown reached zero, pointing it eastward.

The boost initiated. He slammed back into his seat, hardly able to breathe as the cruiser rocketed forward at speeds twenty times its already quick norm. The sky became a blur of motion. Normally, he'd worry about crashing into something, but they were just under the International Skyline. He doubted—hoped—that no Unified Party vehicles would be airborne at a time like this.

When they finally slowed down, their radar showed them as being over the eastern border of Colorado, a good two hundred miles away from where they'd previously flown.

Madame breathed a sigh of relief. Her hand shook at her side. "Cassius," she started. "That was—"

"You're welcome," he replied, folding the override steering back into its compartment and returning the power to her. "Stay at this altitude. I know you like to think you're invincible, but you're not."

He stood.

Eva glanced up at him. "Where are you going?"

"To the back," he replied. "I'm gonna take stock of our supplies. Weapons. Rations. First aid. This isn't gonna be easy."

"Do you want help?"

"No," he said. "Keep her under control." He didn't

meet Madame's eyes. "Make sure she doesn't do anything stupid. And run a functional inventory … make sure those Authority goons didn't rip anything important from our hull." He moved to the door, opening it to reveal the cabin beyond. "Let me know when we're closer to Atlas."

8

Trails of smoke beckon us forward, rising from Portland's Bio-Net like fingers. The city sits on the horizon, right in the center of the cruiser's windshield. Even from a distance, I can see the war raging. Red Pearls continue to fall from the sky, hitting the ground like meteors and instantly transforming into Authority soldiers.

The air is clogged with vehicles around us. People trying to get out, maybe. Unified Party cruisers hoping to fight the battle from above. With every minute we remain airborne, another shuttle comes crashing to the ground. They land in fiery explosions, pelting the earth like broken toys. Most are accompanied by parachutes, thank god, but not all. And the longer we're amongst the fray, the better chance we have of becoming one of the casualties.

The city's cannons, attached on all sides to the Bio-Net connectors, let loose a flurry of blasts aimed at the invaders. But the soldiers are too quick and too small to have much success with something as cumbersome as a cannon.

"Bring us down," I tell Avery.

She grips the steering, hands shaking. "That's what I'm

doing, but we can't do it too fast. Do you wanna crash land like last time we were in Portland?"

"No." I think back to when I'd first left the Academy with her, when Cassius had been in pursuit. Not only had our Academy shuttle lost power, but it did so right over the city, breaking through the Bio-Net and landing in a crowded plaza. We'd been lucky to survive.

I focus on the trails of smoke, drawing ever closer. "I'm more worried about one of those cannons hitting us."

"Trust me," Avery says. "I've got this."

I wanna trust her. I know what a good pilot she is, but there's so much going on around us. Utter chaos.

I watch as the crimson light of a soldier careens across our windshield, less than a mile away. I don't know where it's going, or if it's even in control of its own course, but I dread the thought of one of them clamping onto our cruiser.

The door to the cockpit opens and Skandar strides in. "Man." He plops in a seat behind Avery. "It's hell out there."

Avery's brows rose. "How are the Drifters?"

"Antsy." He stares out the front window.

Before I can respond, an orange panel illuminates at the top of the console.

Avery glances over to the light. "The emergency hatch."

"What?"

The back of the cruiser lurches, as if someone had just dropped a sandbag in the cabin.

"The emergency hatch," she repeats. "It's open."

"I don't—"

I'm interrupted as a pair of green flashes pull to either side of the cockpit. I look out the window to see Talan flying beside us, matching the pace of the cruiser. On the other side is Sem, his green glow equally as strong.

"The Drifters," I start.

"They're out," Avery finishes. "The back hatch is already closing up again. They were waiting for you to leave, Skandar."

He shrugs. "I guess."

I stare at Talan and Sem as they continue forward, overtaking us but losing altitude at the same time. "I didn't know they had any Pearl energy left inside of them."

Avery brings us lower. "Just enough to get to the surface, I'd wager. I guess we weren't moving fast enough for them."

Within seconds, both Drifters are out of sight. They've joined the fight, sure, but they've also left us alone in the process. Maybe they saw something we didn't. Maybe our cruiser was about to be attacked.

"We can't worry about them now," Avery says. "I'm speeding up descent. We'll take a wide, low route. I'll set us down in the shadow of the northeast landing pad. Depending on what's happening on the ground, they'll have either amped up security or seen their checkpoints completely breached, in which case I'm betting it'll be pretty easy getting past. Of course, once we're inside the city, it'll be a different story. Either way, it's better to be safe."

Skandar rests his chin in his hand. "I still say you should let me go with you."

I pivot so that I can see him. "It's gonna be hard enough getting two of us in there."

"Besides," Avery adds, "if something goes wrong, which…chances are…" She trails off. "Anyway, we'll need someone manning the cruiser that can get us out of here fast. I'm fairly familiar with the layout of the city. And Jesse…well—"

"He breaks Pearls," Skandar interrupts. "I know." He sighs. "And I wait in shuttles. Fantastic."

———

Once on the Surface, the Chosen City towers over us, casting an enormous shadow along the entirety of the landing pad. Of course, I can't see much of that now. Avery managed to make a tricky turn underneath the concrete pad, wedging us in between the city and the ground—down with the roaches and spiders, and I'm sure there are many of them out here.

Avery said the northeastern landing pad is the least-frequently used. Passenger parking, basically. And most people on the Surface rely on the automated Chute system to travel from city to city. Not many own shuttles to park, and those that do would have tried to clear out already.

We exit the cruiser and climb up the rocky terrain, settling on the desert ground after a minute of sweaty, arm-straining work. The hot Fringe air crawls inside my lungs. The scratchiness of the air instantly takes me back to the dream I've been having.

The rooftop. Syracuse.

At least the Nevada bunker had been temperature regulated. After so many days down there, my body struggles to adjust to the blast of heat. With any luck, we won't be outside for long.

From this distance, the battle seems muted. Much of the attack is happening in the air now. I'm sure it will be different once we're inside the city, but barring the occasional explosion, we've found a relatively calm place.

Once at the edge of the landing pad, I glance up at the Bio-Net connectors. As apprehensive as I am about breaching a Unified Party stronghold, my body longs to pass the city's walls and enter into the cool, Net-protected atmosphere.

I'm so eager that I don't even notice the obvious until Avery raises a hand and points.

"Do you see that?"

I trace the line of her finger and realize she's pointing at the closest connector. A red circle, right in the center of the metal cross, flashes in quick repetition. I scan the horizon. Every Bio-Net connector's the same. Red, off and on.

"Security breach," she says.

I open my mouth to respond, but end up swallowing my words. Something tugs at me, grabs me by the chest, and tries to pull me forward. I plant my feet on the ground and easily stay in place, but the sensation remains. I've felt this before. I've been waiting to feel it again.

"The Pearls," I say.

Avery stands on her toes to get a look at the city, still far in the distance. "Where?"

"I can feel them already," I whisper. "They're inside. There are a lot."

She grabs my hand and pulls me closer. "Maybe you can reach them from here."

I close my eyes and try to focus on the energy, pinpoint exactly where it's coming from. But each time I grab on, something interrupts my concentration—pushes me away. "No." I let the sensation pass. "There's too much going on inside. We'll need to get closer."

"Figures." She takes a deep breath before releasing her hold on my hand. "Just follow me."

We approach the city slowly, leaving Skandar behind in the cruiser and making our way to the nearest entrance. A short tunnel, surrounded on all sides by rows of flashing lights, leads past the Bio-Net and into Portland. A guard stands watch, turned sideways. A blue laser searches the area around him, beaming down from the ceiling to catch Unified Party identification codes. Avery used to have one before she came up to Skyship. I never did, which means neither of us will be welcome past the checkpoint, especially during a security breach.

The guard notices us before we've even passed through, and holds out a hand. "We're in lockdown." There's a tremor in his voice, a hint of fear I'm not used to hearing from a Unified Party soldier.

Avery moves faster. "Our little brother's still in the city. You have to let us in!"

"You'll be safer outside," he replies.

"Please." Avery approaches him. "We got separated on our way out. We need to—"

"Listen," he interrupts, though I can see he's just as shaken as Avery's pretending to be. "If I were you, I'd take your—"

Before he can finish, Avery delivers a roundhouse kick, knocking him to his knees. In the same motion, she spins to grab a pistol sitting on the desk behind him. "Go, Jesse."

Without a hint of hesitation, I sprint through the laser and past the checkpoint. The stupefied guard attempts to react, but Avery's too fast. She follows behind, grabbing my shoulder and forcing me to the left. We barrel down the nearest street as the alarm sounds behind us. He might call backup. But with everything else going on, he's more likely to forget us.

The city is as messy as the skies outside. Troops of soldiers race down the narrow streets, dwarfed on either side by skyscrapers so tall they block out the sun. The dull red flash of the Bio-Net connectors reflects off the silver sides of buildings. Smoke far above us casts the city in a gray ashiness.

And I know they're here. I can't see them, but there are invaders inside Portland. Like Talan and the other Drifters said, you won't notice them until you're close enough to see the red of their eyes. They could be anyone.

Avery and I bolt into an alleyway and take a moment to catch our breath.

"Close your eyes," she pants. "What way should we be going?"

I nod, and lock onto the Pearl energy. There are still disruptions, but I feel it in the distance. A constant pulse, like an extra heartbeat outside of my body.

I open my eyes and point to the far end of the alley. "In the center of the city. Exactly. Follow me."

I take a step forward just as an enormous blast ruptures the ground two streets behind us. A bomb? Enemy fire? Unified Party defense? There's no way to tell.

My ears ring as the sound of the explosion fades. A cloud of rubble rains over the street bordering our alley and begins to work its way toward us, like a tidal wave of gray.

Avery shakes her head. "We had to pick Portland."

She's right. There may be other Chosens that are in better shape. Of course, we had no way of knowing that. And then again, Portland could be one of the safer places. We're completely in the dark. Guesswork. That's all we've got.

"Come on." It's my turn to lead. We sprint forward as the dark cloud streams in behind us.

All the while, the Pearl energy intensifies. I'm locked on it now. And I'm not stopping until I'm close enough to break them all.

9

From a distance, Skyship Atlas appeared untouched. Upon looking at it beyond the windshield, Cassius was reminded of the last time he'd been onboard, before everything with the Pearls and Drifters had started. The Skyship had inspired awe back then. It certainly was an imposing structure—a tremendous wedge of dark metal floating above the clouds—but in the midst of war, nothing seemed untouchable.

Madame had already contacted the Tribunal through official channels. Now that they were close enough to the ship, she could do so without worrying about scrambled or dropped lines.

He knew the Tribunal didn't like her, but they did respect her to an extent, and a meeting with a high-ranking Unified Party figurehead was nothing to brush off. Their cruiser was granted landing in one of Atlas's docking bays.

Meanwhile, Cassius and Eva sat in the back of the cockpit, as far from Madame as they could manage without actually leaving the room.

Cassius tapped his foot nervously on the ground. "Do you think the Tribunal will listen to us?"

Eva shrugged. "I think they'll be happy for the glimmer

of alliance, even if it's with her. If they understand half of what's going on around them, they better be."

"I hope you're right."

She laughed. "Or they'll just shoot us down without question."

Atlas's immense hull soon overtook the view of the sky outside. Cassius stood and kept his attention forward, searching for any indication of an attack from the Skyship. Even after receiving positive confirmation, he wasn't willing to concede the possibility that this was all a trap.

"Relax," Madame said. "Don't let them see you sweat. Remember last time. It's important not to show weakness. These people thrive on it."

After settling down on Atlas's most secure docking bay, their cruiser was met by a fleet of guards surrounding Representative Chandler, one of the three operating heads of the Skyship Tribunal.

Chandler was an eager, brown-haired man in his mid-thirties. Of all of the Tribunal, Cassius felt the least threatened by him. Even flanked by a battalion of guards, he had an easygoing, almost friendly nature.

Madame disembarked the cruiser first, striding onto the landing pad with instant authority. Whatever his feelings toward her, Cassius was continually amazed with her ability to put on a show for those operating underneath her.

Cassius and Eva followed, arms to their sides, free of any weapons or tech.

Cassius looked over the rows of soldiers. They were modestly dressed in navy jackets and slacks. No body armor, but each had a pistol holstered at their side, ready for action.

Representative Chandler nodded as Madame approached. "Seems like we just did this yesterday, Jessica."

"Trust me." She walked beside him, moving deeper into the ship. "None of us has ever done something like this."

He nodded. "You've come to tell us what's happened, I hope. Who's attacked us. Or maybe this is just another Unified Party trick."

"If you'll listen, I can assure you we're not here to attack anyone."

Chandler stopped, looking her up and down. "Security checks first, Jessica. One can never be too certain with you."

"If you must." Her lips pursed. "But make it quick. We're running out of time. You've already lost a Skyship. From the looks of it, the Chosen Cities aren't faring much better."

"Mmm-hmm."

He ushered them forward, through a series of energy and metal detectors, through a detailed pat-down, and finally to the elevator that would take them to the Tribunal meeting room. Even Eva was thoroughly checked. Throughout the entire process, she didn't mention that she was Skyship. No one seemed to question her on it either.

Once in the meeting room, Representative Chandler

took his seat at the far left podium beside Representatives Buchanan and Leone. As Cassius moved to his place at the table below the Tribunal's three imposing podiums, he was reminded of the last time he'd sat in this room, sent on a secret mission to capture Jesse Fisher and bring him back to Madame. Had he known the chain of events that assignment would set off, he wasn't sure he'd have taken it on. Even back then, it had been prickly between Madame and the Tribunal. Now, with war raging outside, it could end up much worse.

Representative Buchanan—a round woman with harsh features—was the first to speak. "Would you like to tell us about Skyship Altair?"

"That's neither here nor there," Madame responded pointedly.

Buchanan laughed. "Isn't it? Several hundred of our people died when Altair sank. A thousand more have been displaced. Is the Unified Party going to take responsibility for this attack?"

Madame clasped her hands in front of her. "We do not. The sinking of Skyship Altair was the opening salvo in a new war. We can't be enemies now. There is a greater threat."

Representative Leone—a man so old and gaunt that he seemed to disappear when he turned to the side—leaned forward. "*Red* Pearls."

"Of course," Madame replied. "Raining down on Earth, more than you can count. More every hour. It's hell down there. We passed city after city, destroyed."

Buchanan rested her chin on her fingers. "We're aware. These Pearls contain something. Soldiers, of some sort."

"Drifters," Madame countered. "Aliens. Just like the green Pearls. But these ones are not friendly."

All three representatives paused. They turned to one another, whispering. Cassius was too far away to hear what they were saying. Their expressions revealed nothing.

Finally, Representative Buchanan turned to face them once more. "We are aware. Most seem to have hit the Surface, but a few have broken through the domes on the top decks of our ships. There have been attacks. We've taken a few bodies into custody, but our scientists have found no easy means of destroying them. Brute force. That seems to be our only option at this point."

"We have a Pearlbreaker," Madame said.

Representative Chandler's brows lifted. "What's a Pearlbreaker?"

"One of yours," she continued. "A boy, trained at one of your academies."

Cassius turned to face her. He knew how much she'd wanted to keep Fisher a secret in the past. The great lengths she'd gone to capture him in order to further her own agenda. Madame was laying all her cards on the table. In front of the Tribunal, no less.

"Alkine's academy," Buchanan interrupted. "We know the situation well. They've been out of contact. Illegal breach of the Skyline. Unauthorized use of force in Seattle."

"Water under the bridge," Madame said. "This boy..."

this Pearlbreaker...can open green Pearls—the *good* Pearls—
and release our allies in this war. Green Pearl energy can hurt
our attackers. I know both of our governments have experi-
mented with weaponizing it in the past. We'll need to do as
much as we can, as *fast* as we can, if we're to have any hope
in this."

Buchanan crossed her arms. "I don't believe you. You
may think you've flown under the radar thus far, but the
Skyship Community has been keeping an eye on your
behavior for some time. I know what you've been up to in
the past. Experiments with the human mind...a seemingly
unquenchable thirst for Pearls that goes above and beyond
that of a concerned—or *sane*—government official." She
faced the other members of the Tribunal. "If you ask me,
she's finally snapped. Regardless of what's inside, Pearls are
energy. Any attempts we've made at turning it into something else have been middling at best."

"*You* don't have a Pearlbreaker," Madame countered.
"Trust me."

Representative Leone shook his head. "Even if this boy
can do what you say he can, you're asking us to hand over
our most valuable resources to our enemies."

"You were spotted fleeing the wreckage of Altair," Representative Chandler added. "How do we know this invasion isn't some thing concocted by the Unified Party itself?"

Madame bit her lip.

Buchanan smiled. "May I point out that most of these red
Pearls have fallen to the Surface, bypassing our community

altogether? Maybe we let you fight this war and see how it goes."

Madame opened her mouth, but before she could speak, Cassius stood.

"With all due respect," he started, "the Authority won't stop once they've conquered the Surface. They'll come for you, stronger than before."

Madame nodded. "And there isn't any place your ships can fly to escape this."

Buchanan's eyes narrowed. "Attacks on our ships have been minimal and isolated. I'm sorry that the Surface seems to be taking the brunt of this, but—"

"Isolated, *now*." Madame interrupted. "If that's truly the case, it's only because that's the way the invaders want it."

Representative Buchanan folded her hands in front of her. "I don't think—"

A dramatic rumble interrupted her. It came from underfoot, like a chasm was about to open across the floor. Then, the ground sank beneath them, tilting to a diagonal. Cassius held onto his chair. Madame stumbled, catching herself for a moment before falling to the floor in a heap. The Tribunal gripped the sides of their podiums, struggling to stay upright.

"What's going on?" Eva shouted. "Is the ship losing power?"

Nobody answered.

The ground lurched once more. Chairs scattered through the meeting room, colliding with tables and desks. Anything not fastened to the ground tumbled through the air and crashed into the left-hand wall, which had tilted so far that it had nearly become the floor.

Cassius grabbed onto the nearest table leg just as the entire piece of furniture fell along with everything else. It was pointless trying to resist the pull of gravity. He let go and let it take him.

As he was falling, he noticed it, beaming through the slit of a window directly above Representative Buchanan's head.

The sky had turned crimson, like a sunset strengthened to otherworldly vibrancy. It was as if he was staring directly into a red Pearl, so all-encompassing that a beam of it shone through the window and hit the wall on the opposite side.

The sky bled.

That's when the lights in the room snapped off and the ship began to sink.

10

Even through the chaos of the city, I see it clearly.

Portland's core reactor stands in the distance, noticeable amongst the many other buildings for its cylindrical shape, widest at the bottom and stretching up to a narrow point, like a skyscraper-sized missile set upright on the ground. There are no windows or marks in its perfectly smooth, silver exterior.

Inside, there will be dozens of turbines, much like the one at the center of Skyship Academy. They filter and convert Pearl energy into a form that the Unified Party can harness. The process also kills whatever Drifter's living inside.

Hence, my dilemma.

"There." I point to the reactor.

Avery pants. "It's getting worse out here, Jesse."

A faraway explosion punctuates her statement. This time, I don't even flinch. There's too much going on in the city for one little explosion to rattle me anymore. I try to imagine them as fireworks, like there's not even a possibility that any of them would hurt me.

I turn to see a group of soldiers sprint down the street

in front of us. Weapons forward, they're in pursuit of something. They pay no attention to Avery and me.

I'm just about to speak when a beam of red light shoots from around the corner of the nearest building and connects with the soldiers, exploding and throwing them into the air. They scatter in all directions, tumbling backward until they hit the ground, unconscious. Or dead.

Screw my firework theory.

Avery pulls me against the building. We flatten, concealing ourselves as a troupe of dark figures tramples over the fallen soldiers. When they reach the intersection, they separate and move down each available alley and side street, including ours.

We try to make ourselves as invisible as we can. Luckily, the foot soldier moves too fast to notice us. I catch a glint of red in his eye as he barrels past, offset by the dark bodysuit clinging to his thin frame.

We wait for a minute before venturing from the wall. Without Pearl energy, I'm no match for even a single Authority soldier. Seeing one so close is confirmation that we need to move even faster. Getting to the reactor may just be the difference between life and death on these streets.

We bolt forward, past the bodies of the fallen soldiers, through alleyways and side streets. We don't stop once, even as explosions ripple around us, nearing closer with every footstep. I push through the dust in the air, which at times is nearly blinding, and try not to choke as I breathe it in.

Then we reach the reactor. It dwarfs us in its shadow.

I freeze. Avery nearly runs into me before catching her-self.

She struggles for breath. "How do we get in?"

I crane my neck to take in the full expanse of the tower. "Maybe we don't have to." I turn back to her. "How do you feel about standing guard? I'm gonna be out of it for a second."

"You think you can break the Pearls from out here?"

"I hope so."

She nods, then turns to take in the city behind us.

I close my eyes and connect with the Pearl energy. It floats all around me now, so close that it pulls and pushes on my body. Soft touches, but it feels as if it could escalate and yank me into the air—fling me around like a puppet. A familiar warmth bursts deep within my chest. If I let it, it'll spread through my arms and legs and take over completely.

I push my hands into the air and swirl them slowly around like I'm conducting a symphony. Although my eyes are closed, it's as if I can see the Pearls inside the reactor. They're just beyond the thick, insulated walls, waiting for me.

It takes all I can to differentiate between the already-harnessed energy coursing through the reactor and the stuff encased in the yet-to-be-broken Pearls. In the past, I've been able to draw energy toward me, even if it wasn't in Pearl form. I don't want to cause a malfunction in the city's defenses, and manipulating anything beyond the Pearls themselves would do just that.

My eyes bolt open as I latch onto the nearest set of

Pearls. I could break them now, inside the tower, but there's no telling how many people are in there with them. The resulting burst would cause a concussive force, capable of flattening a crowd if they were standing too close.

No. I have to extract them from the building. Delicately, but quickly too.

I survey the outer wall of the reactor. Explosions continue to disrupt the atmosphere around me. I do my best to block them out.

My eyes settle on a security door, far on the right-hand side of the tower. Above that rests a narrow window. It's bound to be triple-paned at least, and bulletproof. But if I can get these Pearls going fast enough, they might be able to burst through.

Avery pulls on my shoulder, threatening to fracture my concentration. "Jesse," she whispers. "I think I see someone coming."

I tune her out, even though I know she wouldn't interrupt me unless it was important. But she's got a blaster. She'll shoot if she needs to.

With one swoop of my hand, I yank the distant energy forward. I imagine the Pearls pulling up from their bindings, flying through the corridors inside like ghostly orbs. If there are workers in the tower, they'll more than likely freak out at the sight of it. But there's nothing they can do. Not unless they find a way to stop me. And nobody would think to look outside ... not at a fifteen-year-old kid, breathing heavy with his arms in the air.

Seconds later and the first Pearl bursts through the window, shattering glass. It's followed by several more, shooting through the sky like sideways comets. There are twenty in total. Together their green glow is practically blinding.

I glance to the side, even as they come at me. My breath shortens as I hold my hands tensed in the air above my head. As the Pearls bob around my shoulders, I'm struck by the sudden sensation that I'm buried under a pile of rubble, fighting to keep the world from falling down on me. Even though the Pearls don't come near enough to touch, their weight is undeniable.

Then come the whispers. That strange, alien language. Words from Haven. Words that, in another life, I would have understood. They form a ghostly chorus, more and more until I'm afraid they'll become deafening.

I don't have much time.

Avery flinches behind me, overwhelmed by all the energy floating around her.

"Get on the ground!" The words force themselves through my clenched mouth. But even without the warning, Avery knows what to do.

She hits the dirt and covers her head, weapon at her side. Once I know she's safe, I begin to lob the Pearls into the air. With a flick of my wrist, I send the first one shooting up to the heights of the towers. When it's safely out of range, I break it.

The Pearl explodes like a green firework. Even in the daylight, the reach and scope of its luminescence is impressive.

I do the same with another. Then two at a time.

Pretty soon, I'm shooting four straight up in the air. Crackles of green energy fizzle into the city's transformers.

Four more. Then the last few.

Each time, Drifters are released. This far down, they look like green fireflies, darting in all directions—narrowly missing towers and sky bridges. They'll fly in a blind panic at first, as their bodies and minds struggle to adjust to the shock of a new world.

Their presence, and the presence of the Pearl explosions, will draw foot soldiers from around the city. But if what Talan and the others say is true, the green Drifters will attack immediately. They have their marching orders. Fight against the Authority. Join forces with the humans.

At least, that's what's supposed to happen.

A curtain of green energy falls on us, dissipated some from the initial burst but still enough to pack a wallop.

I stand, shoulders back, and absorb it. The exhaustion and discomfort in my body fades as the Pearl energy works its way into my system, healing me.

Avery's not so lucky. It comes at her like a hurricane, whipping her hair up around her head and flattening her farther against the ground. When she finally gets up, she looks like she's been hit by a truck.

We stand in silence for a moment, watching the green mist disintegrate into the air. I turn back to the reactor. "There are more, deeper inside."

She bites her lip. "We've only got one lousy blaster…"

I'm about to respond when an explosion thunders above us. I duck instinctively, for the sound of this one is a hundred times louder than any we've heard so far.

Avery crouches, hands on her head, staring up at the sky. "That came from—"

She's interrupted by a crackle, like rolling thunder right above the city. I expect rubble to come raining down on us, but there's nothing. Instead, I see red.

It starts in the center of the sky, like a crimson star just beyond the Bio-Net surrounding the city, and expands slowly in a circular whirlwind, overtaking more and more of our view with each passing second. Before I know it, there is no blue left. The green of the Pearl energy's gone too, replaced by a bubble of red that surrounds the entirety of Portland.

"What's happening?!?" Avery stands just as the winds from the energy burst hit us.

Our hair's yanked into the air. Dust kicks up underfoot. The crackling continues as the crimson seeps ever closer.

I keep my eyes on the sky, arms trembling as I watch the destruction play out in slow motion.

The Bio-Nets—seven hundred pounds apiece—begin to shudder. Previously held aloft by magnetic forces, secured into their places, they succumb to gravity. A moment more and they plunge. Freefall.

Like man-made meteors, nothing stops them as they pelt the city.

11

Cassius raced after Madame.

Skyship Atlas, third-largest ship in the fleet, was crashing to the ground.

It didn't seem real. There was no warning. There should have been alarms, but electricity had shut off. Backup had gone. The temp control ... pressure regulator ... everything had been wiped away. Not that any of it would matter when they made impact.

They careened through the crowded hallway, fighting against a sea of people traveling each and every direction. Though the ship itself had fallen silent, the people had not. This particular hallway reeked of vomit. The screams, shouts, and cries of confusion melted into one panicked stream of sound. And there was no denying the sinking feeling. Cassius had felt it previously, on Altair several weeks ago. The ground remained unstable, tilting in unexpected directions. Just when he thought he'd stabilized himself, it would lurch away from him.

They formed a chain in order to avoid being separated. The Tribunal had taken a different route, leaving everyone else to fend for themselves. They didn't particularly matter anymore, as far as Cassius was concerned. It would obviously take a catastrophic event like this to shake them out of their stupor, but it was too late now.

He felt Eva's fingers separate from his and glanced over his shoulder to make sure she was still with them. He watched her shove another harried passenger to the side, fighting to claw her way closer to Madame and Cassius.

They struggled through, heading to the private docking bay that housed their cruiser. It wasn't that long of a journey, but every second counted. Once in descent, Atlas wouldn't take long to collide with the ground. Ten minutes maybe. If they were lucky.

Just as they were about to reach the door to the bay, the entire hallway shifted underneath them. Cassius attempted to regain balance, but stumbled backward as the corridor collapsed downward into a slide.

The crowd toppled, some as a direct result of the change in angle, some because others knocked into them and sent them over like dominoes. It was like some sick amusement park ride.

People attempted to pick themselves up, using other bodies as leverage, which only exacerbated the struggle. The corridor soon became a pit of pushing and pulling, standing and falling. When Cassius was finally able to right himself, it was only to feel a hand grip tightly around his knee and try to yank him down again.

Luckily, he was strong enough to withstand the passenger's desperate pull. He pried his leg free. He hated to do it, but knew that every moment he spent fighting the crowd was another that brought him closer to certain death.

Together with the others, he pushed through the door and slammed it behind him, hoping that the mob wouldn't follow.

The tiny docking bay was empty, save for their cruiser. Cassius winced. The vehicle could have fit more passengers, but the time and chaos it would take to load strangers aboard would make saving innocents impossible.

Eva froze as soon as they were safely inside. "We need to help—"

Cassius grabbed her by the wrist. "There's nothing we can do. They'll have to head to their shuttles."

"By then it'll be too late," she continued, panic in her eyes. "There's not enough time for everyone to…" She stopped, unable to finish the statement.

Madame sprinted to the cruiser, sliding open the door and jumping into the cockpit.

Cassius turned back to the closed door. His eyes fell upon the lock. Madame must have secured it the moment they passed through, into the bay. A pang of guilt rose in his belly. He was brought back several months, to the wreckage of the Chute train he'd accidentally destroyed on the Surface. Could he really let innocents perish to save himself?

Madame's voice came from behind him. "Open that door and you might as well shoot yourself."

He and Eva turned to see her standing before them.

Cassius swallowed. "What's wrong?"

"The cruiser won't power on," she replied. "There's nothing."

Eva flattened against the door as the skyship tilted once more. "Not even solar?"

"Not enough," Madame replied. "Something's interfering with the system. You can try it yourself. I assure you, it won't work."

Cassius stared past her shoulder, at the red of the sky beyond the mouth of the bay.

"The Authority," he muttered. "That red energy … Wherever it's coming from, whatever it is, it's bringing us down. Sinking the ship."

Eva's breathing began to speed up. "If we can't operate the cruiser, then—"

"Nobody's getting off," Madame finished.

Cassius glanced at the floor, closing his eyes in thought. He shook his head. "Nope. I'm not going out like this."

Madame's eyes shifted nervously around the bay. "Any ideas would be greatly appreciated."

Cassius motioned Eva toward the cruiser. "Rodriguez, check the power again. Double-check it. Triple. If anything happens, shout."

Eva took a step toward the cruiser, then stopped. "We've got minutes … it's not enough … "

Cassius shooed her forward, unable to argue. If the crimson had managed to disable the power on Atlas, it may have clogged smaller ships too. But he couldn't accept it.

There had to be a way out. He hadn't come this far only to be brought down by a Skyship.

Madame gritted her teeth. "Cassius, what are you thinking?"

He laid his hand on his head and closed his eyes, trying to work through it logically. He couldn't give in to emotion at a time like this, as difficult as it was not to.

The cruiser didn't work. That meant that none of the ship's emergency shuttles would function either, not that they'd have the time to reach them. Their docking bay was almost completely empty. A fueling station in the corner, an emergency fire kit nearby. The only thing worth a try was the cruiser, and it was inoperable.

But there were tools *inside* the cruiser.

His eyes bolted open and met Madame's.

"Parachute," he said.

She shook her head. "There will only be two." She glanced behind her, then leaned forward to whisper. "Leave the girl here, is that what you're thinking?"

"No."

She sighed. "Even if we jumped off, the force from the ship would more than likely suck us under. The full weight of Atlas would fall on top of us."

"No," he repeated. "I have an idea." He sprinted to the cruiser, praying he could make it work.

"There are only *two* parachutes!" Madame called out behind him.

"That's okay," he shouted back. "I only need one."

12

The Bio-Net connectors pelt the city. They're the size of ovens. Bathtubs. Boulders. Some take chunks from the tops of buildings, adding to the violent hailstorm of rubble. Others crash in the middle of streets and alleys. They leave craters in the concrete, fling metal and wire haphazardly through the air.

Avery and I take shelter under the concrete overhang that protects the entrance to the reactor, though it's far from guaranteed safety. One of the connectors could easily scrape against the side of the tower on its way directly to our heads. We'd be pulverized before we could even think to move.

But there are only so many Bio-Nets in the sky. I grip the top of my head—like *that*'s going to be any help—and wait for the horrendous collisions to stop.

It isn't long. In seconds the last few tumble to their resting spots. The cascade of oncoming dust and scrap from the tops of nearby skyscrapers begins to thin. Then, everything falls silent.

No explosions. No gunshots. They aren't needed. In one

move, the Authority's disabled the city's protection, not only from the invasion, but from the elements outside as well.

The temperature-regulated air starts to dissipate almost immediately. I feel it warming the moment the Bio-Net connectors stop falling. Soon the Fringe heat will work its way into every corner of this city.

Avery coughs, then waves her hand through the dust to peer through to the streets beyond. "Is it safe? Should we move?"

Before I can respond, the doors behind us fly open. Several Pearl reactor workers run outside, colliding with my shoulder as they push past.

They freeze, taking in the destruction before us. The air's still too thick to see anything but silhouettes, but even through the haze I can see three Bio-Net connectors among the wrecked cityscape—the closest mere yards away.

One of the workers notices Avery and turns to face us, expression aghast. Several seconds pass before he's able to put his thoughts into words.

"What happened out here?"

Avery hugs her stomach, shaking her head. I consider answering for her, but then I realize that the doors are still open behind us. I glance through the opening, teeth gritted. What I'm about to do could be stupid, but there are more Pearls inside, maybe even hundreds.

Avery begins to respond to the man, her words fragmented. "The Bio-Nets...I don't know..."

The other workers turn to look at her. I take a deep breath. It'll be quick. In and out. Break them all. Done.

While they're preoccupied, I sprint through the doorway, toward the reactor.

"Hey!" I hear one of them shout after me, but by then I've already turned the corner. He's out of sight. Plus, with everything that just happened, I'm not too sure any of them would follow me. I think I hear Avery call my name as well, but I ignore her.

I turn all my attention over to the Pearls. They pulse inside my consciousness—dozens of heartbeats growing closer. Louder. They lead me where I need to go.

The corridors are white on all sides, and curved around the top like a never-ending tunnel. I race through them, making changes in direction when the pull of the Pearls commands me. I don't know where I'm going, or where exactly I'll end up.

Thirty seconds into my sprint, a deafening alarm cuts through the air, pulsing through the tunnels. It threatens to break my concentration, but it only lasts for a moment before it's cut off.

It's silent for a moment, before the footsteps.

I spin. I can't tell if they're coming from behind me or in front. Maybe they're not even real. Maybe it's only the Pearls thumping inside me.

I round another corner and run right into an oncoming guard.

We collide in the center of the hallway, knocking each

other sideways. My shoulder plants against the wall. I keep my balance and push forward.

"Stop!"

His voice echoes behind me, so loud that it reverberates along the curved walls. I glance over my shoulder and watch him aim a blaster my way. It's not some dinky pistol, either. It's a full-on, resting-on-his-shoulder bazooka.

I freeze, betting that with everything going on, he'll shoot before asking questions.

But he doesn't know about me.

With a clench of my fist, I latch onto the nearest Pearl.

It isn't far now. I hear its whispers.

A slight swipe of my hand brings it shooting from its hiding spot, around the corner and into the corridor. The green light, so close and reflected against the shiny white around us, would throw anyone off guard. But this guy's wearing some kind of goggles, probably to deflect energy from inside the reactor. The light doesn't seem to bother him.

But the moving Pearl does. I imagine his thoughts at this moment. *How is it floating? Why is it hurtling toward me?*

I don't give him time to wonder.

Four yards from his body, I break it. The Pearl explodes directly in front of my face, surging energy in every direction. The moment it slams into his chest, he topples to the ground. Armor or no armor . . . doesn't matter.

I absorb some of the energy. The rest clatters along the walls, electrifying the entire hallway.

I watch a Drifter begin to form from the ether. I've

never seen it happen so closely before. Sparks collide, growing and congealing into bands of energy that meld together to create legs. Arms. A head. It happens so fast that I barely have a chance to process it.

The Drifter flips sideways and soars through the air, down the corridor, and out of sight. He'll calm down eventually, if the Authority doesn't get him before that.

Free from the guard, I push forward.

I don't have much longer to travel before arriving in the belly of the reactor. A bulky metal door marks my way forward. It's half-open—knocked loose from the Pearl explosion, maybe. Or perhaps the guard was too panicked to remember to close it.

I push my hands over my ears, trying to drown out the noises from inside the reactor. It's not only the mechanical rumbles and whooshes from the machine itself, but the whispers all around me, loud enough now to make concentrating on anything else difficult.

I run through the door.

The chamber stretches high over my head, a dome so big that it feels as if I've entered another city entirely. I glance up. The dark siding of the room must stretch twenty stories above me. Rows of observation windows dot the walls every few levels, but beyond that the dome is completely smooth. Though the metal's as dark and unforgiving as the door I came through, the Pearl energy from within the reactor still manages to reflect, casting what looks like green sparks around the entire perimeter of the chamber.

Directly in front of me sits the actual reactor. It's about half as high as the chamber itself, but impossibly complicated. Thick tubes stretch out at all angles, looping around the room until they attach to the wall at different points around me. Turbines scoop through the air, sounding like whirring helicopter blades amplified a hundred times. The entire structure reminds me of an enormous, upside-down tree, roots coming out of its sides and top while the turbines spin so fast above that I can hardly see them move at all. This is a far cry from what we've got aboard Skyship.

The chamber's deserted. I'm not even sure it's completely safe to be here. My eyes dart around the room, from window to window. There might be officials staring down. They'll order more guards, if there are any available. Hopefully the chaos outside stole most of their attention.

I can't see the Pearls, but I feel them. Hear them. They're close enough to break, for sure.

I kneel on the ground, conserving as much energy as I can. I cup my hand and stretch it in front of me, like I'm waiting for someone to drop something in. My eyes close. I listen to the whispers without trying to decipher their otherworldly language. I don't have to use words to let them know I'm here.

The Pearl energy pushes closer to my body. I imagine every last bit of green streaming from the reactor toward my waiting hand.

I collect the Pearls—mentally catalogue them—and connect to as many as I can. Each one steals more of my attention until I can't focus on anything else. I feel my knees give way as I sink farther to the ground.

Too much.

I don't know if I can do it.

My shoulders shake, pushed around by waves of energy. I feel my hair bristle above my head as more and more Pearls cram their way into my consciousness. There's not enough room. There's not enough of me.

The whispers are so loud now. They're hardly whispers at all. Yelling. Pained screams, begging me to do what only I can.

I don't know if there's any coming back from this.

Just as it feels as though I'm going to pass out, I let go.

Boom.

The entire chamber rumbles with the force of an earthquake. The turbines lurch to a stop as green energy erupts everywhere, so bright that I can see it with my eyes closed.

I feel the ground give way beneath me—enough to forge a small crater below my feet.

The shouting decreases as my body floods with all that's floating around the room. I know there are dozens of Drifters circling above my head. But I can't open my eyes. I can't do anything.

The room heats, so hot that I fear it'll sear my skin right off. I've never felt this much energy at once, so close with nowhere to go.

Then I realize it. The dark siding, the reflective metal. It must be a shield to keep the Pearl energy in. Reactors are built like this, Captain Alkine once told me. Sealed, so no energy can be lost.

There's nowhere for this to go.

A trickle of green forces its way out the open door behind me. The rest bounces around the chamber, trapped. Some feeds back into the turbine, starting and stopping the blades in loud stutters.

Everything else comes at me. Point blank.

I open my eyes. All I see is green.

It's the last thing I sense before falling forward, head connecting with the ground.

Out.

13

Cassius finished strapping the parachute around the three of them. It didn't have enough bands to secure them all, so he had to pull some extra rope from the cruiser's cabinets and weave it in. He tied the material in several places, hoping that the force outside wouldn't be able to rip them all apart. But he didn't have the luxury of time. It would never be his best work, given the constraints he was struggling under.

He and the others stood back to back, forming a human triangle. Cassius had fastened their bodies together so tightly that he found it difficult to move his own shoulders.

"Madame's right," Eva shouted from his side. "Once we pop the chute, who's to say the ship won't just drag us down with it?"

"Trust me." Cassius led them closer to the edge of the docking bay, taking awkward tiptoe steps since he couldn't stretch out his legs all the way.

A deafening blast issued all around them—the sound of the air being ripped from the innards of the ship as it plummeted.

He prodded Madame's shoulder. "Pull it as soon as our feet lift off the ground. I'll do the rest."

"But that's not how—"

"You always taught me to follow your lead," he interrupted. "Now it's your turn to follow."

He knew that she wanted to argue. As brave a face as Madame put on, she wasn't used to this kind of action. This sort of situation—jumping and praying—was Cassius's thing. For better or worse.

More important, he could do things that she couldn't. And this kind of escape was going to rely on his specific talents. If it worked.

They couldn't run so close together, positioned the way they were, so they continued to inch along the ground, fast as they could without tripping, until they reached the point of no return.

Once close enough to the edge, the force from the rapidly passing air became too much. It tugged up at them like a claw, sucking their hair straight above their heads. Cassius felt the sleeves of his shirt pull up. His feet lifted from the ground.

With a great lurch, the sky plucked them from the docking bay and sent them spinning into clear air. The upper lip of the bay nearly connected with Cassius's shin. He used the close proximity to kick off, pushing them farther from the sinking Skyship.

Behind him, he heard the snap of the parachute being released. All at once, they shot upward at dizzying speed.

Cassius fought the wind's forceful blows and craned his neck to see the chute unfold above them. They whipped diagonally, at first away from the ship and then closer. This wasn't the typical emergency escape. Parachutes were made for cruisers and shuttles. Skyship Atlas was too big. It created wakes in the air, pushing them around in a nauseous seesaw, drawing them closer.

His arm tensed. He cupped his fingers into a fist and reached up through the air. His shoulder forced against Eva's. The wind threatened to slam his arm back to his side, but he fought through until it stretched all the way above his head.

It was time.

Focusing the energy inside of him, he let his fingers spark. A flame ignited above his hand, growing slowly until it climbed a foot in height. Eighteen inches. Twenty.

The wind wanted to tear it away, shift it sideways so that it would burn through the ropes, keeping them attached to the parachute. Gritting his teeth, Cassius kept hold of it, forcing the flame into a ball around his hand, steady in the center of all the chaos around him. Sweat dripped from his brow, eaten by the wind before he could even think to wipe it off. He felt his muscles tremble with the added exertion.

But it was working. They began to rise.

Like a hot-air balloon, the parachute trapped the heat from the fire. Even so, the tiny hole at the top let much of the hot air through, so Cassius had to keep the flame burning high, at least until Atlas was far enough away from them.

They rose slowly, but not at a constant rate. The atmosphere pulled up and down—turbulence they had no guarantee of surviving. Their parachute wobbled through the red-tinted sky as Atlas plunged ever farther below them.

Soon, a deep rumble came from the Surface, so loud that it nearly broke Cassius's concentration. A series of fire balls erupted below them, spreading along the desert landscape as Atlas ripped apart. The heat from the explosion swelled toward them, catching in the parachute and sending them even higher.

Cassius caught glimpses of the catastrophe below him—snapshots of fire and rubble—but never enough to get a full picture of the wreckage. He wondered how many passengers were still onboard during impact. It was worse than Skyship Altair had been. Bigger ship, more casualties. If nobody had been able to escape via shuttle or cruiser, how had anybody gotten to safety?

Had anybody gotten to safety?

He thought about the Tribunal. Enemies, maybe, but he couldn't imagine them all snuffed out so suddenly. It didn't seem real.

Cassius clenched his fist, extinguishing the fire. The parachute dipped down immediately.

Atlas had crashed off to their right. If the wind started to push them toward the blazing wreckage, he'd conjure another flame to steer them to safety. Right now, all he could do was let his arms fall to his sides and close his eyes, unwilling to look down.

When he refocused on the ground, they were less than a mile from the Surface. He could see people now, running away from what was left of the Skyship. He imagined that they'd piled at the edges of the upper docking bays, jumping off just before the explosions at the center of the ship had spread to engulf them. Others had fallen to the ground on parachutes, only they'd already landed—most much closer to the wreckage than Cassius's steered chute would bring them. Most had undoubtedly been crushed.

"Look!" Eva's voice pierced his thoughts.

She wriggled her arm free and pointed to the sky, off in the opposite direction from the crash. Cassius turned his head. At first, he didn't notice anything. He squinted, shielding his eyes from the oncoming wind. Then he saw it.

The red in the air began to dissipate—fold back into itself. Normal blue sky replaced it, starting from far in the distance and racing closer to their parachute.

It stopped. The sky was blue again. Everywhere but one spot, directly in front of them.

As if being pulled by a magnet, the red energy swirled together, churning like an enormous whirlpool in the sky. Cassius half-expected to watch a tornado form out of thin air.

Something did emerge from the whirlpool. But it was no tornado.

A metal object—so seamlessly silver that the sun beamed a blinding reflection off its hull—protruded from the center of the portal, growing in size as it came down upon the earth. First it was narrow, like the tip of a missile, but it soon expanded into a wide, oblong shape. A rocket, without windows or wings or tail fins. In seconds enough had popped out that it dwarfed everything around it. Cassius could hardly see past the metal siding of the craft. It dropped several miles away from them, sending shockwaves through the sky. Their parachute blew sideways in its wake.

Cassius watched in horror as the strange vessel fell closer to the Surface. He expected it to explode just like Atlas had, but instead of dismantling, it worked its way into the ground like a drill, sticking in the earth at a diagonal. The red whirlpool above evaporated. The ship stopped moving.

Cassius couldn't take his eyes off it, and with good reason. Within seconds, he and the others would land back on the Surface, inches away from the vessel. They were heading straight toward it.

14

A slap wakes me.

I jump and grab hold of some sort of plush handle to my side. When I open my eyes, I realize I'm sitting with my back against the wall. A cramp right between my shoulder blades makes twisting uncomfortable. My entire body aches with bruises.

My eyes part to see Avery crouched before me, hand recoiled and expression worried. She winces. "Sorry. I figured you were already beat up enough. What's another slap?"

I wiggle my jaw. It feels displaced. Nothing feels right.

Beyond Avery, the narrow space we're both in seems to be completely empty. It's not like a normal room—too long and constricted to make much sense as anything but a closed-off hallway. The metal walls are barren, dark and scuffed up beyond saving. It's unnervingly quiet, except for a constant rattle underfoot, like I'm sitting on top of a generator or engine.

"Avery." My voice comes out weak and strained. "What's happening?"

She sits back, though a sudden shift in the ground almost throws her to the side. "Thank god you're alive."

"Did the Drifters … did the Pearl energy make it out?"

Her jaw clenches. "Don't worry about the Pearl energy."

"I lost consciousness … " I shake my head. "Back in the reactor chamber. The energy … the Drifters."

"I know." She lays a hand on my knee, mostly to stop me from talking. "Listen Jesse, none of that matters right now. They've got us."

I search her eyes, trying to understand. "Who?"

She glances nervously to the other end of the room. A door. I hadn't noticed it before. "Who do you think?"

My heart sinks. "The soldiers?"

She nods. "The Authority."

"But—"

"The explosion from the reactor must have drawn them to you," she interrupts. "Jesse, I did what I could. I tried to stop them. When they surged on you—grabbed what I thought … " She pauses, shielding her face from view. I can tell she's fighting back tears. "What I thought might be your lifeless body. I wouldn't let them take you without taking me, too. I was sure they were gonna kill me. But they didn't. And now you're alive too."

I peer around the room, hoping to find anything besides blank walls.

"The door's locked," Avery says. "I already tried. They left about five minutes ago."

"Where are we?"

Avery bites her lip. "Some sort of train. Transport, I think. It's definitely not the Chute. They hijacked it and brought us onboard. I've got no idea where we're headed."

I stretch my arms, wincing as bolts of pain shoot through my limbs. Suddenly the rumble underfoot gains new significance. We're moving. "Why didn't they just kill us? It's worse this way. It means they're planning something."

Avery glances at the door, hand shaking. "The entire city's gone to hell. Should be in complete ruins by now. I saw the buildings crumble, Jesse, as we were being dragged to the train car. Then, just after the Bio-Nets fell, the sky bled. It was as red as the Authority Pearls. What are we up against?"

"It's worse off than we thought," I reply. "And I was stupid enough to think that freeing a few dozen Drifters would have any effect. If they can take down a city like that—"

"You did what you could," she interrupts. "We're alive. We learned. Now we just need to stay alive."

Before I can respond, the door bursts open and a pair of foot soldiers stride through, similar in height and design as the one that nearly killed me in the bunker. On first glance, it would be easy to mistake them for human, but as they turn to appraise us, the gleaming red of their eyes is more than enough to dehumanize them.

Avery grabs my arm and pushes her body against mine. We press against the wall, unable to look away from the soldiers.

They speak to each other—words I can't comprehend,

but ones that mirror the desperate sounds of the pleas from inside Pearls. The native Haven language is twisted as it spills from these soldiers' mouths in deep, guttural phrases.

They're unarmed. Once I get past the initial horror of seeing them so close, this observation registers with me. Not that the guy down in the bunker had been armed, either. And not that I have any Pearls around to use as an offense.

Where did Talan and Sem go? What about Skandar?

These questions ricochet in my mind as my panicked brain tries to work out what to do. There is no help in this train car. Only Avery and I. Sure, we've overcome a lot together already, but neither of us is the least bit physically imposing when it comes down to it.

Once the soldiers have finished communicating with each other, the one on the left advances. Avery lets out a yelp as he grabs her by the arm and forces her to her feet.

That's all I need to see. The sight of her manhandled by this guy gets me standing, even though pain nearly collapses me once more.

"Let go of her!"

The soldier doesn't seem to understand. Or maybe he does. He clenches her tighter against his body, eyes blazing crimson.

"Jesse," she says through a half-suffocated windpipe. "No!"

I ball my fists, determined to fight. I know I won't last long, but I can't just stand here and watch Avery crushed to death.

The enemy Drifter smiles, wide enough that I get a look at his teeth. The second approaches me. I tilt away, legs apart, ready to punch.

What the hell do I punch? His body's covered nearly head to toe in armor. I don't stand a chance.

Just then, the entire back wall of the train car rips open. I fall against the metal behind me, watching in horror as the train's ripped apart. The back end peels off with ruthless efficiency. Once gutted, the entire square of metal flies onto the tracks in the distance, thrown by an unseen hand.

The first soldier drops Avery. She collapses, gasping for air.

A man jumps, from above the train, into the opening he just created. He stands there, framed by the jagged hole. Train tracks disappear behind him as he grips the frame, feet firmly planted.

He wears a baggy gray shirt, so dark that it's nearly black. His legs are partially covered by some sort of armor—badly worn and cracked in several places. His head is shaved, and he wears a deep frown. I only see one eye. The other is covered by some sort of patch. From this distance, it looks as though it's been sewn into his skin somehow. His bulky shoulders heave with exertion.

When he speaks, his voice rumbles with the same force as the train engine. "Jesse Fisher."

He knows my name.

Releasing his hold on the door frame, the man stomps into the room.

The first soldier springs into action, lunging at the man before he can say or do anything else.

I watch as the stranger deflects his attack, kneeing the soldier in the gut and swinging him back through the opening. The Drifter hurtles onto the tracks outside, quickly forgotten.

Seeing this, the second soldier comes at the man, only to be met by a colossal fist, shattering the Drifter's helmet. Before the body can even hit the ground, the stranger grabs the soldier by the neck and pounds him into the opposite wall, hard enough to leave a dent in the metal. The soldier falls to the ground in a heap, unconscious. Probably dead.

The armored man turns back to me. "Come with me, Jesse." His good eye narrows. "We have things to do."

I back away. "I don't—"

Before I can finish, he sprints toward me, impossibly fast. I attempt to counterattack, do *something*, but in less than a second he's whipped his arm up around my shoulder. We stay still for just a moment. Then the ground falls away from us.

We're out the back opening and in the sky before I even realize we're flying.

15

Cassius's feet nearly collided with the strange vessel. They plummeted so close to its hull that he could clearly see his terrified expression reflected back at him against the silver metal.

Their parachute landed on the ground in a mess, mere yards from the base of the ship. Madame undid the bands holding them together. Cassius was too shell shocked to do much of anything.

When they were freed, he fell to his knees, hands in the dirt. He breathed heavy, exhausted from conjuring and maintaining a flame for so long.

Eva stood and staggered away from the enormous ship. They'd landed right in front of it, positioned so that it rose up in a diagonal away from them. Even at an angle, the vessel seemed taller than any building Cassius had ever seen. When he stood and peered up, it looked almost like an endless silver slide, stretching into the heavens.

Behind them lay a pile of dirt and rock, exhumed from the impact of the ship's pointed nose burrowing into the ground.

"What is it?" Eva asked after a few moments of silent observation.

Madame neared closer to Cassius, resting her hand on his shoulder. "Did you see where it came from? One moment the sky was clear. The next ... "

"It's the Authority," Cassius whispered, the strength of his voice stolen by their daring escape. "It has to be."

"We're too close," Eva said. "If there are Drifters inside, we're in trouble."

Cassius didn't take his eyes off the metal. He waited for it to shift or transform, for some sort of door to appear and release whomever was inside.

But all was silent. If the ship was occupied, there certainly wasn't a sign of it.

Far behind them, the ruins of Atlas smoldered. A cloud of smoke rose into the air, adding to the haze caused by all the dust in the Fringes. Beyond that, they were too far away now to hear or see anything of note. Too far to help any of the survivors, either. The Fringe heat started to get to him. Madame pointed up.

"Look at the sky."

Cassius peered into the blue. "I don't see anything."

"Exactly."

His heart fell at the realization of it. Usually, when standing on the Surface, he could see at least two or three Sky-ships, even if they were little more than small dots. Without any clouds, he should be able to notice them immediately.

But the sky was empty. No Skyships in the distance. No shuttles or cruisers.

Atlas had sunk. So had everything else.

"They immobilized it all." Madame's voice was quiet. "Brought it down in one quick move. They turned this into a ground war."

Eva shook her head. "We don't know that for sure. The Skyships are ... well, they're designed to withstand things like this."

"Things like what?" Cassius began walking away from them. "An alien invasion? Obviously the Tribunal didn't see any of this coming."

He moved farther away. His reflection distorted as he neared the shiny siding of the vessel. Carefully, he reached forward and pressed his hand against the metal. He closed his eyes, half-expecting to be shocked or burned or something.

Instead, it felt perfectly normal under his fingers. The only thing that struck him as slightly off was the temperature. In comparison to the atmosphere around him, the metal felt pleasantly warm, but not hot. He knew that normal metal—even after a few minutes in the Fringes—became almost unbearable to touch.

"Cassius." Madame's concerned voice came from behind him. "I wouldn't."

He turned. "Wouldn't what? Touch it?"

"You don't know what kind of defenses this craft may be equipped with."

"I don't see anything." He glanced behind him again, eyes tracing the length of the vessel. The top end climbed beyond his vision, growing hazy the farther away it stretched.

"Exactly," she whispered. "Just because you don't see it doesn't mean that everything's safe. There could be invisible traps."

He turned back to the ship, pressing his hands on the metal once more. The temperature hadn't changed. "I want to see what's inside."

"No," she said. "We have a mission, Cassius. A plan."

"You mean *had* a mission," he responded. "It didn't work. Time for Plan B."

"You know fully well that we have no Plan B."

He leaned in closer, staring at his expression in the silver reflection. "We do now."

Eva stepped up beside them. "We need to contact the others. Tell them what's happened."

"Go ahead," he replied. "You've got a com-pad, don't you? Call up Fisher. Meanwhile, we're here. Could be the base of the enemy. We could be right in the thick of it. Maybe it's the opportunity we've been waiting for."

Madame laid a hand on his shoulder. "And if we were to attempt a break-in, how do you suppose we get in? I see no doors."

Without responding, he began to skirt the perimeter of the ship. It was nearly as wide as a city block, so he moved fast. Fast enough to be out of earshot.

But Madame wouldn't let him. She followed close

behind, pecking at his patience with little annoyed noises. Starts of sentences that she couldn't finish.

Halfway around the ship, Cassius felt the metal tremble under his fingers.

Shocked, he bolted back and stared at the underside of the vessel, which now climbed above their heads, dwarfing them in an enormous shadow.

Something blossomed far above them. Cassius watched as a ring of steam issued from the perimeter of the ship, half a mile up. It emanated from somewhere within. Streams of white clouds flowed along the surface of the metal, far enough in the sky that it didn't immediately threaten them. Still, something was happening. Cassius wanted to see it closer.

The steam stopped suddenly. It evaporated in the air, silent and invisible.

Madame took a step back, keeping her eyes on the ship. "What was that all about?"

Cassius shook his head.

Before he could speak, something new issued from the metal.

It dripped from within—long black torrents that spilled down the sides of the craft like an overflowing cup. It clung to the metal as it descended. At the angle it fell, it should have dripped right down to the earth, but something held it in place.

"Oil?" Madame squinted to better focus.

"No," Cassius said. He knew exactly what the substance

was. Only one thing could be so pure in its void of color, so otherworldly in its movement. He'd fought for his life against it only weeks ago. Under the control of the right Shifter, it was incredibly dangerous.

Ridium.

He'd recognize it anywhere. Impossibly black, it came down in thick tendrils—dozens around the perimeter of the ship. It didn't exist naturally on Earth, only on Haven. And it could be used for almost anything. Most notably: killing.

It slid down in silence until it reached the ground. Cassius backed up, pushing Madame with him. He feared it would stretch toward them and engulf their bodies. Instead, it plunged into the dirt, coursing under the crust until it disappeared completely.

Madame slid in front of him to get a better look.

"It's everywhere," Cassius said. "Matigo had it buried on Earth during the Scarlet Bombings. The red mist may have covered the atmosphere, but it was black seeping in our soil. He can control it. Build weapons. Slice us in two. Anything. I'd step away if I were you."

She turned to glance at him, confusion on her face. "This is the substance that once formed your bracelet, isn't it?"

He nodded. "And if there's a Shifter around, we're as good as dead."

Eva came rushing around the corner of the ship, careful not to get too close to the still-streaming Ridium. "I tried calling Fisher." She glanced at the thick stuff, face souring. "What's it doing now?"

"Another Ridium deposit," Cassius answered. "We shouldn't stay in one place for too long, though. Remember what happened outside of the swarm?"

Eva winced, glancing at the ground. "Black blades."

Cassius remembered watching Matigo's son, Theo, summon the element from the ground, fatally stabbing a group of Skyship Agents in the process. "We don't want to end up like them."

She took a deep breath. "Fisher wasn't there, Cassius." She bit her lip. "Nobody answered when I called."

"You try Avery?"

"Nobody," she said.

"Skandar?"

"I tried every line I could think of trying."

Madame backed away from the vessel. "They were on the Surface, at least. The Authority couldn't have brought them down."

Eva shook her head. "You better be right."

As the last of the Ridium cascaded into the ground, everything fell still.

Cassius balled his hands. "We're not safe out here, but we can't fly, either. We're going inside." He gritted his teeth and conjured fire. "Get behind me."

"Are you crazy?" Madame said. "It's a shot in the dark, Cassius."

She was right, of course, but he'd learned never to

assume he knew anything about how Haven or the Authority worked.

Sparks along his fingers ignited into a small fireball, searing the air around him. A blast at this close a range might be enough to make a dent in the ship's surface.

He'd never find out. Before any fire left his hand, the wall collapsed in front of him.

Or rather, it opened up.

Metal folded on itself, though Cassius noticed no lines or seams as it moved. It was almost as if it disappeared—evaporated—right before their eyes.

When the last of the metal had retreated, they were left with an oval-shaped opening, the size of a large door. Beyond that were a set of stairs, rising steep into the darkness of the vessel.

It was too easy. A trap?

He turned to Madame to ask her.

He didn't get a chance. An incredible suction issued from beyond the door, sudden and very powerful. It took Cassius off guard. Nobody could do anything.

His feet soon left the ground, no longer under his control. One by one, they were sucked through the door and into the ship.

16

I muffle a scream as the stranger drags me through the sky, propelled so fast that my mind can't keep up with the horror and adrenaline pumping through the rest of me. My stomach doesn't even have time to be sick.

He released my shoulder some time ago, and now grips onto my hand as he pulls me onward. Terrified of falling, I clutch both hands around his fingers. His grip is steel tight, unwilling to let me go.

The world tilts and flips underneath as he brings us in a sudden loop, heading back down to the Surface.

Three feet away, he releases his hold on me.

I collide with the dirt, rolling on my side several times. When I finally settle, my clothes and hair are covered in brown dust.

I lie on my stomach, exhausted both physically and mentally. The seesaw sickness of my sudden escape/kidnapping catches up to me and threatens to bring nausea with it. Instead, I cough, which only sends more dust up my throat as I gasp for air. By the time I work my way to a sitting position, the man is standing right in front of me.

He stares down, intense curiosity in the one eye that's

not covered by the patch. After a moment, he offers a hand to help me up. When I grab hold again, I'm brought to my feet with a great lurch, faster and stronger than I would have done on my own.

"What the hell?!?" I start shouting without even realizing what I must sound like to the guy. "You left Avery back there! She could be—"

The man holds up a hand, palm out. I flinch. The gesture quiets me mid-sentence, just from the intensity of it. The next words come out far more reserved. "We have to go back and get her. She's important to me."

Without a word, the stranger brings down his hand, then turns and moves away, feet tromping through the dust. I glance behind my shoulder. We're surrounded by desert in all directions. I can't even see hints of Fringe towns in the distance. Nothing but flat, brown land and equally brown hills, though they're so out of reach I might just be imagining them.

I shift my attention back to the stranger. "Hey!" I stagger after him. "Hey, what are you—?"

He plants his feet and turns. He's laughing.

"What's so funny?" I stare up at his face. The top of my head comes up to his shoulders. I feel like I'm standing in a hole. "This isn't something to laugh at. Those things back there were gonna kill us. Avery's still—"

"You can take a moment to regain your bearings." His voice rumbles through me, like he's amplified somehow— wearing a mic. It's not that he's loud, because he isn't. But there's a presence in the way he speaks, kind of like Captain Alkine back home.

"Wh-who are you?"

His half smile settles into a frown.

"You're a Drifter," I continue. "Obviously."

His expression remains fixed.

I rub a cloud of dust from my shoulder. "And a totally psychotic one, from the looks of it."

He crosses his arms, appraising me for a moment before speaking. "What were you doing in that train?" He turns and continues to tromp through the desert.

"I didn't plan to be there." I follow him. "We were kidnapped by the Authority."

He stops. "I saw what you did in that city, Pearlbreaker."

"Yeah. It wasn't enough."

"It was something," he says. "But you're right, not nearly enough." He resumes his pace.

"Are you just gonna keep walking like this?"

"We gain nothing by standing still," he replies. "We need to find your brother."

"No," I say. "We need to find Avery."

The man sighs. "I needed to get you away from those soldiers. There wasn't time to carry both of—"

"We go back," I interrupt. "It's not up for discussion."

"Do you suppose that train will simply stop? Your friend will be carried away with it, Authority or no Authority."

He's wrong. I know Avery well enough. She won't stay

in that open train car, captive. Either she'll bust through the door or jump out the back.

"We need to find your brother," the man repeats.

I glance up at him, doing my best to match his pace. "Cassius? How do you know about him?"

"Every Drifter knows about him," he says. "*And* you."

"So you are a Drifter, then. With the Resistance?"

The man laughs again. "You're too trusting. Where is Cassius now?"

"He's on Skyship Atlas."

"Too trusting," he repeats, shaking his head. Then he stops and points at the blanket of blue above us. "Look above you. Do you see anything in the sky? Your ships have been leveled—pulled to the ground. Defeated."

I bring my eyes away from the sky, looking up at him once more. "You're here to help?"

"I'll do what I can," he says. "But there's only one way to end this for good. And I need the both of you together."

"You still haven't told me who you are."

He frowns. "We can retrace our steps, if we must. Find your friend. Then, we need to talk about your brother. When I developed the Pearl technology, I allowed for a failsafe—"

"Wait." My head spins. I stare at his face, but his head's bowed, obscuring much of it. "*You* developed—?"

"Yes, Jesse." He raises his head and his eye meets mine. "For my sons."

"Then you're—"

"It's comforting to finally see you," he interrupts, "after so many years apart."

We're silent for a moment, which is fine because I can't even form words. Instead, a chuckle spills out of my lips. I don't even realize I'm doing it, and I'm not quite sure why, either.

My father's brows rise, and for a moment I think that he's going to scold me. Then he smiles.

I swallow. My mouth is dry. "You're not serious. No way."

His smile fades. "I don't joke about such things. Of course, you don't know me well enough to understand that." He pauses. "My name is Savon. Number three-thousand-thirty-eight. I've been waiting to find you. For as long as I can remember."

17

The suction receded and Cassius found himself deposited in a dark, circular room. Whatever traction beam had pulled them into the strange vessel had known not to pull them too far. He landed feetfirst on the ground. Even so, he found himself crumbling under his own weight. He crashed to the ground before his body adjusted.

Eva laid next to him, forcing herself up. "The gravity's different. How's that possible?"

Madame straightened her back. She was the first to stand completely. "We're inside of an alien ship. I'd think anything's possible."

Cassius spun slowly around, taking in their surroundings. They'd landed in the center of a wide disc. On first inspection, the material below his feet looked like a simple, dull metal. But when he put weight on it, he found that it was somewhat pliable, conforming to his every shift in balance.

The walls were of a similar material, lit by a dim ring that emanated from somewhere in the middle. Behind him, stretching into the darkness, was a ramp. No signs or symbols to tell him where it led, but the only other way out was the doorway they had come through.

Madame moved to his side, struggling with the increased gravity. "We'd do best to escape while we still can."

"No way," he replied. "We're inside. We've got a chance to do some damage."

"Or get ourselves killed," she countered. "An attack without strategy is a guaranteed—"

"Then leave if you want. Doesn't matter to me."

"Cassius..."

He stepped closer to the ramp, marveling at the cushioned substance under his feet. It felt like stepping on damp moss. He tapped his foot on the ground. The floor was hard. Foamy, but hard.

Eva followed behind, cautiously glancing around. "I should've grabbed a weapon. We're unarmed."

"I don't see anything to fight against," Cassius whispered as he took his first step onto the ramp. The metal became tough and unyielding. In a way, it reassured him. At least it didn't feel like the entire thing was going to pull him in.

He quickened his pace. The ramp provided no railings or edges to grip onto, but he managed to ascend its steep slope with ease. The extra gravity kept his feet stuck to the ground each time he planted them.

The farther he worked his way up, the more the light behind him disappeared. Stretching his arms in front of him, he hit a corner, then turned to accommodate the twist. The ramp's slope lessened until he arrived on a flat platform.

A dim red light blinked several feet ahead, hanging in the darkness.

Looking behind him, Cassius realized that turning the corner had disconnected him from the chamber below. He glanced back at the flashing red. It looked almost like a tiny Pearl, but from what he could tell it was flat—a circle affixed to a wall or door.

Without hesitation, he moved forward and laid his hand over it. Nothing.

He feared warmth or, even worse, electrical shock. Maybe a trigger for some kind of attack.

Still...

Taking a deep breath, he pushed on the red with the palm of his hand.

Immediately, the wall crumbled before him, revealing cracks that expanded into a full, door-sized rectangle. He shielded his eyes from the oncoming glare. Compared to the pitch black around him, it felt like a sudden stab in the eyes.

He heard Madame's voice from far below. "Cassius, is everything okay?"

He let his arm fall from over his eyes and peered into the corridor beyond. "I think so," he muttered back.

Chunks of wall laid in front of him on the floor. He watched in amazement as they began to tremble, then slink into the corridor. The pieces danced along the floor before they were sucked into the far wall, melting and disappearing into metal. In seconds, they were gone. The ship had fed on itself.

He cautiously stepped through the opening. The corridor was remarkably silent—the kind of stillness that made him instantly anxious. Where were the people? Where was the rumbling of the temp control or the humming of onboard computer systems? From what he'd seen on the outside, the vessel was big enough to house hundreds. Yet there hadn't been a single sign of life since it landed.

He reminded himself of the streams of Ridium that had coursed into the ground from the vessel's outer walls. Maybe that was its only purpose. But it didn't make sense. There were already large deposits of Ridium under the surface of the Earth from the Scarlet Bombings long ago. How much did the Authority need?

Someone grabbed his shoulder, startling him from his thoughts.

He jumped, despite himself, and turned to see Madame. Despite clenching his shoulder with her hand, she didn't make eye contact. She stared intently at the corridor beyond.

"Last chance, Cassius," she whispered. "The deeper you go—"

He pulled forward, away from her. She followed into the hallway, along with Eva. The moment they had all safely emerged from the darkness, the opening behind them sealed.

Beads of what looked like liquid metal sucked into

place, like some sort of invisible vacuum had pulled them together. In less than a second, there was no door left.

Eva banged her fist against the newly formed metal before turning. "It's a trap."

Cassius shook his head. "If it was a trap, we'd be dead by now."

As if on cue, he felt his foot begin to sink into the ground. Unlike the strange gravity in the dark room, this time the metal came up at him, wrapping itself around his ankle. He tried to kick free, but the grip was too tight.

"What the—?" Eva stumbled sideways before the ship cemented her in place.

"It's alive." Cassius looked down at his feet, watching the metal fall still. He could see the tips of his boots, but nothing from there to his ankles.

Madame grabbed hold of her knee and tried to pull herself up, to no avail. "That's ridiculous. This can't be—"

"I was in a ship like this," Cassius said. "Before Altair. Theo made it from Ridium. He could control the entire thing."

Eva wriggled her body, trying to break free. "But this isn't Ridium."

The walls shifted sideways. At least that's the way it looked to Cassius at first. The entire journey up to the corridor had disoriented his mind. It took a moment before he realized that the walls hadn't moved at all. It was the floor.

The ground shuttled them along, pushing all three

forward through the corridor, their feet never leaving the ground.

The floor slanted upward. They turned a corner. The metal underfoot shifted to accommodate every move, like a conveyer belt that wouldn't let them go.

"It isn't stopping!" Madame held her arms out, afraid to lose balance.

There were no windows in the vessel, and every corridor looked the same. They sped up. Soon, it became impossible to tell how far they'd ascended.

Cassius noticed the turns in directions become more and more frequent. Each level of the ship decreased in diameter until every move felt like part of a circle. Too much of this and he'd be sick.

Finally, after several dozen of these loops, the ship released its hold on them.

Cassius was thrown forward. He reached out his hands to break his fall. The corridor spun.

Eva brought herself to her knees, rubbing her bruised shoulder. "And the point of that was...?"

"Disorient us," Madame said. "We've no weapons, and now we don't even know which way is which."

"All of these corridors are identical." Cassius stood, closing his eyes to catch his bearings. Then, he strode to the nearest wall and laid his hand against it. Immediately, the entire thing gave way. Beads of metal dripped in a crater around his hand and spread quickly until he'd carved a large opening.

He stepped back, eyes wide. "It's responding to my touch."

Eva moved to his side. "It didn't do anything when I banged against it."

"You're from Earth," he replied. "It must be designed to—"

"Watch out!" Madame grabbed his arm and forced him to the floor, just as a missile launched from somewhere beyond the opening, straight at them.

They hit the ground as the dark missile blasted into the wall behind them, shattering into a thousand black daggers.

The pricks of Ridium rained down, clinking against the metal floor like broken china.

Cassius pulled himself forward on his belly, past the opening, before any of the knives could lodge themselves into his body. Eva rolled to the side, evading most of them.

Madame didn't have time.

Cassius heard her cry out in pain as one of the daggers connected with her leg, slicing through flesh on its way to the ground.

Frantically, he pulled her forward, away from the chaos. Rushing to her side, he watched the last of the Ridium wriggle from her wounded leg and melt away from her, leaving a trail of dark blood.

"Cassius!" she cried.

"Your blazer." He motioned for her to hand it to him, keeping one eye on the blood now gushing from her leg. He wasn't sure if he'd ever seen Madame bleed before.

He helped her out of her coat, then rolled it up to fashion a tourniquet and quickly tied it around her leg.

She pulled herself to a sitting position against the wall, breathing hard.

"You'll live," Cassius said.

Eva scrambled around the corner, away from what was left of the Ridium missile. "We're dead. This is suicide."

"It's not." He stood, glancing to his right. They stood in a small room, connecting the corridor they'd come from with another. Everywhere he looked had the illusion of sunlight, but he couldn't tell where it was coming from.

"I can't walk, Cassius." Madame grimaced. "It would only—"

He nodded. "Let me try something." He moved to the opening and laid his hand on what was left of the wall. Instantly, the hole closed up and they were sealed in. He turned back. "I can definitely control it."

Madame stared at him with a pained expression. "What are you saying?"

"I have to see what else is in here. We've come this far."

She frowned. "Did you hear me? I can't walk!"

"Then stay here," he countered. "You're safe enough. Clearly there's nobody here to find you."

Eva winced. "Except that giant missile that just about pulverized us."

"Stay with her," he said. "Make sure no one comes. I'm going up. If there's a chance I might be able to do something here—"

Eva shook her head. "This isn't what I signed up for. Since when do I care—?"

"Stand guard. Or you'll deal with me." He took a deep breath. "Give me fifteen minutes, okay? If I'm not back by then, you can come looking for me. You can even leave *her*." He held up his hand. "Or I can seal the two of you in here, with no way out."

She sighed, then took a seat across from Madame.

Cassius nodded. "I thought so."

Then, without giving either the chance to argue, he raced from the room and around the corner, eyes open for missiles or anything else the Authority might throw at him.

18

I back away from Savon. "This isn't real. How can this be happening?"

"Jesse—" He holds out his massive, gloved hand. It's like he could crush me with it.

"All this time ... every Pearl that fell ... I thought it might be the one that brought you to Earth ... "

"Calm down," he coaxes.

"Calm down? My father ... the guy I didn't even know existed anymore ... shows up out of the blue and you want me to calm down?"

He shakes his head. "The excitability comes from your mother. Look, if we were in a position to sit down and have a long, in-depth talk, I'd be happy to do so. As it stands ... " He stops. I glance up and watch him stride toward me, arms out. Before I realize it, he's got me in an embrace. His bulky arms squeeze tight around my shoulders, so much that I can't really lift my arms and hug him back.

I remember one of the Academy teachers spending an entire afternoon telling us about what they called the "emotional stages" of trauma. Death wasn't exactly a rare thing in our line of work, so they'd wanted to prepare us for anything.

No one's died. But even so, I feel like I'm traveling through a hundred stages—landmark after landmark in the space of a few minutes. Shock. Excitement. Intimidation. Disbelief. Even a little bit of anger. My mind doesn't know how to fit my father in. Try as I might, the thought of him standing here won't sink in completely.

He lets go of me, steps back, and stares. I can't meet his gaze for more than a second, even though I want to.

"What about…" I start. "What about Mom? Is she with you?"

"No," he replies quickly. "We were separated before we left Haven. We lost contact." He pauses, bowing his head. "I don't know, Jesse."

"Do you think she—?"

"I don't know." He cuts me off in a way that signals the end to the conversation.

I shake my head, trying to push away the increasing dizziness I feel. "This is a lot to take in."

He gives an awkward smile. "Did you think I'd been killed? Come now, you should expect better from your father."

"I didn't know what to think." I briefly meet his eyes. "Oh, man…"

He lays a hand on my shoulder. I practically crumble under him. "Jesse. I can't pretend to know what it was like for you, all these years raising yourself."

"I wasn't—"

"You and Cassius were alone. Dependent on the whims of humans your mother and I never had the opportunity to meet. You're incredibly strong. Incredibly resourceful. I couldn't have done what you have."

My shoulders tense. Nobody's ever spoken to me like this. No one's ever called me strong, or looked up to me as a survivor. I don't know how to take it, but I know that it ignites something inside of me that I've never felt before.

"I ... I only learned about you a couple months ago."

He brings his hand back to his hip. "Then there's a lot for you to know. But stories will have to wait. We need to find your brother and make a stand against the Authority. It's the only way."

"But—"

"Don't tell me you're the kind of man who takes the easy route," he interrupts. "Who shirks his responsibilities." I shrug.

Savon nods. "I thought not. Even without my direct influence, you've still got my blood running through you. That ought to be more than enough."

"I don't—" I pause, stumbling on my words. "How did you find me?"

He looks to the sky. "I came to this world several days ago. Confused and unbalanced. I didn't know how I'd find you or Cassius until the explosion you unleashed in that city. It was a happy coincidence that I was close enough to feel it. That much Pearl energy doesn't go unnoticed, especially by the one who created it."

"I … I drew you to me?"

His good eye meets mine, staring.

"Well," I mutter. "If I knew it would've been that easy … "

"Nothing's ever easy. And nothing happens just because."

An awkward silence hangs between us. I picture the man in the photograph, the one Cassius and I had found on our first trip to Seattle. I can't believe I hadn't recognized him sooner. The eye patch is new, probably the result of some battle on Haven, but the basic features match. This is my father. The guy I've been waiting to find ever since I learned my true identity.

And now that I've found him, what am I supposed to do?

I never allowed myself to imagine this moment. I could've rehearsed it, scripted something to say. But even if I had something written down, I'm sure the words would fail me now. I was so used to being a ward of the Academy.

Savon grabs my shoulder again. "Listen, Jesse. I don't want to be a distraction. I know this is sudden, and I know we've been separated for many years, but we're going to have to pull ourselves together. Stay strong in the face of this invasion." He pauses. "Do you know where Cassius is?"

I force my mind to stop circling my unfinished thoughts. Cassius.

Even thinking his name gives me an anchor—pulls me back to the reality at hand. "They were headed to Atlas."

I catch myself. "But if the Skyships sank ... oh god, they might have been on the ship!"

"We'll go there regardless," Savon responds. "We might be able to help." He steps back, as if he's prepared to walk across the entire country to get there.

"But—"

"We don't have a lot of time."

"Avery," I continue. "You promised."

He stops. "Yes. Your friend."

"If we can stop and check—"

"Tell me this," he interrupts. "Do you have access to transportation?"

"You mean a shuttle?"

He nods.

I think back to Portland—our descent to the outskirts of the landing pad. Then I remember Skandar. "Oh my god." The words fall out of my mouth before I realize it. "What if the Authority got Skandar?"

The question doesn't seem to register with my father. Either that, or he just chooses to ignore it.

I stare up at him for a moment, then back to the ground. "We might have a shuttle. My friend back in Portland has our communicator ... a direct link to Cassius. If he's okay, he'll answer. That's probably the best chance we have of finding exactly where he is."

Savon appraises me in silence before speaking. "Very well. Stick out your hand."

"What?"

He moves his own hand forward, spreading apart the fingers. "Just do it."

Hesitantly, I raise my right hand and hold it outstretched. It's like we're about to do some weird alien handshake. Of course, under the circumstances, that might be *exactly* what we're about to do.

He clears his throat. "Have you driven?"

"I don't know what you mean."

"Ships, shuttles, transport."

"Oh." My mind flashes back to training modules—the few times I've actually taken the wheel on Academy ships. I don't have the heart to tell him how unsuccessful I was. "Sure."

"This is similar." He pushes the palm of his hand against mine. Instantly I feel a suction, like our skin is melding together. The last time I felt something like this was when Cassius and I first met on the rooftop in Syracuse. After the strange suction of our hands, I'd started developing my Pearlbreaking powers.

"What are you doing?"

"I have limited Pearl Transport Energy left inside of me. Most Drifters would have used theirs up within minutes, wasting it all in a blind panic. But I'm not most Drifters. Not only can I harness it, but I can transfer some to you."

The suction quickly amps up. Another few seconds and it's all I can do to keep my feet on the ground. But standing in front of him, I don't want to slip even an inch.

"It feels warm," I manage. "Like when I break a Pearl."

He nods. "It's exactly the same. Only up until this point, you haven't been taught how to harness the energy for flight."

"Flight?!?"

"The effects will be short-lived," he continues, "but it'll be enough to give you the boost that I'm currently enjoying. Now, pretend that your body is a shuttle. If you'd like to move left, roll to the left. If you want to slow down, lower your feet. Straight arms and legs will allow for faster transport."

I swallow. "I'm not so sure this is a good idea."

"I'm not going to carry you again," he says. "Not when this option is available to us."

"But you haven't seen me in action," I interrupt. "Sometimes I have trouble *walking*."

"You're my son. I have the highest expectations."

"Well ... " I stop myself. If I was talking to anyone else—Captain Alkine, Eva, Mrs. Dembo—I'd have no problem telling them the truth. I'd freely raise my hand and admit that I'm a klutz ... a total screwup. But the way he looks at me, the *no-is-not-an-answer* glare in his eye, makes it impossible.

The suction settles down. When it stops, we're forced apart. Savon seems to expect it, and has no trouble standing his ground. Meanwhile, I'm thrown backward, off my feet. I land on my butt, several feet away.

Savon ignores this. "Ready?"

"I don't kno—"

He raises his right hand into the air, as if conducting

music. Instantly I feel a tug on my shoulders. Before I can react, I'm yanked into the sky, tumbling up in curlicues.

"What the hell?"

Savon darts into the air beside me. "Straighten your body! Concentrate!"

The words barely register as they're whipped away by the wind. Still, I manage to force my legs down. It feels horribly unnatural to extend them without feeling anything underfoot.

This at least stops me spiraling. But it's not enough to correct my ascent completely. My arms plunge in diagonals at my sides. When I move them closer to my body, I speed to a breakneck pace. This freaks me out, so I open them again, which slows me so suddenly that I nearly suffer whiplash.

I don't look down. I know that the ground is mass far away by now, but I don't want to see it. It's easier to picture this as a simulation, that if I were to press a button the whole thing would fade away and I'd land safely on a cushion.

Savon loops by, stopping right in front of me, matching my pace.

"Relax." He shouts to be heard above the wind. "The more you panic, the more difficult you'll make this on yourself. I'm about to release my hold on you. Focus on staying airborne. Trust that the energy will guide you."

I wince. He doesn't give me a second to prepare before he brings his hand back to his side. Immediately I take a slight tumble, sinking toward the ground. It's my fear of falling that eventually steadies me. I ball my fists and concentrate on the energy whirring inside of me. I imagine it as a protective shield, a solid disc beneath my feet. I picture green strands of energy forming from the top of my head, pulling me up like ropes. And before I know it, I'm level with my father once more.

I'm doing it. I'm actually flying.

Savon laughs, then points toward the horizon on the right. "This way. Do you think you can follow me?"

My entire body shakes. I keep my arms stretched away from my body, feet firmly pointed down. "I can try."

"Don't try," he says. "No son of mine *tries*. We *do*."

With that, he hurtles forward through the air, until he's a distant speck.

I close my eyes, take deep breaths, and try to steady my nerves. When I feel less like I'm going to puke up my life, I tilt forward. Then come the arms. Before I know it, I'm a pointed arrow, bolting through the sky just as fast as any ship.

Only there's nothing to protect me.

Cutting through the air is painful, like my body's drilling through a wall. I keep my head forward, my eyes force closed, so I have to look down.

It's not that I haven't fallen from heights before. I have, and far more often than anybody my age should have. But those times, I never had the luxury of staring at the Surface so long, unencumbered by windshields or glass.

The brown land stretches below me like a vast, dirt-ridden carpet. I see Fringe Towns every so often, though they look like ant farms from so high up.

I wait for my body to lurch downward—for the Pearl energy to fail and send me plummeting to the ground. But each second that passes brings with it more security. The nerves begin to die down. The uncertainty all but vanishes, replaced by an exuberance—the kind I haven't felt in months. For a moment, I feel brave.

I venture a glance forward to see Savon. He's nothing but a dark dot from my view, but I'm getting closer to him. Against all odds, I'm keeping up.

I laugh, even though the wind sweeps it away immediately. Despite the things that have happened, despite the danger and uncertainty that's surrounding us. Despite Avery and the others. I can't help myself. I feel bad about it, but I can't stop.

I point my fingers and go faster. I dip right to turn, then back again.

In moments I'm side by side with Savon.

If I can do this, I can do anything. Me and my father, my father whom I thought I'd never see again. We're unstoppable—higher than any bird. We have the sky all to ourselves, and a vantage point above any enemy.

We'll fight together, me and my dad.

The Authority's not going to know what hit it.

19

Crash.

The noise caused Cassius to freeze. He'd nearly scaled the entire vessel without trouble. It was too good to last.

He balled his fists at this sides, ready to conjure fire if needed. His breathing caught up to him, shallow and exhausted.

The corridor became quiet once more, even as the echo of the strange crash rippled through the spiraled corridors.

A figure stumbled forward, from around the corner. Cassius took one step back before stopping himself.

The Drifter reminded him of the one that had found its way into the Nevada bunker. Darkly dressed, with indentations on the armor that stretched from his shoulders to his wrists. But the way he slouched and staggered, Cassius realized immediately that he'd been weakened. Disoriented.

Once in clear view, the Authority foot soldier straightened his back. For the first time, Cassius could see his crimson eyes.

Cassius raised his chin, refusing to show weakness. "Who are you?"

The soldier planted his feet, fingers clenching and unclenching. Nothing more.

"English." Cassius shook his head. "You've got no idea what I'm saying, do you?"

As if in response, a black orb—the size of a bowling ball—began to form behind the soldier. He'd most likely had Ridium stored in a belt or pocket, though the substance appeared to have been pulled from nowhere.

The dark sphere lobbed at Cassius.

He ducked, moving to the side until his shoulder pushed against the wall. The ball flew well over his head and froze in the air, several feet behind him. He turned to watch it burst and expand into a flat surface—a dark wall that perfectly fit the width of the corridor, sealing any possible exit.

"So you're a Shifter." Cassius turned back. "I've been waiting to fight one of you guys again."

He felt the sparks move between his fingers. Another moment and his fists burst into flames. It felt good to let loose without concern. A proper brawl.

The soldier summoned another stash of Ridium from behind him, forging a black whip that shot through the air like a viper.

Cassius crouched, dodging the Ridium and pushing off against the wall to deliver a jet of fire, engulfing the soldier's body.

The soldier staggered back. The whip melted into drips on the ground.

Cassius raised his fists to deliver another blow.

The black drops flew up at him, pelting his back. He fell to his knees as the Ridium coalesced around the soldier's body. It easily snuffed any remaining flames before spreading to the soldier's extremities, encasing him in a shiny shell of black. Cassius had seen it happen before. Theo had pulled the same trick on Skyship Altair. It had made him nearly unstoppable.

Gritting his teeth, Cassius pushed up and sprinted toward the creature. He kept his elbows out, protecting his torso, and rammed into the soldier's chest. Barreling forward, he didn't pause to see what effect he'd had. Instead, he rounded the corner.

The sharp turns of the corridor grew more constricting. He used the walls as a guide, trying to keep himself from getting too dizzy.

Another soldier.

He almost ran into the second guy, but caught himself just in time to deliver a roundhouse kick.

The Drifter went down immediately, but he knew the first one would still be a problem.

Sure enough, a narrow band of Ridium shot after him, coiling around his wrist with incredible strength.

It yanked, pulling him back with enough force that it felt like his arm was going to pop off. A second tendril wrapped around his neck, choking him. He hit the floor. The coils dragged him on his back, toward the waiting soldier.

Cassius tugged at the Ridium frantically, stealing precious breaths when he could.

The first soldier said something to the second in the Haven language. He had a slick, oily voice—snakelike, but harder. More menacing.

Pressing his hands on the Ridium that constricted around his neck, Cassius let his body explode. He'd been aiming for something more focused, but ended up with a blast not unlike the first time he'd burst into flames, back in his dorm room at the Lodge.

The fire engulfed the entirety of the corridor, knocking away both soldiers. It did little to the walls, which seemed to absorb the brunt of the blaze until the flames dissipated altogether.

When it was over, his clothing was tattered and seared. He let his arms fall to his sides and heaved air into his lungs. He lay there a moment, too exhausted to move.

The corridor fell silent again. The soldiers were dead.

When he was finally able to lift himself, he staggered to his feet, ripped an annoying strip of what used to he his shirt sleeve from his shoulder, and moved forward.

The soldiers had attacked instantly, without provocation. They'd been guarding something.

One last turn and the hallway expanded into a wide, circular room. For the first time since entering the vessel, there were windows. Wide portholes wound all the way around the large space, offering a 360-degree view of the world outside.

Immediately, Cassius could tell that something was wrong. While the windows to his left offered an unencumbered view of the sky, the ones on his right looked straight down at the brown Surface.

He remembered seeing the ship from the outside. It had landed at a diagonal, drilled into the ground. The sight from the windows instantly threw him. The floor underfoot clearly wasn't level, but something about the gravity made it feel so.

The room itself was nearly empty, save for an oval platform that rose from the ground at the center. A faint glow issued from the platform, hitting the low ceiling. Though Cassius couldn't see much from his position on the sidelines, he imagined a variety of recessed electronics or computers inside. He'd need to investigate.

He glanced around, making sure that no more soldiers were on their way. He couldn't imagine that a ship so enormous would have been guarded by just a pair of Drifters. Wasn't there an alarm system? Backup of some kind?

Cautiously, he approached the center platform. He kept his footsteps silent.

Once he was close enough to grip onto the edge, he leaned over and took a look at the source of the faint light.

Just as he'd suspected. Computers.

Or at least he assumed they were computers. He couldn't tell exactly *what* they were. Some flashed, but not from screens like he was used to. The lights seemed to come directly from the surface of the platform itself. More than that, they circled around on top of the metal, like small fish or tadpoles. Like they were alive.

Amongst the moving glow rested several stationary, diamond-shaped lights. They shone darker—almost like the black abyss of Ridium, yet somehow reflective. Cassius couldn't quite understand what he was looking at. He'd never seen a color like it on Earth.

He reached out a finger to touch the nearest diamond. A ridge of textured material surrounded it.

He winced, expecting an electric shock or pulse of light. Nothing happened.

He pressed harder. Maybe it wasn't a button after all.

He ran his fingers up and down, then tried to catch one of the strange moving lights. They began to pulse. He stepped closer, watching the platform's strange rhythm. It was captivating, so much so that he forgot to glance behind him.

Then, everything stopped. The pulse died. The lights froze.

He watched a sinkhole form in the middle of the platform. He had to remind himself that this was metal he was looking at. It behaved like sand. Quicksand. For a moment, he feared it would keep expanding—swallow him up along with the lights.

Instead, the platform blossomed.

Cassius stumbled back. A pillar as thick as a tree trunk grew from the opening at the center, on its way to the ceiling. As it silently spread upward, compartments around the perimeter slid open, revealing shelves of tiny metal cubes.

Cassius recognized them immediately. The Drifter Ryel had carried one before he died.

Senso-cubes, used on Haven to catalog important memories of life on the planet.

When activated, each tiny cube displayed an immersive recreation of whatever memory it stored. He remembered being sucked into a particularly harrowing scene several weeks ago. That was the first time he had heard the voice of Matigo, the Authority's leader. Unfortunately, his voice and body had been obscured.

The thick pillar shuddered to a stop as soon as it touched the ceiling of the room. Cassius peered up, wondering just how many cubes were inside, and what they meant. Were they catalogued by the Authority themselves, or stolen from members of the Resistance? Either way, they could contain valuable information. They'd been stored carefully, hidden within the seemingly impenetrable vessel. Regardless of what memories were inside, Cassius knew that they must be important. Or dangerous. But beyond that, any snapshot of his home planet was important to *him*.

Cautious to dodge as many frozen lights as he could, he lifted himself onto the platform.

That was when he felt it—a cold, sickly sensation in his gut.

He paused, unsure of what had suddenly changed. He looked to his feet, then glanced at the lights below him.

They were moving again. They swirled around his ankles like a whirlpool.

The rest of the ground soon joined them, rumbling with the furor of an earthquake. The walls shook.

Cassius spun, trying to make out what was happening. The room remained empty of soldiers, but the metal shifted, alive.

Then a rupture spread across the ceiling. Crack and boom, so loud that it resonated in his chest.

He froze.

The ceiling exploded.

20

Savon and I are so silent that Avery doesn't even notice us until we set down in the center of the Chute tracks.

I open my mouth to say her name. But before I can make any more than a small noise, she turns, strides toward me, and pushes on my chest.

Taken by surprise, I stumble back and nearly collide with my father. The optimist in me was expecting a hug or maybe even a kiss. Instead, she kicks the dirt, clearly rattled from spending time alone in the Fringes.

"God, Fisher!" She swats me again. "Just when I think I've got you back, you get yourself kidnapped again. I can't keep doing this!"

"It's okay." I grab her shoulder. "Avery, I'm fine."

She shakes her head. "I jumped from the train. Is that the stupidest thing you've ever heard? I don't know what I thought I was gonna do when I landed here. Drag myself to a Fringe Town? There aren't even any in sight!"

"Calm down," I say, pulling her closer in a tight embrace. "Here."

"You've gotta stop it," she whispers in my ear. "We can't

keep getting torn from each other. I was sure you were gone. I was sure I was gonna die alone out here."

"It's okay. I'm back, and I wasn't ever in any danger." I release my grip on her and glance over my shoulder. "Avery. This is ... I can't believe I'm saying this ... this guy is my father."

The words feel strange coming out, like someone else is saying them.

Avery pivots, wiping the dust from her face as she stares at Savon. "No way."

"It's crazy, right? He followed me from the city. He's actually here, Avery! Right when we need him."

"That's ... " She grabs my shoulder, her terror beginning to fade. "That's amazing, Jesse."

Savon gives a slight bow. "A pleasure to meet you. I'm afraid—"

"You broke from a Pearl? You came all the way from Haven?"

He crosses his arms. "I'm afraid we're on a schedule. I know you have many questions, but now"—he glances at the skies—"while we're exposed like this ... now is not the time."

Avery raises an eyebrow. "So, you're the guy who sent Jesse to Earth?"

Savon nods.

"Hmm ... " She glances back at me before appraising him once more. "I've got some things I wanna say to you."

"And I'm sure I'd love to hear them when this is all over." He pauses. "You're not Haven-born."

"Yeah, so?"

"If I give you Pearl energy—provided I have any left to give—it would likely kill you. It certainly wouldn't give you the ability to fly. I'll have to carry you."

Avery shoots me a confused look.

I bite my lip. "We sort of … flew back to you."

Her eyes narrow. "*You* flew?"

"I know," I say. "It's weird. But trust him, he's family. He won't drop you."

She sighs. "Honestly, just get me out of the Fringes. Where are we going?"

"Back to Portland," I reply.

"Goodie." She frowns. "My favorite."

―――――

I remember exactly where our shuttle was parked.

It's not there.

We touch down on the Surface, just below the landing pad, which is remarkably unscathed compared to the rest of the city. Avery stumbles forward as Savon lets her go, disoriented from the breakneck pace we took on our flight back to the city. I'm beginning to flag, myself. I feel the energy fading inside of me. Even though the thought of flying doesn't horrify me anymore, I'm not sure I'd have enough power to do it for much longer anyway.

This late in the afternoon, the sun is unforgiving. It heats the dirt to the point where it becomes painful to stay in one place for too long.

Savon stands behind us, not sweating or winded or visibly uncomfortable in the least. Meanwhile, my heart is doing loop-de-loops and my lungs are working overtime to keep up with my rapid breathing. I can almost hear the sizzle of my skin being burnt.

Avery turns, shaking her head. "My god, look at the city."

I steal a moment to take it all in. Portland lies in ruins behind us, skyscrapers pulverized into piles of rubble. The gleam of the fallen Bio-Nets is visible in the distance. I don't see signs of movement or fighting. I'm not even sure if the Authority is still active in the area. It's a massacre, plain and simple. We were lucky to escape with our lives. I pray that Skandar wasn't amongst the casualties.

Savon strides forward. "If your friend has any sense, he would have retreated."

"It's only been a couple hours," Avery says. "But you're right. Once Skandar realized we were missing, he wouldn't have stuck around to die."

I turn and scan the view ahead of us. "Maybe he left us something. A sign. A message."

Savon rests his hands on his hips. "Perhaps you overestimate him."

"We'll see." I lead the way down the sharp slope of the rock, slinking under the lip of the landing pad. It reaches over us like a makeshift roof. Up the hill on the other side is a cliff that looks down on the Columbia River, a shallow body of water that connects, eventually, with the Pacific Ocean.

"You're sure this is the right place?" Savon asks.

I'm about to respond when a distant explosion ruptures the sky beyond the concrete ceiling. Instantly, I duck and cover my head. Avery does the same. Savon stays still, eyes narrow.

As I crouch low, I consider what a horrible idea this is. Even if the battle's over, that doesn't mean the city's completely deserted. One strategically placed explosive and the landing pad collapses on our heads. The good news is, we're far enough away from the city walls to be of any interest. The explosion issued from far in the distance.

I scan the dark expanse of the landing pad's underbelly, spinning to take it all in. "Skandar? Talan?" I shout their names. My words echo along the support beams. I can practically feel my father bristling at the sound of my too-loud voice, concerned that it will draw unwanted attention. I turn to face him, making a point to whisper. "There's nothing."

A ringing clang disrupts the darkness behind me. I jump sideways, turning to stare in the direction of the sound. It's too deep and dark to make out any details from here.

Avery backs up until we're side by side. "What was that?"

Savon pushes his way in front of us. "Behind me. Now."

The clang repeats, louder and closer. Metal against rock.

I keep my voice low. "Is it fighting? Above us, in the city?"

"No," he whispers. "It's close. It's here." His attention doesn't break as he stares at the obscured landscape before us.

Then I see them. Two at first, but soon joined by more. Red pinpricks of light cut through the darkness, floating closer.

Eyes. Six pairs of them, though there could be more farther back.

I think about that last night in the Nevada Bunker. Just one foot soldier had nearly done me in. A half dozen, in such a confined space with no defense, will be slaughter.

"Let me handle this." Savon pushes us both back with such force that I struggle not to fall over. As I'm steadying myself, I watch him bound forward into the darkness. A flurry of sounds follows. First frantic footsteps, then blasts of some sort of words I've never heard before. Shouts, yells, but no gunshots.

I stay frozen in place, scared to move any closer. Every once in a while, I see flashes of outlines, though it's impossible to tell if they're the Drifters or my father.

Then one's thrown toward us. Avery pulls me to the side just as the lifeless body of an Authority foot soldier slams into the ground where we'd been standing.

I grit my teeth. It's six against one. I have to help my father.

I move forward, but Avery restrains me before I can

get very far. "Wait," she warns. "Can you see it? They're no match for him."

As my eyes begin to adjust to the darkness, I realize that she's right. Savon attacks the soldiers with brute force, delivering bruising blows in every technique imaginable. At points, he even hovers above them, coming down with the strength and speed of a jackhammer. It's astonishing to watch, and more than a little intimidating. I'm just relieved that his attacks are focused on *them*.

I take a meager step forward, just as the landscape falls silent. Savon steps out of the darkness, shoulders heaving with exertion. As his face pulls free of the shadows, I notice a bloody scratch above his good eye. It's the only sign of a wound.

"It's finished," he says. "I'm afraid there are cracks in the landing pad. Everywhere. When those soldiers don't return, more will come looking. It isn't safe here. And more than that, it isn't helping us find Cassius. If there's no communicator here, there's no point in staying any longer than we must."

"I just—"

Something hits my right shoulder, interrupting me. I turn, just in time for a pebble to fly right at my face.

"Ow!" I stumble into my father's side. I quickly straighten my back, realizing how ridiculous a tiny rock is compared to what he just did.

"Jesse! Avery!" Skandar's voice comes from the edge of

the pad. He stands where the sun meets the shade of our makeshift cave, a second stone clutched in his fist. "It *is* you!"

Avery beams. "Skandar!"

He's too far away for me to see his expression clearly, but that doesn't last long. Without giving me a chance to respond, he bounds inward. "I thought you were dead," he says, hands resting on his knees as he leans over. "When the Bio-Nets—"

I look up at my father, smiling. "He didn't leave. See? I knew he wouldn't."

Skandar winces. "This place. Man, this place is lost. It's totally gone. I've been hiding out in the—"

"Do you have the shuttle?" I interrupt.

He inhales. "That's what I was about to say. Around the corner. Talan said hide it, so that's what we did. Then he ran back into the city. I … I haven't seen him since."

Avery smiles. "We're just glad you're okay."

"Oh man," Skandar continues. "I didn't know what to do. I can't get ahold of Cassius. I couldn't reach you. Everyone left and I … I didn't know what to *do*." He pauses, then stares up at Savon for the first time. His eyes narrow. "Who's this?"

"This is my father, Skandar."

"Your who?"

"My father," I repeat.

Savon crosses his arms. He gives Skandar a slight sneer, though it's not entirely menacing. It's almost as if he's putting on a show.

"Oh." Skandar looks away, realizing that he's staring. "Okay. Stranger things have happened, right?"

Savon wipes the blood from his forehead. "You have no communicator, I take it?"

"I do," Skandar replies. "I mean, I *have* it, but so far it's not doing me a lot of good. You can head back to the shuttle and try, but all I'm getting is static." He turns back to me. "I heard the Skyships fell, too. Is that true, Jesse?"

I nod, and leave it at that.

He winces. "This is bad."

"I'll try the communicator." I turn to Savon. "If it doesn't go through, we can fly to Atlas and take our chances."

He nods. "Getting airborne is the first step. This place is crawling with foot soldiers. For now, we move. And keep moving before they catch up to us."

21

Cassius ducked and prayed for the best. It sounded to him as if the entire room was coming down. He'd surely be buried beneath rubble in seconds, if the floor didn't cave in first.

He gritted his teeth, expecting the worst. All it would take was a strike in the wrong place and he'd drop. Unconscious, or maybe worse.

Instead, the room fell silent.

He stole a glance at the ceiling. The sight made him question what he'd just heard. Everything above him remained solid, the same as it had been moments before. He stood, cautious not to make any quick movements. Then he saw the movement. No screeching or grating, just a constant plunge.

Like a video on mute, played in slow motion, the ceiling caved in.

It disassembled at a steady pace, sucking in everything below it. Cassius watched the top of the platform's trunklike pillar surrender to the sinking metal, disappearing into its embrace. Soon, every one of its senso-cubes would also fall victim to the vessel's dismantling. He wondered if the entire room—the entire *ship*—had been one huge, advanced hologram. That was the only explanation he could come up with, except holograms were notoriously weightless. He wouldn't have felt the solid ground beneath him, or been able to climb level after winding level.

Cassius felt panic rise in his gut. He pushed it down, knowing that he needed to escape with as many senso-cubes as he could. The last time he'd traveled inside on the Resistance's recorded memories, he'd learned invaluable information about Matigo and the Authority. If these were indeed stolen cubes, he couldn't let them be destroyed.

Lunging forward, he grabbed a handful and thrust them into his pockets. They were small—not much bigger than a standard die, but easily scattered. They chilled his skin, like they'd been kept in a refrigerator for hours.

Once he had as many as possible stuffed into his clothes, he bounded from the platform. The ceiling had already fallen much closer. Thirty feet of airspace shrunk to ten. Maybe less. He was reminded of the trash compactors back at the Lodge. Too much closer and it would squeeze him flat, hologram or no hologram.

He sprinted forward, heading for the doorway he'd come in through.

He cleared it with mere feet to spare, and whipped around the corner. His feet pounded metal, faster and faster as his lungs threatened to give out.

The ceiling silently sunk above him like an accordion being squeezed. Entire levels disappeared. One more turn and the observation deck had been swallowed up completely. Disappeared.

What had he done?

A sudden spike of horror nearly stopped him in his tracks. Madame and Eva. They were still in the ship.

He couldn't remember exactly how many floors he'd scaled after leaving them in the room. The fact that everything inside the vessel looked identical didn't make the prospect of finding them any easier.

He stole another look at the rapidly descending ceiling. It seemed to move faster now, as if taunting him. Too much longer and it would overtake his pace. He couldn't stop to take a breath—not even for a second.

"Madame!" He shouted, not caring if there were other Shifters to hear him. The ship's destruction happened in such complete silence that she and Eva wouldn't get any warning before it was too late. "Where are you?!?"

His words echoed through the gray hallways. He called again, his voice hoarse from the exertion of constant sprinting. His rattled brain forced him to consider the consequence of slowing down. Would he be disintegrated into nothing, like the rest of the ship? Would it tear off his head first, before consuming the rest of him?

The thoughts threatened to slow him down. His body wanted to collapse and fold in on itself, too shock-addled to keep going. But Cassius wasn't the kind to give up without a fight. He never had been, even as a kid. And if he was going down, it wasn't gonna be some insane spaceship that took him out.

He descended two more levels. The circular corridors widened into longer stretches. It bought him time. Seconds.

He nearly tripped. Just as his legs were about to buckle underneath him, he turned a corner and saw them.

Eva stood in the center of the corridor, hands nervously drumming her sides. Madame leaned against the wall next to her, leg dressing damp with blood.

Eva took a step back when she saw him. "What's going on?"

"Run!" He barreled forward, passing them without waiting for a response.

Madame turned. "Cassius!"

Eva grabbed Madame's arm and helped her stand straight. "Something's wrong."

The something became apparent seconds later, as the ceiling came crashing down on them. Cassius tried to remember exactly how they'd entered the vessel in the first place. He hadn't left Eva and Madame too far from the ground. They must be close now.

He ventured another look above him. There wasn't time.

He remembered the way the walls of the vessel had seemed to melt away when he'd touched them. Maybe he could use the same strategy to get them out.

Stealing precious seconds, he leapt toward the nearest wall. His brain spun, which made it difficult to tell what direction pointed to the outside world and which would only lead him farther into the chaos of the ship.

Madame hobbled to his side. "What did you do?"

"Shh." He laid his palm against the wall and focused on getting out. He didn't know exactly how to communicate with the vessel, so instead of trying to figure it out, he channeled his panic through his shaking fingers.

The ceiling moved closer. The wall didn't budge.

"Come on!" Eva urged. She was right to be panicked. Seconds more and they'd be smashed dead.

He closed his eyes, pushing hard against the metal. He let all his weight fall against it, muttering desperate pleas under his breath.

Then, all of a sudden, the wall gave way. The smooth coolness disappeared beneath his hand, replaced with nothing. Unable to stop himself, he toppled forward into the sky.

Opening his eyes, he realized that the ground outside was coming up fast. They were close to the Surface—close enough to survive the fall—but not quite as close as he'd hoped.

He twisted his body, forcing his feet down. He'd need to land without snapping his neck or injuring any other vital body part.

It worked. Sort of.

His feet hit the ground first, but his body quickly crumpled on top of them. He stumbled forward, face in the dirt.

The others followed. He heard the sounds of their feet

slamming into the Fringe landscape. Madame let out a cry of anguish, likely falling on the very leg she'd injured inside the vessel. At least she made a sound. That was better than dead.

He flipped over, lying on his back. A thousand aches caught up to him, merging into one all-consuming void. The hot ground underneath lulled his muscles into complacency. He forced his eyes open against the blazing sun, but had to squint immediately.

Rolling onto his side, he watched what was left of the vessel collapse into itself. In seconds, it had completely disappeared. Utter silence.

He couldn't fathom how it had happened. An object so big couldn't have vanished completely. It had to have gone somewhere. Turned into something.

Challenging his brain this way allowed him to focus on something besides the pain. He wasn't sure he'd be able to get up, let alone stand. But giving up in the middle of the Fringes was a death sentence. It would be all too easy to be lulled to sleep from the heat.

Eva groaned beside him. "We're alone."

She didn't have to say anything more. Cassius knew exactly what it meant. They were stranded, miles away from anything of use, and without transport of any kind. It was only a matter of time before the desert swallowed them up.

22

Avery whips back to look at me from her seat in the pilot's chair. "I can't get it airborne. It just…the cruiser won't fly."

This has been our third attempt. Every time it's the same thing. We'll crank up the acceleration, lift off, and glide for a minute or two. Then the system shuts down and we're forced to make an emergency landing. It was scary the first time. Now it's just infuriating.

Savon stands at the side of the cockpit, expression grim. "It's as I suspected, then. The Authority have disrupted your airspace. We won't be able to sustain flight."

"We've still got our wheels," Skandar starts. "Maybe we can roll?"

I glance over at him, "Across the entire country?"

Avery sighs. "At least we've managed to put some distance between us and the city, even if it was just in fits and starts."

"Not good enough," my father replies.

Skandar stretches. "At least the temp control's working, huh mate?"

I grip the back side of my seat, wishing I could squeeze it until it broke. "If we can't fly, we might as well get as far as we can on the ground. I mean, if we're gonna be stuck in here anyways."

Avery turns back to the controls. I feel the rumble of the engine immediately. "Taxiing," she says. "Now what?"

I grab Cassius's communicator from the floor, flipping it on. It hasn't been much of a help so far, but we're about due for a miracle.

The ground lurches beneath us as the cruiser's wheels hit a rock. This thing is not a tank, and Fringe landscape is notoriously bumpy.

I hold the communicator close to my ear, pressing the alert button several times to get Cassius's attention. It doesn't patch through. All I hear is static.

"I told you, Jesse," Skandar starts. "I tried already. Nobody's answering."

I swallow. "If they were on Atlas when it sank..." I can't finish the sentence.

Avery reaches above her to lower the cockpit temperature. "Even if they were, they'd find a way to escape. The three of them together? They're like a mini army."

Savon crosses his arms. "Your brother is alive."

"How do you know?" I set the communicator down.

"You'd know if he wasn't," he responds. "The connection between the two of you has always been strong."

I turn to look at him. "Like our connection, right? Like how you were able to find me."

Savon nods, then takes a seat in the remaining chair. He rubs his forehead, bowing low in thought. "It's the only thing that's kept me going. The two of you were like satellites, pulling me in. I kept my distance at first, watching. I wanted to see you in action, see what you'd do. It wasn't until the Authority captured you—"

"Wait," Skandar interrupts. "The Authority got you?"

"Just for a little while," I respond. "But if it wasn't for Savon, Avery and I could be dead right now. He saved us."

Avery turns. "You mean, he saved *you*."

"My apologies," Savon says. "I trust you'll understand a father's protective instincts. I didn't know the two of you were close."

I take a deep breath. For the first time since he broke me free from the Chute car, my mind has a moment to catch itself. We have breathing room, if only for a little while. Time to talk. Time to ask the questions that are on my mind.

"Tell me more about Mom." The words come out before I realize what I'm saying.

Savon's expression doesn't change. His attention lingers on me for another moment before he moves to glance out the front window. "I ... have not heard from your mother since landing on this planet."

"I know. But she came down with you, right?"

"Before me," he responds. "Minutes, only. Of course, that doesn't mean we'd land side by side on Earth. Or at the same time. *Or* that we'd land safely at all. Every Pearl is a risk."

I scratch at a piece of dry dirt affixed to my arm. "Is she like you?"

"What do you mean?"

"Like, a warrior?"

Savon laughs. "Jesse, I'm a scientist. It was the Authority that forced me to fight." He pauses. "But your mother is strong-willed, and resourceful. She'll be all right. I have confidence in that"

I offer a slight smile. "Can you sense it?"

"I know it to be true," he replies. "Inside. It has to be true. But I'm afraid we won't know for sure until the Authority is defeated."

"But if you came out of a green Pearl," I start. "That means that I freed you. Maybe you were one of the Pearls in Portland's reactor."

His brows rise. "No, it was before that. The exact details are a blur to me. But it's true. I owe my life to you. So many of us do."

"What if Mom's still inside her Pearl?"

"At least she'd be safe."

"No," I counter. "You don't know what people do to Pearls here. She could—" I can't finish the sentence.

His expression hardens. "She wouldn't want you to think like this. I know it's hard to cope. But trust me, she'll be waiting when this is over. We made a pact, her and I, right after we sent you and Cassius to Earth."

I imagine them, standing together on Haven after sending their only children away. I have snapshots of memories floating in my head—the sounds and light as I was thrust inside the Pearl that brought me to Earth. But they don't add up to much more than disconnected images. "A pact?"

He nods. "That nothing would keep us from finding you again. True, it had to be done. Getting you off-planet was crucial to your safety... to everyone's safety. And I can understand how our decision might have seemed selfish to you. Without a comprehensive understanding of the war and its effects on our planet, you can't possibly understand the choices we were forced to make. But I am here now. Your mother will follow. Nothing will keep us from our sons. Even King Matigo himself."

His words hit me like a meteor. But more than that, it's the way he looks at me. There's desperation in his eyes, and more than a hint of the sacrifices he's been forced to make in his life. It strikes me suddenly, how little I know about him. If we defeat the Authority... *when* we defeat the Authority... I want nothing more than to get to know him. Not as some hazy legend from another planet, but as my father.

Skandar smiles. "A happy ending, right?"

Avery sets the auto-taxi and takes a seat beside me, rubbing my shoulder. "I'm so happy for you, Jesse. This is what you've been waiting for. A family."

I lay my head against her and glance back at Savon. He's right, of course. Thinking about the possibility of my mother being alive isn't going to help win this war. That's small scale. It might not seem like it to me, but I'm not just fighting for myself anymore. I'm fighting for the entire world. It's been my single greatest challenge since I first discovered what Pearls were: force my mind to expand beyond what's immediate and personal. Bigger picture. Bigger than me.

The communicator beeps.

Without hesitation, I bolt upright and pull it to my ear. "Cassius?"

Static. For a moment I wonder if I'd imagined it.

I glance at Avery. "You heard a beep, right?"

She nods.

Another beep fractures the silence.

I play with the volume, making sure that it's not some kind of mechanical function that's keeping his voice at bay.

"Cassius?" I picture him in the middle of a city-sized pile of rubble and wreckage, limbs missing, hanging on for life. In other words, I picture the worst.

But it's not Cassius I hear at all.

"Fisher?"

I nearly drop the communicator. My palms begin to sweat immediately. The gruff tone of his voice. Nobody's voice runs through me the way his does.

I set the communicator at my side and stare at Skandar, then back to Avery. "It's Captain Alkine."

Nobody says a word. I haven't heard from Alkine for weeks, ever since leaving the Academy back in Siberia. I hadn't left on good terms. Hell, I hadn't even left through a *door*. Alkine had thrown me in the ship's brig after he caught me sneaking out. Multiple times. One red Pearl explosion later and I was falling out the window, into even more trouble than I'd imagined.

Alkine's voice comes from the communicator again, loud enough to understand even several feet from my ear.

"Fisher," he says. "Is that you?"

I swallow, and notice my arms shaking. Why does he affect me like this? I'm sitting in the middle of an invasion. Attacks could come from anywhere. I could be killed in the next few minutes. Yet just the sound of Alkine's voice has me more worked up than I've been in days.

Finally I grab the communicator and pull it close. "Y-yes…"

"Thank god." His response comes quickly. "I never thought—" He pauses. "Jesse, do you know how long we've been looking for you? We've tried every piece of Skyship tech—even Unified Party stuff—to break through to you."

"I…I…" I can't form words beyond that.

"Thank god you're safe. Thank god we were able to find your frequency."

I look over to Savon. He crosses his arms, eye slit.

I bite my lip, wondering what he's thinking. He doesn't know who Alkine is, or the history shared between us. It's probably better that he doesn't know.

Alkine's voice softens, just a little. "Jesse, you're still there?"

"Yes." I keep one eye on Savon.

"Where are you?"

I hesitate before speaking. "The States."

"In the thick of it," he replies. "No surprise."

I can't deal with this. The Academy's a world I left behind. It's bigger picture now, just like Savon said.

But Alkine continues, pulling me back. "It's happened, hasn't it?"

"Sir?"

"The invasion." He pauses. "What we've been trying to prevent. What we tried to keep you from."

"I don't know—"

"Listen," he interrupts. "We're on our way. Just tell me where you are."

I picture the Skyships falling to the ground, one by one just like Savon said. Then I remember our own cruiser, forced down after just minutes of unsteady flight. "You can't," I say. "The Authority ... they've done something to the sky. No one can fly."

"That's nonsense. We're flying right now."

"Over the U.S.?"

"No, but soon enough. We're over the Pacific. All controls are normal."

I swallow, wondering how much I should tell him—how much he'd be able to handle. But I can't help myself. "The Skyships," I start. "The Skyship *Community*. They're all gone."

"What do you mean, all gone?"

"Sunk," I reply. "They crashed. The skies are clear."

There's a long pause on the other end. Alkine's not one for long pauses. I wonder if he believes me.

After a moment, his voice comes back. "We'll go as far as we can. Get to the coast, Fisher. Find a shuttle and head over the Pacific. We'll be waiting for you."

"But—"

"The coast, Jesse. You can't do this without a Skyship. We're here to help. We *want* to help." He pauses. "And keep your communicator close. I want you in constant contact, okay?"

I don't respond.

"Okay, Fisher?"

I look up at Savon. He wears a deep frown, but says nothing.

"Yeah," I mutter into the communicator, then quickly shut it off.

Bigger picture. I think I suck at that.

23

Somehow, without Cassius even realizing it, his eyes had closed. He had succumbed to the Fringes. After all that running—daring escapes, the battle with the Shifters—the desert had swallowed him up.

He wasn't sure how long he'd been out, but certainly long enough for Surface Stroke to have set in. It was the number one rule in the Fringes: don't give up. Don't close your eyes.

But he wasn't dead. Death would carry with it less pain—a pleasant numbness, he imagined. He felt the dull aches flare up around his body, sometimes in the same spot, other times in completely different areas. His skin throbbed with the heat of a bad sunburn. He was still lying on his back, arms at his sides, but not on the ground.

He opened his eyes to find a large panel stretched over him, several inches from his body. It wasn't metal. He could tell that immediately. Maybe some sort of reinforced foam.

His back rested against a slab of the same material. Yeah, it had to be foam of some sort. Whatever it was, it didn't conduct heat. If anything, it was pleasantly warm. He ran his fingers along the material. Lightweight, slightly porous. It had been constructed specifically to endure the heat.

Between the roof and the floor of the coffin-sized container, Cassius could see a thin stripe of empty space through which he watched the brown dirt of the Fringes speed by. It startled him at first. A roll to either side would send him through the narrow slit onto the ground, but whatever device or vehicle he lay captive to was moving too fast. Hitting the dirt would surely break a bone or two. Plus, he'd only roll back into the Fringes.

The slit of empty space did have its use, though. Air streamed through on both sides of him, made cooler by the rapid forward motion of the strange casket.

He took a deep breath, shaking his arms and legs to make sure they still worked. There weren't any ropes or shackles keeping him in place. In fact, the entire structure seemed overly flimsy, like it could give way at any moment if he made the wrong move.

But Cassius wasn't about to lie back and wait.

Bending his knees, he raised his feet and kicked at the overhead panel. Without much resistance at all, the entire thing flipped open. He craned his neck to watch hinges above his head squeal shut. The panel retreated out of sight, revealing a solid rectangle of blue sky.

He bounded up from his back, crouching on bent knees—and almost toppled forward, right into the desert.

He perched at the back end of some sort of vehicle. Two identical holding cells flanked him, one on either side.

The back end of the transport formed a three-pronged pitchfork. Cassius crouched in the center, staring out at the rapidly passing landscape. There were no cities in sight. Not even Fringe Towns. Only endless brown.

Keeping his balance, he peered around the edge of the flipped-over panel to see a pair of drivers. They sat in low-backed chairs, side by side behind a wide steering wheel. The entire vehicle looked like some thrown-together shuttle. But instead of flying, they hovered several feet from the ground.

A skimmer.

He'd seen such technology from the Unified Party, used when shuttle travel was too burdensome or risky. But from the looks of it, this skimmer had been tinkered with, which meant that those probably weren't Unified Party drivers at the helm.

He crouched low again, eager not to be seen. He was surprised that the drivers hadn't noticed the overhead hatch fly open. Then again, the noise from the wind as they cut through the Fringe Desert was loud enough to cover up most other sounds. He hadn't gotten a chance to look, but he wouldn't be surprised if the drivers were wearing earplugs of some sort.

He glanced from side to side at the two chambers that bordered his. Madame and Eva. It had to be. Neither were awake, though. Both of their hatches stayed firmly in place.

His mind flashed back to the disappearing Authority vessel they'd come from. He felt around in his pockets, searching for senso-cubes. Two handfuls remained. Whoever was driving the skimmer must have picked them up quickly, not even taking time to search them. But why?

In truth, he wasn't so interested in the whys. His captors had transport out of the Fringes. He was alive. Now only one question remained: should he try to bring down the drivers and take control of the skimmer, or play dead and wait to see where they were being taken?

He reached up and pulled the panel back into place, hoping the drivers wouldn't see it moving. He'd learn more if he waited, though it killed him to do it. Plus, it would give Madame and Eva time to wake up. He'd keep his guard up and be ready to attack if the situation called for it. After all, his body needed rest. He didn't trust that he'd be able to put up much of a fight in his current state.

He lay down, resting his hands against his thighs. The tips of his fingers brushed across the outline of the senso-cubes in his pocket. Unable to resist, he pulled one free and held it above his head, inches from his face.

It was only slightly bigger than a six-sided die, with ornate lines carved into its surface. Last time one of these had activated, it had been just as Fisher and he were falling out of a ship in the middle of the sky. It froze them—seemed to freeze time itself.

Cassius wasn't sure exactly how it had activated, just as he wasn't sure how he'd moved the walls of the Authority vessel hours ago or how the entire thing had seemingly crumbled into nothing. Elements native to Haven seemed far more malleable than ones on Earth.

As he was considering this, a flash of light overtook the chamber. The cube, through no fault of his own, had activated.

His head spun, giving him the sensation of movement even though he knew that his body remained in the vehicle, completely still.

When the disorientation concluded, he stood at the edge of a vast pit of darkness. A black sea stretched before him, small enough to swim across, but just barely.

He spun to see what looked like miniature gray mountains all around him. The landscape reminded him of pictures he'd seen of the bottom of the ocean. Desertlike, but wholly different from the Fringes. And despite the large pool of darkness before him, everything else looked so dry that it could crumble.

Complicated, curling sculptures of porous rock created a landscape without any flat surfaces. Cassius took a step forward and felt the brittle ground underfoot. He turned his attention back to the deep blackness before him. He recognized the material instantly. Ridium. He stood beside a pit of it.

He'd heard others talk about the Ridium pits on the southern end of Haven. This was where the element came from, before Matigo and the Authority had depleted it. But the real question was, why was he seeing this now? If the memory had been kept captive by the Authority, it had to have some meaning.

His surroundings were completely silent. Even the Ridium, which bubbled every once and awhile, remained quiet. He stared into the abyss, wondering how deep it stretched. If he were to step inside, would he sink or be able to stand on top of it?

Just then, he noticed a man in the distance, slowly walking along the shore of the Ridium pit. He hadn't moved up until now. His dark-gray garb blended almost too well with the rocks. Cassius crouched instinctively. He had to remind himself that he was as good as invisible inside this memory.

Taking a deep breath, he ventured forward, watching his step as he looked for safe, relatively flat, places to put his feet.

With every step, the man drew closer. His graying hair belied his body, which was tall and fit. In some ways, he reminded Cassius of Fisher's Captain Alkine. The man had obviously seen battle. Or at the very least, rigid training exercises.

When the man's toes were close enough to touch the Ridium, he stretched his arm out to his side. Cassius watched as his wrist began to move. The man's hand looped in circles, faster and faster until it seemed like it would spin off. Cassius had never seen someone move in this way. The rest of the man's body remained completely still. It was as if his hand was possessed.

The Ridium trembled before forming waves, which

crashed onto the rocky structures, swallowing the man's feet. He seemed to be unfazed by it, continuing to twirl his hand as the Ridium coursed over the landscape.

Cassius watched in horror as the substance ate away at the rock beneath it, swallowing entire structures whole. Within moments, the man had carved a sizable swath of flat, lifeless ground. As he guided the Ridium back into the pit, he left the scenery decimated. If Cassius had been standing closer—if this had been more than a memory—he would have likely been covered as well. Smothered, even.

He'd seen this type of thing happen before, up on Skyship Altair, when Theo had dismantled all of the ship's circuitry by sending Ridium coursing along the ground. Was this a clue as to what the Authority was planning? The way the black stuff ran down the sides of their vessel and burrowed into the ground in the Fringes—would it come back up again to smother everything in sight? The Authority had already prevented ships from flying. If people couldn't get off the ground, there'd be no place to escape it. Everyone would be buried.

With this thought, the memory whisked away from him. The landscape disappeared like a runny watercolor painting and his eyes opened, revealing the tight chamber inside the skimmer yet again. Surprised by his sudden line of thought, he dropped the senso-cube. It hit his chest and rolled down his side, sucked out of the opening between the chamber's panels. Cassius didn't try to hold onto it.

The image lingered with him. He imagined Ridium

coursing along the ground of the Fringes. A flood. There'd be no surviving it.

He'd stay silent, but alert. Whoever their drivers were, they had to stop somewhere. When they did, he'd be ready. Flood or no flood, the Authority was going down—one foot soldier at a time.

24

"Captain Alkine."

The words stick in my throat. They feel old, like remnants from another life.

I take a deep breath, tapping my fingers on the side of the communicator.

Avery rubs my knee. "Do you trust him?"

I shoot her a confused look. I keep forgetting that when she was back at the Academy, it was as a double agent for Madame. Sure, Alkine and I have history, but I don't think she's ever felt comfortable with him.

"Listen to your friend," Savon says. "Running away is not an option."

"He never said anything about running away," I reply.

My father shakes his head. "We have a plan."

"Yeah," Skandar laughs. "And it involves rolling across the entire country at about forty miles an hour. Some plan."

"They have a Skyship," I add.

Avery's brows rise. "Provided it stays airborne. And provided Captain Alkine doesn't try to hold you hostage again."

"Cassius is more powerful than any ship," Savon says.

I glance at him. "You mean that?"

"Every word."

I shrug. "I know what he can do—"

"You don't," he interrupts. "You've seen a fraction of it, maybe. It's the same with you, Jesse. You didn't know you could use the Pearl energy to fly until I taught you. There's more inside of both of you than you'll ever know. I need my boys at my side. Not some human-made ship."

Skandar stretches. "No offense, man, but have you ever *seen* a Skyship before?"

Savon ignores him, standing and striding to the control deck.

I set the communicator aside. "What are you doing?"

"Seeing if we can speed this up."

"We can't," Avery responds. "Trust me, if we could, I would've done it already."

My father shakes his head, hands resting on the edge of the console. "Human technology," he mutters. "We're a rolling appetizer for any squadron of foot soldiers that find us. There was a time back on Haven—before you were born, Jesse—when a Resistance transport vehicle was set upon by a horde of Matigo's men. Their weaponry was far more advanced than ours. No one survived." He pauses. "Earth is a ball of dirt, hundreds of years behind other civilizations. None of your technology will withstand what the Authority's capable of throwing at us."

I stand, arms crossed. "So what are we supposed to do?"

"Bring Pearls." He turns to meet my eyes. "Bring them

toward us. Bathe us in energy so that we can take to the skies and end this."

"What about my friends?"

He frowns. "For your friends to live, you have to leave them."

I feel Avery clutch my arm. "It's okay, Jesse. We've survived worse. If you really need to get Cassius, then get him. Skandar and I can call Alkine, as much as I hate to do it. We'll be okay."

"Indeed," Savon replies. "This is only the beginning. Things will get worse, and soon."

"But I—"

I'm interrupted by a rumble underfoot. To be fair, the cruiser's been unsteady this entire time, rolling over rocks and potholes, but this is different. This feels distant somehow, yet getting closer.

The cabin lurches to a stop before jolting forward once more. Avery and I are thrown off our feet for a moment. I turn to see Savon's good eye widen.

"No," he says.

Avery glances around the cockpit, as if some part of the cruiser's malfunctioning. "No? What's that supposed to mean?"

Savon shakes his head, unwilling—or maybe unable—to respond. Instead, he turns back to the control panel. "Shut the vehicle down."

"What?" Skandar stands at the back of the cockpit. "Why?"

"Just do it," he says. "We have to get out."

Avery looks at me for confirmation. I grit my teeth, staring at my father. He's rattled, but I have no idea why.

I turn back to Avery. "Do it."

With an exasperated sigh, she rushes to the console. We stop moving almost instantly. "Why the hell are we stopping in the middle of the Fringes?"

Her answer comes in the form of a second rumble, closer and fiercer than the first.

Savon moves to the back of the cockpit, throwing open the door. "I can't protect you in here," he says before striding into the cabin.

I follow behind, eager to find out what's happening.

Any sane person would hit the button to open the side exit, but apparently Savon doesn't see it, because he grabs onto the secured handle and rips open the door, lock and all, before bothering with buttons or controls.

Intense Fringe heat blankets us immediately, forcing my eyes shut. A gust of wind pounds the side of the cruiser, throwing clumps of dirt and sand into the cabin. Savon doesn't seem to mind. He bounds from the ship, landing with a thud on the ground outside.

Avery and Skandar move behind me, shielding their faces from the oncoming flurry.

The cruiser shakes beneath us again, so furiously that I have to grab onto the wall to stabilize myself. Another second and I'm out, landing on the dirt in an unstable mess.

Turns out it isn't just the cruiser that's rumbling. The entire ground rattles beneath me.

I move closer to my father. "What is it? What's happening?!?"

"Look." He points at the horizon beyond us. At first, it's hard to see anything past the hazy screen of heat in the distance, but then I see it, bubbling up from the ground. Ridium sloshes to the surface, crumbling the earth as it pushes upward. Worse yet, it's moving forward.

"The Authority's caught up to us," Savon says, extending his arm. "Get behind me." He motions. "All of you. Now!" I turn to see Avery and Skandar bunch behind me, coerced by Savon's urgent command.

We huddle together, watching my father stand tall in the face of the oncoming tide of Ridium. It sloshes over the ground with incredible speed, swallowing up every rock and bush in its path. A few more seconds and it will swallow us up too.

The ground rumbles with renewed fury, forcing all three of us to our knees. Savon stays in position, somehow resisting gravity. He stretches out his arms, like he's going to catch the Ridium. He's concerned, I can tell, but not terrified. Looking at him, I'm not sure he's ever terrified.

I wanna scream up to him, tell him that there's no way we can survive this much Ridium headed toward us at once, but I can't find my voice.

Instead, I watch as he brings his hands together in front of him before throwing his arms out to his sides in a "T" shape. Instantly the Ridium splits into two distinct streams, each of which flows past us in a wide arc, close enough to see clearly, yet far enough that it won't hurt us.

I gaze up at my father in awe, watching his arms tremble with the exertion of controlling so much Ridium at once. He's a Shifter.

My father, the Shifter.

And for the second time today, he's just saved my life.

I take comfort in this for a moment, which is foolish because it means I let my concentration wane. I don't see the tendril of Ridium shoot from the wave beside me. I don't notice it rush toward my shoulders.

I only notice after it's hit me—pounded into the square of my back, hard enough to throw me face-first into the dirt. Hard enough to knock the consciousness right out of me.

25

The land skimmer continued to push forward, moving in a remarkably straight path across the desert. There was no telling when or where it would stop, and Cassius feared it would be too dangerous to sneak another glance outside of his holding capsule.

He lingered on the idea, but eventually conceded that jumping into another senso-cube memory was the best use of his time. There was no telling which cube would hold the answers he sought.

He pulled the next cube from his pocket, allowing the alien coolness of its surface to ease the sweltering heat around him. When his palm felt more relaxed, he held the artifact over his head and closed his eyes, trying to do whatever he had managed with the last one. He focused on unlocking it with his mind—pointing all of his thoughts to what might be inside.

Within seconds, he was standing in the middle of a forest. He looked up to see a sky much like Earth's—dark but colored with the last hints of sunset. He marveled at his ability to use his legs, to be thrust into a standing position from his cramped posture in the capsule.

Trees stretched all around him, tall and straight as if they'd each been created in the same mold. The air was warm, but not uncomfortably so. A panorama of small noises surrounded him—chirps and creaks that could be coming from all sorts of creatures. He wasn't too sure he was eager to meet any of them. After all, who knew what kind of life Haven supported beyond Drifters.

Cassius raised his head to stare at the canopy of trees. He'd never seen so many in one place. The memory must have been recorded prior to Haven's devastation—before the planet had lost most of its resources.

The underbrush rustled behind him. Cassius turned to see a man running directly at him. No, it was more than running. *Sprinting.*

The man's eyes were wild with fear. His hair was wet, matted to the scalp. A thin T-shirt stretched over his narrow body, stained with dirt.

Cassius was about to dive to the side until he remembered that none of this was actually taking place. Even though the cube took over his senses, it was only a memory. He stood his ground, letting the ghost of the guy pass right through his body.

He spun to watch the man disappear between trees. Another moment and he'd be completely out of sight.

This was an invitation to follow.

And that's exactly what Cassius prepared to do, until he noticed the red energy beaming through the brush behind him.

He froze, remembering the look of terror on the man's face. The guy was being chased. This red light, whatever it came from, pursued him. Cassius's breath tightened as he waited to meet the pursuer.

The red energy grew closer. Soon, it formed the silhouette of a Drifter.

A second figure emerged from the trees. Cassius sidestepped to the nearest trunk. Even though he was perfectly safe, something about this encounter made him feel like he needed to get out of the way.

The red Drifter was unlike any other he'd encountered. For one, it was a woman. Her dark hair billowed behind her as she mirrored the man's path with unerring speed. Crimson energy cocooned her slight frame, like she'd just burst from inside a Pearl.

As she sprinted past, Cassius bolted from the tree and followed her. He couldn't believe how quickly she moved. Even at full speed, he still lagged behind.

The trees rushed past in a blur as Cassius forced his body to move faster. His lungs burned. Muscles shook.

Then, the woman froze.

Cassius ran through her right shoulder before managing to stop himself.

In front of him lay the scared and exhausted man, foot caught in a piece of root that looped up from the ground. He'd tripped and hurt his leg. Bad luck.

Cassius back-stepped, leaning against a tree to watch the woman crouch and pull the man up to her eye level.

She held him an inch off the ground, dangling his body in the air. Unreal strength. The man must have been twice her weight, at least. She wasn't winded. She was calm. Assured.

Her red eyes focused directly on the man's terrified face. Her lips tugged into an intense frown.

"Jorbun," she started. Her voice was lighter than Cassius expected. "Number seven thousand and eight. A pathetic number." English rolled easily from her tongue. Like Pearls, the senso-cubes processed and translated language.

She removed a hand from the man's shirt, easily keeping him aloft with one slim arm, and retrieved a device from her thigh. Some kind of scanner, from the looks of it. She pressed a button and four prongs popped out from the sides of the small disc, like the legs of an insect. Once finished, she clamped the device onto the man's chest. He howled in pain as the prongs dug into his flesh, burrowing deep until the metallic device melded with his skin like an emblem. The man whimpered, trying to control himself. His legs shook.

"Jorbun the messenger. The great communicator." The woman smiled. "The Authority heard your broadcast. I'm sure you would be happy to know that. Matigo sends his regards." She dropped him to the ground, where he collapsed in a heap, unable to right himself. "Unfortunately for the Resistance, we cut the commercial stream fifteen seconds in. All your rousing and nobody beyond the enemy even heard it." She took a step back. "But there was a benefit to your caterwauling. We were able to trace your safe house and find you. That's a big catch for us, Jorbun. You're a voice. And voices are very important."

Jorbun looked up at her from the ground. Cassius could tell it was killing him to lift his head. He wasn't sure what the pronged emblemlike device was, but it was clearly messing up his body. He couldn't move his legs. His back slumped unnaturally. Still, he met her eyes. "Just kill me, if that's what you want."

The woman crouched in front of him. "But Jorbun, that's not what we want. The Authority prizes a voice, especially a defector."

He forced a smile. "I'd rather die than defect."

She sighed. "I'm giving you an opportunity. You'd be a fool to refuse."

"I don't want any part of the Authority. Matigo can go—"

"Shh," she interrupted. "We don't want to hear that. Just go to sleep, Jorbun. We've already got what we need."

His eyes widened. "What do you mean?"

"The Authority thanks you." She laid her palm on the disc embedded in his chest, eyes intently focused on his. "And before I kill you, I want you to know this." She smiled. "We've found them."

His eyes widened. "Wha-what?"

"Yes," she said. "Your leaders. Savon and Adaylla. King Matigo has found them. Soon, there will be no more Resistance."

Suddenly, energy from her hand streamed into his

body. Cassius saw it boiling underneath, blistering his skin as it coursed through his torso, into his limbs. Skin began to tear, ripped off from the inside in chunks. He fought back nausea as he watched the man torn inside out. Beams of red poked through holes in his body, arcing into the sky like lasers. His face exploded.

When it was done, there wasn't a body left. It was a pile of scraps, littering the forest floor. The smell was almost too much to bear. Cassius moved away, trying not to breathe in the rancid air.

The woman, unimpressed and unbothered, reached forward and retrieved the device from the center of the pile. After wiping off any remaining residue, she held it an inch from her lips and whispered, "I have seen the error of my ways. I, Jorbun—number seven thousand and eight—have joined our beloved Matigo in the pursuit of a new home. I encourage my listeners to do the same." She stood and ran her finger along the backside of the disc. Moments later, Jorbun's voice emanated from within, echoing her words.

I have seen the error of my ways. I, Jorbun—number seven thousand and eight—have joined our beloved Matigo in the pursuit of a new home. I encourage my listeners to do the same.

Cassius understood immediately. Her message would be relayed to the Resistance, disguised as one of their own. The Authority's war was not only a physical one, but mental as well.

The woman smiled and returned the device to her hip. Then, without taking another look at the mess of scraps at her feet, she bent her knees slightly and rocketed into the sky. The canopy shifted as she cut through the forest and disappeared.

Blackness.

Cassius's eyes flew open.

He felt sick as the image of the torn-apart man stuck in his head. But more than that, the woman's words stuck with him.

We've found them. Savon and Adaylla.

Those were the names of his parents, though he'd never met them. The leaders of the Resistance.

It was hard to feel much about either one of them, since he knew so little. Even so, he prayed for their safety. A part of him hoped they'd come down to Earth and help fight against the invasion. They'd know what to do. He'd be rid of the constant guesswork. He needed a leader.

His thoughts were cut short when the skimmer slowed to a stop. He felt the ground come up at them, rattling his chamber.

Wherever they were, they'd reached their destination. In a few moments, the Authority foot soldiers would come to open Cassius's prison capsule.

He took a deep breath. It was time to fight.

26

I awake in the center of fire. A vast whirlwind of flames rushes past me at all angles, so thick that I can't see anything past it. I make out faint outlines, silhouettes moving beyond the burning walls, but I can't tell what they are.

I stand, turning to look for an exit. I expect heat, so staggering that it would burn the life out of me. Instead, there's nothing. No hot, no cold. I feel balanced, at peace somehow. Protected by the flames.

I step forward and reach out a hand, wondering what will happen if I touch the fire. My fingers shake as I extend my arm farther. The fire tenses, as if waiting for my touch. When my skin finally dips beneath the flame, it's like plunging my hand into room-temperature water. I leave it in place for a moment, marveling at my newfound invulnerability.

Then a figure breaches the fire wall.

I pull my hand to my side and turn to see Cassius, barreling toward me. He's already passed through the flames, with only a few yards before running into me.

"Cassius!"

He doesn't respond. He doesn't slow his pace or change

his direction. He keeps coming, too fast for me to move out of the way.

Our eyes meet. His mouth stays shut, his expression plain, but focused.

"Wait!" I reach out a hand, as if that'll stop him.

He runs right into me. As soon as our skin touches, his body fizzles to phantomlike transparency. Another moment and he's gone. My hand is still outstretched, stopping nothing.

The flames continue to loop and twist around me, but something's different. Something's changing.

I lower my hand and watch the color spread through the cyclone.

Green. Pearl green.

———

A detonation wakes me, this time for real.

My father's hand wraps around my waist. I lie slumped over his shoulder, carried through the Fringes like cargo, bumping up and down with every footstep he takes. My head spins. My heart pounds like it's about to explode. I don't know what's going on or why we're running.

Another explosion, closer this time. A hailstorm of dust shellacs my face. I manage to shield my eyes, but swallow some of it. I cough, struggling to see the landscape around me. I don't see the cruiser, but I do notice the silhouettes of soldiers. They sprint by too fast to make out details, and move in all different directions. I can't tell if they're chasing us, surrounding us, or something even worse.

Savon hoists me farther up his shoulder, but this time I'm awake. I reach out with my leg, accidentally kicking him in the thigh. A moment of surprised exertion on his part sends me toppling over his side. He holds firm to my bottom half, but the rest of me dangles. My hands touch the ground and support my torso, dragging in the dust for a painful, disoriented moment. When Savon realizes that I'm conscious, he allows me to right myself.

I topple onto the ground and land unceremoniously on my butt. The pain and nausea catches up to me, but there's no time to dwell on it.

I push up, trying to get back to a standing position amongst the chaos. The outlines of soldiers zip by overhead, flying like Savon and I had a few short hours ago. Are they the ones dropping bombs? Are they shooting at us? There's no way to tell. The Fringe dust, kicked up now to storm-like levels, obscures most details around me.

Just as my leg feels like it's about to collapse, a figure darts by and grabs my hand. As my arm's hoisted around her neck, I realize it's Avery. She supports me going forward, though says nothing.

I glance at her face, but can't see much as my vision fractures. She's covered in dirt from the cloud around us. That much is for sure.

I don't see Skandar anywhere.

The air around us burns so hot that I know it won't

be long before we all collapse from the exertion in such extreme temperature. Avery'll be first, having to help me along as well as care for herself. I can't let that happen. I don't know what happened after I was knocked unconscious, but now that I know I'm alive—if barely—I have to do something.

And there's only one thing a guy like me can do.

I close my eyes, hoping that Avery's got enough strength left to support the both of us.

We're on the ground. That, at least, will help me. I've been able to draw Pearls to me before, though never under such beaten-up circumstances.

I try to ignore the explosions and choking dust, even though I could be hit from any angle, and lock in on any Pearls that might be near. I haven't seen or felt one since Portland, which is a bit alarming, but they must still be falling. And if they're within reach, I can use them.

The first Pearl pops up in my consciousness almost immediately. I feel it shifting course as it speeds toward me. I keep all my attention focused on it, even as the ground war rages around me.

It comes hurtling toward me so quickly, I'd imagine no cruiser or ship could keep up with it. I reach out my hand, even as the other arm tightens around Avery's shoulder, and bring it to my fingers. I watch as the green orb cuts through the dust cloud, muted but undeniably awesome in its power.

This is going to have to be different. Savon said I could

control the energy much better than I had before. There have been times when I was able to channel it certain directions, even mold it into razorlike fragments.

I don't think I need to be that specific here, but I don't want to hurt any of my friends, either. Savon could probably take it, but a blast in Avery's direction would surely finish her off. And I don't even know where Skandar is.

I stop the Pearl, mere feet from my fingers. A volley of blasts hits the ground beyond it, fired off from an unseen soldier.

I spread my fingers slowly, imagining a hole in the Pearl that I can pry open.

The orb crackles in front of me. The Drifter inside whispers, but I ignore it.

My hand tenses on Avery's shoulder. She stops as she notices what's happening with the Pearl.

I pull away, then step in front of her, using both hands to control the energy. Bands of it snake their way toward my fingers, instantly empowering my body from the inside.

I don't have a lot of time. This needs to happen now.

I mirror the hand movements I saw my father do when he controlled the Ridium stream. My fingers touch as I stretch my arms out in front of me. The Pearl pulses.

Then, I release it.

The Pearl explodes in a spider web of green strands—a million lightning bolts fired in all directions.

I watch as soldiers fall from the air like dead flies, crashing to the ground with thuds and snaps.

The green energy fires full strength for only a moment, but while it's happening, it looks dangerously like the green bolts of flame at the end of my dream.

I watch as a Drifter blossoms from the middle, then bursts through what's left of the dust cloud, into the sky.

The explosion calms, replaced with an eerie silence as the cloud begins to dissipate, pushed away by the force of the energy.

My chest heaves as my shallow breathing threatens to force me to the ground. But inside, I feel renewed. I needed that.

I sink to my knees, and turn to see Savon come toward me from the left. He grips a fist in one hand, cracking his knuckles. I notice blood drip down one cheek, though the patch over his eye remains intact. He, like all of us, is covered in dirt.

"That's how you fight," he says, stopping inches from my side.

I glance up at Avery. She rests her hands on her knees, coughing. I don't think she can talk. Not yet.

"Skandar!" I stand, spinning to try to find him.

His cries of pain eventually draw me to him. He lies on his back several yards to my right, cradling one arm with the other, shouting in anguish.

Despite my exhaustion, I run over and drop down on my knees beside him. His entire body's caked with dirt, though the whites of his eyes are wide with panic.

"My arm!" he shouts, so loud that I'm afraid the Authority will hear him and come back to finish what they started.

I look down at his left arm. He grips it with his right hand, clutching tight so that it won't fall into the dirt.

Then I notice it. The sheen of the blood is dulled by the dust, but it pours from him all the same. A mangled hand lies in the distance, sliced cleanly from the rest of him. He lost it. I don't know how, but it's been chopped off completely.

"Skandar." I grab his shoulder, panicked. The blood continues to flow into the Fringes, pooling beside him. He's in shock. It won't be long before the wound turns fatal.

I grit my teeth, looking around for help. Our cruiser's so far in the distance now that I can't even see it. There's nothing I can do. We're stranded, and he doesn't have much time.

27

Footsteps sounded outside the skimmer. Cassius heard the sound of boots tromping around the perimeter. Soon the steps were joined by words. Haven language.

The Authority, just as he feared.

Cassius didn't know why they'd stopped—or even where they were—but he had one advantage over the soldiers. They didn't realize who they'd stuffed into their capsule.

Most likely they assumed him a helpless boy. But he'd had time to prepare, to regain his strength and gather sparks. He'd need them. He'd need all the fire he could muster.

The footsteps grew closer. Cassius balled his fingers into a fist, feeling the energy stream from his chest, down his arm. Both hands grew hot as embers. He wouldn't be able to hold it for long.

The capsule flipped open.

A pair of bald, muscular men stood before him, looking down as if they were staring into the inside of a coffin. Cassius tensed, ready for attack.

Before he could do anything, he watched as both men were pulled back, out of sight. Cassius stood, alarmed at what else might be in the Fringes.

To his shock, there was no monster or alien or big, bad enemy. There was only Madame.

Somehow she'd crept out of her own capsule and caught both soldiers by surprise, yanking them backward by the scruffs of their collars.

A pair of shots rang out, breaking the silence of the Fringes. With expert aim, Madame fired a pistol, sending a beam of Pearl energy right into the hearts of the soldiers. Cassius recognized the weapon instantly as standard Unified Party issue, though it had obviously been modified with Pearl energy. Somehow, she must have been secretly carrying it ever since they left the bunker. He shouldn't have been surprised at her resourcefulness, yet he still found himself shaking his head.

The soldiers were no match for the unfiltered Pearl energy. They fell to the ground immediately, unmoving.

Madame lowered the weapon, glancing at Cassius. "Nobody sticks me in a cage."

He didn't respond. Instead, he grabbed onto the edge of his capsule and jumped out onto the sand. The sparks along his fingers died down, though part of him still wanted to let loose a torrent of fire.

"Cassius." Madame rushed toward him. "You're safe."

"How long have you been awake?"

She holstered the pistol under her shirt. "Long enough for my anger to turn to action."

Cassius looked past her, at the bodies of the fallen soldiers. "I could've taken them."

"Of course you could have," she responded, "but why waste your talents when a simple gunshot will do?"

He met her eyes. "I suppose you carried that thing along in case the opportunity for a double-cross presented itself."

"Don't be silly," she said. "The days of fighting against each other are over."

"Hmm."

The thwack of the third capsule being kicked open interrupted them. Cassius turned to see Eva crawl out of her prison, rubbing the back of her neck and cursing. "Great," she muttered under her breath. "More Fringes. Just what I wanted to see."

He was going to respond when Madame grabbed his shoulder. His first instinct was to pull away, but instead he turned back to her.

"Cassius." Her eyes traced a path behind him. "Turn around. I think I know what caused us to stop here."

Without a word, he spun to take in the length of the vehicle. But the skimmer paled in comparison to the structure behind it. He nearly toppled over with shock at the sight.

Not far from the front end of the skimmer, a black arch stretched several hundred feet in the air. It dwarfed everything else around them—like a sharp, black rainbow. He only needed to take one look at it to know that it had been constructed from Ridium.

The vast shape stood silent and still, overlooking the

Fringes like a sentinel. Being so close to Ridium made Cassius uneasy, even though there weren't any weapons or soldiers in sight. Still, he knew it was dangerous. Even by itself.

He turned away from the monument. "What do you think they were going to do to us?"

Madame shook her head. "Who says it had anything to do with *us?*"

He stepped back, eyes falling upon the structure again. He kept his attention there, even as he spoke. "I've never seen Ridium sculpted into a shape like this."

Eva joined them. "It reminds me of the St. Louis Arch. I mean, before they brought it down." She sighed. "How long were we out?"

No one answered her, for it wasn't clear to any of them.

Madame turned to survey the vast desert around them. After a moment, she pointed to the north. "Look, I see the outline of a Chosen far in the distance. It's so hazy. There'd be no way to tell which city it is." She paused. "I think we're best off seeing if we can fire up the skimmer and take it north."

Cassius moved farther away, starting to round the corner of the skimmer. "There's something about this thing . . ."

"I wouldn't," Madame warned. "Remember the vessel? Don't tempt fate, Cassius."

"She's right," Eva added. "All this open space makes me nervous. I can't get the sight of all those Skyship Agents being sliced to death when Theo developed his powers."

Her words conjured images in Cassius's consciousness

immediately. He remembered Matigo's son pulling the black substance from the earth like daggers, stabbing an entire battalion of Shippers in one move. But this was different. This arch, whatever it was, seemed so quiet. Peaceful, even.

"All right," he said without looking at either of them. "Head to the control deck. See what you can do. I just want to check this thing out real quick before we go."

Madame stepped to his side, clutching his shoulder. "Cassius, be careful. Remember what happened last time you 'just wanted to check something out.'"

He moved away without a word, taking quick strides around the length of the skimmer and sprinting the rest of the way. The heat threatened to slow him, but he'd been waiting to move for a while. He wasn't going to let it stop him completely.

He arrived in the shadow of the arch and slowed to a walk, craning his neck to marvel at the sheer size of it.

If he held out both arms as far as they would go, he'd just about get the width of one of its legs. It appeared to be completely solid, like a sculpture cut from obsidian.

He stepped forward cautiously, extending a hand to touch the surface. He wasn't sure what would happen, but he knew that he needed to feel it. It had been the same way with the bracelet of Ridium that had once been fused to his wrist, which Madame had foolishly given him back when he'd been hunting Fisher. The material had always fascinated him, even more so when he knew how dangerous it could be.

He pressed a finger against the blackness before letting his entire palm rest against the substance. It was hard to the touch, and cool, unlike the rest of the Fringes. Not as cold as the senso-cubes, but definitely abnormal.

He was reminded of the first memory he'd witnessed back in the skimmer—the Haven man flooding the rocky basin with an unending supply of Ridium. It had been a thick liquid then. This was rocklike.

He noticed movement overhead.

Quickly, Cassius recoiled and took three steps back, looking straight up at the underbelly of the arch. He scanned the length of the structure, searching for changes. At first, he didn't notice anything. He had to concentrate hard to see the Ridium quiver.

It happened directly above him, at the highest point on the arch. Bubbles, at first. But soon, something began to emerge from the blackness.

It dropped down like a spider on a string of web, carried lower by sticky coils of the substance. As the Ridium began to part, Cassius could make out a human form, though there was no doubt in his mind. This wasn't human.

He watched the creature descend, held airborne by several thick arms of blackness, like chains on a swing set. It was a figure of complete, polished blackness. No facial features, no clothing or shoes beyond the tight layer of Ridium.

Cassius backed away, keeping his eyes on the figure the entire time.

The others saw it too.

He heard the skimmer engine rev up and glanced over his shoulder to see Madame ushering him back to safety.

"Cassius! Quick!"

He stepped back through the desert, unable to pull himself from the sight in front of him.

The figure slowly descended all the way to the ground, coils of Ridium keeping it steady. Cassius wasn't sure if the creature could see him. There didn't seem to be any awareness beyond the movement. For all he could tell, it was operating blindly. Were its eyes covered? At least when Theo had worn a suit of Ridium, he'd kept a spot open for his face. The lack of any features at all made this creature far more intimidating.

The arch remained still and silent. Blackness from the figure's shoulders oozed up in tentacles, joining the solid rainbow of Ridium. One remained, feeding into the creature's back like a tube, fused together with the body.

Cassius bumped into the front of the skimmer. He felt a hand reach over his shoulder and grab his arm. He turned to see Eva, trying to lift him up. He laid his foot on the vehicle's bumper and jumped, allowing her to guide him into the benchlike seat at the front of the vehicle. They had no roof. Apart from a curved windshield, it was like riding an old-fashioned horse and carriage. They'd be open not only to the elements, but to whatever this creature was going to do.

All at once, the arch of Ridium crumbled.

It did so without a sound, much like the Authority vessel had miles back. The blackness shifted into liquid, melting into an "m" shape before pooling on the ground in a thick mess. The figure stood in the center of it, unmoving. Cassius knew that it had made this happen, just by thinking it. This creature was a Shifter, and unlike any he'd seen before.

Without hesitation, Madame hit the accelerator and steered the skimmer in the opposite direction, making a tight turn away from the Ridium pool.

Cassius buckled himself onto the bench, nearly flying out the right side of the vehicle in the process. He kept his attention on the Shifter, craning his neck uncomfortably as they sped away.

"What is that thing?" Eva gawked behind her, shoulders trembling.

"Faster," Cassius coaxed.

Madame swore. "I'm trying."

It was obvious she was already pushing the engine to its limit. Skimmers usually moved at a good speed anyway, and this one seemed to have been augmented— most likely by Fringers. But it could be moving at 300 miles per hour and it wouldn't change the facts. They were hopelessly outmatched.

Cassius watched behind them as the black figure rose into the air, held aloft by a wave of Ridium underfoot. He knew what was going to happen next.

"We're in trouble," he muttered.

Madame turned to him. "What's happening back there?"

"He's coming after us."

With that, the figure surged forward, as did the immense pool of Ridium. It moved across the Fringes with horrifying speed, like a sentient puddle of oil. A tidal wave.

It would outrun their skimmer in minutes.

28

"Skandar." I grab at the dirt beside me in frustration, not knowing what to do. "Oh my god."

He looks up at me, eyes half shut, voice groggy as unconsciousness threatens him. "Is it bad?"

I grit my teeth, forcing tears back into my eyes. I turn and shout. "Avery! Savon!"

They're beside us in a moment. I watch Avery cup her hand over her mouth. Savon stands still, arms crossed.

"Help him!" I shout, though in reality I'm not sure what anyone can do out here.

Savon shakes his head. "He'll bleed out if we leave him long." He pauses. "Your ship is too far."

I watch as Skandar's eyes flutter closed. "Can't you ... can't you do *something*?"

Savon crouches at his side. "It's a clean cut. Ridium, most likely. It needs to be cauterized. A tourniquet will slow the bleeding, but not by much."

"What do you need?"

He lifts a hand. "Wait."

I stand, anxiously watching as Savon concentrates. I can barely look at Skandar. In one moment, hundreds of memories come flying into my brain. Times at the Academy, goofing off as kids. Conversations. Dares and one-ups. It can't end like this.

Just then, I notice a sliver of darkness inch its way out of the ground beside Skandar. A thin snake of Ridium coils along the length of his arm, then wraps tightly around the wound, cupping his blood-stained wrist. It fuses there, just as the Ridium bracelet had done on my own arm some time ago.

I glance back at my father. He lowers his fingers, finished controlling the substance.

"That'll hold," he says, "for a while. But it won't save him."

I run my hands through my hair, panicking. "We can't stay out here. He'll die."

Savon reaches under Skandar's body and stands, holding him in his arms. A few incomprehensible mumbles and Skandar's out. I check to see that he's still breathing.

"The best we can do is trudge back to the shuttle," Avery says. "But to be honest, I'm really feeling it now. I'm not sure how much longer my legs are gonna stand."

Savon turns, appraising me. "Are you okay?"

"It's not me I'm worried about."

"Your head," he continues. "That was a nasty hit . . . enough to knock you out for several minutes."

I glance at the sky. "Where did the Authority come from?"

"Everywhere," Avery answers. "At least, that's how it seemed."

"They descended on us like locusts," my father adds. "If we are being tracked, I don't know—"

He's interrupted as a shadow falls over the Fringes. I wince instinctively, though I don't yet see what's approaching.

A small ship rushes by overhead, not far from us. It kicks up a gust as it passes, then turns to circle around again. Nothing special in normal times, but the fact that any ship is airborne after the Authority took the skies is miraculous.

Savon steps back. "They've found us again. Prepare yourselves!"

"No." Avery holds a hand over her eyes to block the sun. "No. Jesse, look!"

I follow her gaze and fixate on the ship, struggling to see what she sees. As it veers closer, I recognize the familiar markings on its fins. The Skyship emblem.

My heart jumps at the sight of it. It's like spotting an oasis in the middle of the desert. I don't know who's piloting the ship or where it came from, but it's as close to salvation as we're gonna get.

I stagger forward, waving my arms. But the pilot already sees us. The ship descends.

"Jesse!" Savon shouts. "What are you doing? That craft should not—"

"It's okay!" I continue waving my arms, even as the ship nears the ground. "It's friendly!"

He doesn't respond. After our earlier conversation in the cruiser, I'm sure he's not thrilled, either. But none of that matters right now.

I rush forward as the ship lands, shielding my eyes from the dirt as the wind briefly kicks up again. I come to a stop feet from the ship's nose and wait, not knowing who or what will come out at me, but knowing that it has to be better than this.

The cockpit opens.

I watch Captain Alkine bound out from the pilot's seat, feet hitting the ground with a reverberating authority.

I haven't seen him in weeks. He wears a dark pair of goggles, which he moves up to reveal his weathered, concerned face. His graying hair's pulled back behind his head like usual. In a dark battle suit that covers every inch of his skin, he's not dressed for the Fringes.

I gawk for a moment before running at him. Before I know it, I've wrapped my arms around his midsection in a tight embrace. I don't know why I do it. I certainly didn't expect to. It's not me at all. It certainly wouldn't have been me a month ago, when I was doing everything bad I could think of to escape his grip. I've never thought of him as anything else than a leader—captain of the ship. We've sparred, verbally and physically. But now, I can barely let myself release him. Maybe it's the stress of everything that's just happened. Maybe I just want to be home again.

His hands fall to the side. I feel him squirm away. "Fisher," he whispers. "Fisher, it's okay."

I pull away, more than a little embarrassed that I just crumbled in front of him. As much as the touchy-feely isn't me, it's even more not-Alkine.

"No." Thoughts bombard my mind too fast to put into words. "Skandar. You have to help Skandar."

Alkine's attention shifts as he notices Savon for the first time. Instantly, he backs away, hand moving to the holster on his belt. "Who's that? Is that one of 'em?"

"He's hurt." I ignore him. "He's going to bleed to death if you don't—"

I watch as several more Skyship Agents spill out from the side of the ship. I recognize them all, though I couldn't come up with their names or ranks.

"I understand." Captain Alkine motions his troops forward. "We've got an emergency medical supply onboard, but we'll need to get back to the Academy."

Savon hands Skandar over to the nearest agent, wiping his hands clean of bloodstains. "His hand is over there in the dirt, if you're so inclined."

I keep my eyes on Alkine. "He's gonna be okay?"

"Amputation, you say?" He pauses. "If it's clean . . . it shouldn't be too much of a concern."

Savon crosses his arms. "The Ridium will hold until they can figure out something to do with him."

I crane my neck to see Skandar's unconscious body being hoisted into the ship. Alkine sidesteps, obscuring much of the sight. "You haven't answered my question, Fisher. Who is this man?"

"It's . . . it's my father."

"Your what?" Alkine gives me an expression like he's

just been punched in the gut. "You found—? I mean, that's the guy?"

Avery moves closer to my side, wiping the sweat from her forehead. "Crazy, isn't it?"

Alkine's lips purse as he glances at her. "I figured you'd be mixed up in this, Wicksen. I don't even want to know what you've been through. You look terrible."

"How did you find us?"

"We pulled your coordinates outside Portland when we spoke over the communicator. You weren't there when we arrived, but we knew you couldn't have gone far. We combed the Fringes looking for you." He grips my shoulders, looking straight into my eyes. "There were moments where I thought I'd never see you again, Fisher. I can't believe…" He squeezes harder. "I drove you away. It was incredibly stubborn of me. I've never been the listener I should be."

"But how is your ship flying? The Authority did something to the sky."

Alkine moves back. "Didn't affect us. I guess that's what we get for hiding on the other side of the world. Now get inside the ship. We can talk more on the way. We need to move fast."

I turn to look at my father. He stands, arms crossed, quietly sizing up Alkine. I have to remind myself that the two of them have never met before. Of course Savon would be suspicious. We were just attacked by enemies from the sky. Now some ship comes down and wants to take us onboard? It's all new to him, but I don't have time for arguments. Not when Skandar's life is on the line.

An agent steps out from the shuttle to get Alkine's attention. "Captain," he starts. "We're powering up."

"Yes," Alkine responds. "Come on, Fisher."

I nod, looking back at Savon. "I know we need to find Cassius, but this is the best way. And we can't—"

I'm interrupted by a shocked cry of pain. I turn to see the Academy Agent, impaled by a blade of darkness coming up from the ground. It retracts back into the dirt so quickly that it appears to simply vanish. The guy topples face forward, a mess of blood and flailing limbs. He's dead in seconds.

Alkine grabs my arm and pushes me toward the ship. But before he can move me too far, my father blasts forward, throttling through the air until he's knocked Alkine sideways and has me in his arms, pushing my back against the ship's wall.

"Are you okay?" Savon's eye is wild with fear.

"The ground," I start. "It's happening again. Ridium…"

Savon nods. "You're sure this man is who you say he is?"

"Of course I'm sure!"

Alkine picks himself up. "Into the ship, Fisher."

Savon turns to face him, releasing his grip on me. "It's not safe."

"Of course it isn't," Alkine responds. "That's why we're getting out of here. *Into the ship*, Fisher."

I move forward, but my father grabs my arm again. "It's

convenient, isn't it? Your captain finding you in the middle of nowhere?"

"Listen," I say. "I understand why you're freaked. But I don't want to stay down here when that stuff could come up at us any minute."

He glances up. "The skies are not safe, either. Or did you forget the ships crashing down around you?"

Captain Alkine flips open the side entrance to the ship's cabin. "I think we'll take our chances with the skies." He motions me in.

I lock on to Savon's good eye. "I have to go with Skandar. You do too. I need you."

He grits his teeth. "I pray you're not walking into a trap."

"I'm stronger with these people," I continue. "This is where we need to be. This is how we'll find Cassius too."

Savon curses, then releases his hold on me. "So be it."

Alkine ushers Avery inside the ship, then looks back at me. "Now that *that's* settled … in with you both. We have a lot to discuss, and I'd rather discuss it in one piece."

29

"Can't this thing go any faster?" Eva shouted, though Cassius could barely hear her over the oncoming wind as the skimmer powered forward.

He ventured another look behind them. The Ridium-encased figure floated in midair, pushed forward by the slushy substance at blistering speed. It was almost as if the creature was surfing. Cassius had never seen someone ride Ridium like this. Even a Shifter.

Madame cursed. "If I give it any more, the entire skimmer could break down."

Cassius grabbed hold of the back of his seat and unbuckled himself.

She clutched his arm. "What are you doing?"

"Trying to find something to slow this guy down." He wrestled away from her. Keeping his grip on the seat back, he jumped over toward the rear compartments of the vehicle.

"Cassius!"

He brought himself low against the skimmer, knowing that the wrong move would send him flying off, right into the very enemy he was trying to escape.

He'd studied these vehicles before, back when he was at

the Lodge training to become a Pearlhound. Of course, the ones he was familiar with were the standard Unified Party models. Who knew what had been done to this thing.

He pawed around for the emergency hatch. The Unified Party wasn't keen on sending out their troops without backup weaponry in case of a Fringe scuffle, and Cassius knew all the places to check for it.

Keeping one hand on the back of the seat, he unlatched the panel beside him and let the wind blow it open.

It was empty. They had nothing to fight back.

He forced his memory back to the battle with Theo. Madame's firepower from her government cruiser had been enough to stop the boy in his tracks, but Cassius didn't have the luxury of military-grade missiles at the moment. Once again, he'd have to make due with what was available.

He pulled himself back toward the seat, keeping his grip tight while balling his opposite fist and urging forth fire. He'd stoked it already before Madame had taken care of the Authority soldiers, so it wasn't difficult to get it flowing through him.

The blackness continued to surge forward, lapping at the back of their skimmer. Tendrils climbed from the goop, mere feet from grabbing onto the vehicle and pulling it back.

Cassius felt the heat surge from his fist, carried along by the wind, whipped back into the darkness.

It met their pursuer head-on, slamming into its body and spreading through the width of the black puddle. Like fire on oil, it burned bright for a moment, but soon dissipated into nothing. The creature continued its pursuit, unabated.

The skimmer shifted underneath them, thrown briefly to the side by a sideswipe from the Ridium tentacles. Cassius held on, but barely. The creature released the vehicle and wound back for another attack.

This time the Ridium coursed straight forward, past the capsules at the rear of the skimmer, past the fuselage and engine, and right toward Cassius.

He didn't have time to react before the tendril wrapped around his midsection and pulled him back. His neck strained with whiplash as his body lifted up and away from the skimmer, feet dangling in the air.

He couldn't focus on anything except the darkness before him. He heard the skimmer pull away. The sounds from its engine grew more distant by the moment.

He was twirled upside down, whipped around in nauseous circles before being flipped right-side up again.

Then, everything stopped. He regained his bearings, even as the Ridium tightened around his waist. A pair of eyes began to form before him as a layer of blackness sheathed away. Two red dots—pupils—met him head-on.

But it wasn't the eyes that really got to him. Underneath, blooming from the darkness like a half moon, was a smile. Murderous in intent, and wide. Gleaming. The sight of it said more than any words could have. This creature had him right where it wanted him.

All at once, the Ridium coursed forward.

It hit him like tar, splotched along his body. The moment it made contact, it latched onto his skin as if millions of tiny little fingers were grabbing at him. Cassius felt the central coil around his waist loosen. It hardly mattered anymore. Ridium crawled all over him.

His eyes widened. He tried to scream, but it wasn't long before the substance had worked its way up his neck, spilling closer to his face. He felt it on his chin. It touched his bottom lip, pulled at his hair as it slid down his forehead.

His arms were yanked to his sides, forced against his body like he was being wrapped up by a spider. He tried to kick, but the Ridium had grabbed hold of his feet as well.

His last chance was his fire, not that it had done much for him moments ago.

But before he could summon anything, the Ridium crawled into his mouth. At first, he choked on it. It tasted of harsh metal as it worked its way down his esophagus. Soon, it contracted enough so that he could breathe, but he still felt it crawling around inside him, like a cold serpent winding its way down to his stomach.

His eyes were covered. He existed in complete darkness. All sounds outside were muffled to the point of incomprehensibility, the Fringe heat a dull afterthought.

Then something astonishing happened.

His eyes bolted open, and he could see. The Ridium hadn't left his body. It hadn't uncovered his face, but he could see just the same.

The world was a prism of browns and silvers and a few colors he'd never seen before. The ground, which had been dull and lifeless before, now thrived with an added layer of reflective, almost sparkling elements. He could distinguish individual particles in the air, swirling around him like he floated in the middle of a blender. And more than this, he could see *through* it. The ground had become one layer of many, each accessible with no more than a thought. A catacomb of unending business stretched below him.

But most of all, he could see the Ridium.

His gut churned as he watched it course underneath Earth's surface, like a river gathering steam. It was everywhere, moving in patches, ready to strike whenever necessary.

Before he could think on it for too long, he felt his body press downward. His torso folded in as his knees rose to meet it. The Ridium encasing his body forced his hands down to his legs, gripping his shins and pulling up until he'd curled into a human ball, floating in the sky. Like a giant Pearl.

He began to spin, faster and faster until he wasn't sure where he was anymore. He couldn't control it. The element had fused so completely that it had melded with his brain, forcing his body in whatever direction it deemed necessary.

He straightened out again. He looked down. He was several yards from the ground now, suspended helplessly in the air.

He looked up. The stars shone brightly, even though it was still daytime. He'd never seen the solar system like this before. It was as if he could zoom in and judge distance between planets—see layers and cross-sections of stars he'd never known existed before.

The Earth's atmosphere became like a swamp. So much happened in the air, now. *Too* much. Dots and lines and transparent nets of material roped through his vision, sweeping across the sky like an entirely new race. The shock of it smothered any discomfort or terror he felt.

Still, he wasn't able to enjoy the sights for long. Within seconds the Ridium pushed on his feet. His entire body shot like a bullet into the air.

The world vanished below him, a gridline of unending curiosity. In front of him was space, and only space.

And he wasn't slowing down.

The stars reached out to touch him. He reached back.

Earth fell away from him, a tiny ball underfoot. The blue sky was swallowed up by a black, empty void as he catapulted into space.

He should feel cold. He should be struggling for breath. He felt nothing.

He stopped, floating in a netherworld between the planet and the solar system. It was like a vast, dark ocean—never ending. Pearls surrounded him on all sides, streaming downward. Some red, others green. None were close enough to touch, not that he'd be able to do anything with them if he could.

The Ridium continued to encase every square inch of his body. Just like on the Surface, he could see through it.

It offered some sort of alien lens, different than his normal eyes, in which everything looked fuller. If he concentrated, he could see around objects, look at their backsides without even moving. He gained a complete sense of distance—how long it would take to fly to the moon, to Mars or Saturn or beyond. It all seemed so attainable now, somehow.

But it wasn't to be. Seconds later, he felt the gravity of Earth begin to tug on him. He fell backward, slowly at first but gaining speed. All the while, he had an unencumbered view of the Heavens. It was the most striking, and most terrifying, thing he'd seen in his life.

He stretched his arms and legs apart and let himself go, like a falling star. Once he hit Earth's atmosphere, the descent was bumpier. He felt the wind resistance push up on him. Flames began to dance along the contours of his suit. Any meteor his size would have burned up. But somehow, the Ridium protected him.

He fell faster and faster, unsure of when—or where— he would land. He had faith that the impact wouldn't hurt him, but that didn't mean that his descent was peaceful.

The minute he entered blue sky again, he noticed the particles. The world was swimming with them. He wasn't sure what they were, but he became keenly aware of the thickness of the atmosphere. If he was any lighter, he could swim through it. Had the Authority put this stuff here when they opened their portals? Or had it always been in the air, invisible to the naked eye?

He landed right where he'd started, surrounded by the

skimmer and the pile of Ridium. The ground gave way immediately, leaving a human-shaped crater in the hard rock.

He lay still for a moment, in shock. As the Ridium began to drip from his face, carving a hole for his eyes, nose, and mouth, he noticed Madame and Eva, staring down at him from the edges of the crater he'd created.

No one said a word at first, though their expressions spoke loudly enough. In all his years at the Lodge, he'd never seen Madame look so surprised before. She usually knew exactly what to say and do. Suddenly she looked small, eyeing him from above. He couldn't believe that he used to fear her.

Eva wasn't the skittish type either, but her wide eyes and open mouth told him that she'd just witnessed something that shook her to her very core.

Finally, Madame spoke. "Cassius?"

Before he could respond, the Ridium pool above him whipped into a drill-shaped coil and burrowed into the ground. He tilted his chin so that he could watch it disappear beneath the surface. Without the Ridium covering his face, he lost track of it once it got too deep into the Earth's crust. The air became unclogged and plain. Everything snapped back to normal. More or less.

He pulled himself to a sitting position. It was surprisingly difficult, even though he felt no pain from anything that just happened. But he felt heavier, like his extremities were pulled down by weights, like he wore a full suit of armor.

Eva's mouth closed into a concerned frown. "Are you all right? How far did you go?"

He looked up at the stars. "I was in space," he muttered. "I saw the planets. Stars. Moons. Everything."

Her eyes narrowed. "That's impossible." But her words didn't carry much weight. Impossible wasn't in their vocabulary any longer.

"You're alive." Madame reached down. "And you stopped that thing from killing us. That's all that matters. Let's get you out of here."

He grabbed her hand, nearly pulling her down with him in the process. The truth was, he didn't need her help to climb out from the crater. The more he got used to it, the better equipped he felt to handle his body. His new body.

"You're covered in the stuff," Madame observed. "Can you ... can you take it off?"

"I don't know." He paced several steps into the desert, marveling at the protection the suit seemed to offer from the elements. Even if he could remove it, he wasn't sure that he'd want to.

"That creature sucked you up," Eva said. "The Ridium ... you just disappeared into it. It was horrifying to watch."

"It *felt* horrifying," he replied, "at first. Then it just felt kind of numb. And then ... good. It felt good."

He held his hands in front of his face, consumed by the incredible tightness with which the element seemed to grab him. He could clench his fists, rub finger against finger, and it hardly felt like he was wearing anything at all. A second skin.

Once he was finished staring, he noticed that the Shifter—the other Ridium-encased figure—had vanished, along with the black goop that had trickled into the ground.

"I feel … " Cassius spun to take in the entirety of the desert. "It's like I can sense the stuff everywhere. I can—" He clenched his fist and watched as a coil of Ridium burst through the ground in front of him, winding into the sky before it arced downward again and crashed into the ground, loosening into a wave of thick syrup. He pulled his hand to the side, reaching out his arm. The ooze shot through the Fringes in sharp daggers, puncturing the dirt where they landed.

"Whoa," Eva said. "You're a … a … "

"Shifter." He turned to face them. "I can make it move. I can reform it. Just like Theo. Just like Matigo."

Madame grabbed his shoulder. "But you—"

"Back in the memory," he interrupted. "The first senso-cube Fisher and I discovered … we heard Matigo talking about his son, Theo. He said the kid needed to be submerged in Ridium before heading to Earth. It triggers something, I think. I'm like him now. Everything's different. The *world* is different."

He concentrated on the Ridium around his face and felt it ooze back over his eyes. His vision became more complicated again. The particles in the sky reappeared, along with the vast amounts of Ridium underfoot. "I can still breathe," he said, "and talk. Even with this stuff over my face."

Madame stepped back. "Pull it up again. You look... I need to see your face. I can't convince myself that you're not suffocating in there."

He ignored her. "The Authority Shifter thought I'd die... thought I'd be smothered in the stuff. But there was enough of it. All I needed was to be covered completely. All this time, I never knew..." He looked down at his feet, seeing through the first layer of the Earth's crust. "But it's worse than we thought. The Ridium's everywhere. You wouldn't believe how much they've got stored down there."

Madame followed his gaze. "You can see through the ground?"

He nodded. "There's an entire layer, ready to be pulled to the Surface by a Shifter. Way too much for just one of us to use." He paused. "Back in the skimmer, when they were transporting us, I activated another cube and saw something. They can manipulate Ridium like water. I think they're going to bring it all up at once, Drown us."

Eva glanced nervously at the ground. "You're sure?"

"It's a guess," he replied. "But I don't know what else they'd do with so much of it." He glanced at the sky. "We have to stop them, but we can't stay here."

He closed his eyes. Suddenly the whole world was on offer to him. All he had to do was think it.

He visualized Ridium pooling up from the ground. Even though his eyes were closed, he could see it as clearly as if he were staring right at it. He saw the coils reach up and form a ball of perfect, uninterrupted blackness. He saw the ball flatten into a disc, then arch back up to create indentations—seats—for three people. He saw a protective guard form at the front, capable of blocking any oncoming Fringe dust.

When he opened his eyes to look upon it, he saw a vehicle. It was a sort of skimmer, formed of nothing more than Ridium. Forged by his imagination.

He lowered the makeshift vehicle to the ground as the others stared at it in quiet disbelief.

"Step in," he offered, settling his construction with a motion of his wrist.

Madame glanced at him, then back at the vehicle. "Are you … are you sure? What is this thing?"

"I know what I'm doing," he replied. "It'll hold. It's solid."

Taking a deep breath, Eva stepped forward and climbed onto one of the indentations toward the back. "It's like a surfboard," she remarked. "A fat surfboard. You're freaking me out, Cassius."

"It's a little nicer than a surfboard," he shot back before climbing into the front-most indentation. It held him without any give. The moment he sat down, it conformed to his body, like he was always supposed to be there.

Madame joined them last, carefully climbing onboard and allowing the substance to melt up and embrace her figure. "Marvelous." She ran her fingers across the black surface. "Cassius, I can't believe this."

He planted his fingers in front of him and knocked on the Ridium twice.

Seat belts grew from the vehicle and wrapped safely around all three of their waists.

He looked over his shoulder. "I'm going to move fast," he warned.

Madame's brows tensed. "How fast?"

"Fast enough that you might get some bugs in your teeth." He smiled. "So no more talking."

With that, the vehicle moved upward, so smooth and constant that it hardly felt that they were moving at all.

Then, with a snap of his fingers, the vehicle shot forward. The Fringes became a blur. They were off.

30

The Academy ship speeds into the air, moving faster than I've been able to all day. Skandar's back with a few of Alkine's Agents, who are doing all they can for him with what's available in the ship. I sit next to Alkine in the cabin. Savon rests behind us.

"We've climbed to maximum altitude," Alkine says. "We should be safer up here, I hope. From what I've seen, the Authority's been hesitant to fight too far above the Surface."

I stare out the front windshield. "I thought we'd be stuck on the ground forever."

"It looks like we picked you up just in time," he replies. "What happened down there? One of my men, gone. That thing from the ground . . . was it some sort of landmine?"

"I wish it was that simple," I say. "It was Ridium—the same substance that took Agent Morse and August Bergmann. The Authority controls it. It brought down Skyship Altair too."

Alkine grunts. "You've got a lot to tell me. We've been in the dark, essentially. Once the e-feed cut out and the

Chosens stopped broadcasting...we knew something was wrong. Just didn't know how bad it was."

I glance over my shoulder at Savon. He reclines on the bench at the far end of the cockpit, head bowed. "But it can't reach us all the way up here, right?"

He looks up, frowning. "I wouldn't be so sure. Anything's possible with the Authority."

"Then we'll move faster," Alkine says. "Jesse, I know that we didn't leave things the way that we should have. I see the reluctance in your eyes, even now."

"Just save Skandar," I interrupt.

"We will. But after that, I don't want you to get the idea...just because you've found your father—"

He's cut off by a swarm of dark-clad soldiers, zipping across the length of the windshield some distance away. Authority. Maybe the same ones who attacked us on the ground.

Alkine shakes his head, then steers the ship away from the soldiers' assumed path.

Savon turns to look out the window. "They don't expect to see humans airborne. They thought they'd dismantled all of your resources. Had they the firepower, they would've returned to finish us off."

"The Academy's just past the west coast," Alkine says, "not far from our coordinates before this whole thing with the Pearls started. We're over the Pacific. Off their radar, hopefully."

Savon frowns. "For now."

Alkine shakes his head. "The world's gone crazy. I've never seen the skies so quiet before, or so many trails of smoke coming from the Surface.

"We're on our own," I mutter.

Alkine laughs. "You'd think we'd be used to it by now."

———

When the outline of Skyship Academy finally pulls into view, I'm flooded with memories. It was only six months ago that Eva, Skandar, and I had flown up here from Syracuse—three loser trainees who'd just flunked their first Surface mission. I knew nothing of this war back then. The only battle I could relate to was the one waging inside of me.

Flash forward and the Academy's the only Skyship still airborne. It's a weird sort of irony. We've never been much of an imposing ship. We're no Atlas or Polaris...just a small school with a couple thousand passengers. Of course, that number had been cut in half when we split to hide out in Siberia. There are probably even less now.

Still, it's home. And right now, in the middle of all of this, just the sight of it gives me the boost of morale I've been missing for weeks now. For a brief moment in time, I'll no longer be some runaway combing the Fringes with no hope of finding what I'm looking for. The Academy brings order, and relative safety.

I glance at our altitude display. It's just below 65,000 feet. That's a lot higher than most Skyships venture. The unending blue of the Pacific stretches before us, sunlight glinting off the surface. After so long in the Fringes, the sheer size of the ship seems impressive. It hovers before us like a castle in the sky—wider than several city blocks and taller than even the most impressive Chosen City. I long to head up and breathe the cool, recycled air of Lookout Park, or walk along the quiet corridors. Unfortunately, those are luxuries that'll have to wait.

I know Alkine's game plan. He's a soldier. He likes strategy—emotional disconnect from the situation. Kind of like Cassius. He'll want meetings. Battle plans. I've never been able to do that kind of stuff so well. He's like Savon in that way. They're all worried about the bigger picture, what I *should* be worried about. Instead, I just want Skandar to be all right and for my father to stay with me until the war is over.

Alkine's words break me from my thoughts. "I'd expect a bit of a welcoming party, Fisher. They've missed you."

I take a deep breath. "Yeah, right."

"You think I'm kidding?"

The door to the cockpit opens and Avery strides forward. "He's going to be fine." She directs the words to me, knowing that I desperately want to hear them. Then she turns her attention to the fast-approaching Skyship. "You know, for a while back there I never thought I'd see her flying again, and over American soil, no less."

"Are you okay, Avery?"

"Fine," she responds. "Nothing a little rest won't cure. If I'm so lucky."

I turn to look at my father. He remains at the back of the cockpit, head bowed and eyes closed. I'm not sure if he's sleeping or just charging himself up again. Whatever the case, I decide not to disturb him.

Alkine levels us out and flips a switch on the ceiling. "Five minutes. Prepare yourselves for a lot of noise and a lot of faces."

We watch in silence as the Academy pulls closer. Our ship heads to the lowest level, an open docking bay ready for our landing. As we continue to approach, I notice my body start to tremble. I don't know what it is, but the sight of the bay makes me feel sick. I stand, wiping my forehead.

Avery notices. "Is something wrong, Jesse?"

I shake my head. "I'm fine."

But I'm not. My heart races. Breath tightens. If I continue to let this get to me, it'll be a full-blown panic attack.

It's full circle. Seeing the Academy again, realizing that I'm really going home, brings this entire war into focus. Before, it was like I was on some long odyssey in another world. I'd managed to separate all of the traumas of the past few months from the rest of my life. But looking at the Academy like this, floating nearly where it had been before I learned the secret of Pearls, is like déjà vu. But I've changed, and my circumstances have *definitely* changed.

Avery moves beside me. "Jesse—"

"It's okay." I take a deep breath, tilt back my head, and

stare at the ceiling for a moment. It's going to be fine. We're going to win this. My father's here. I'm not alone.

I keep my attention on the interior of the cockpit even as our ship sets down inside the bay. Then I hear it.

The sound of the crowd starts as a dull roar and continues to build as the ship's cabin door opens. They'll take Skandar out first, straight to the med center to get fixed up.

Alkine shuts down the power to the console and stands. "I'll go first. Make sure your father is close by your side. We don't want people getting the wrong idea." With that, he opens the cockpit door, letting in the full clatter from outside, and strides into the docking bay.

Savon wakes from his meditation for the first time. He looks at me with a blank expression before stretching and moving to his feet. "This is your domain, son. I will follow."

Avery grabs my hand and squeezes, and together we move from the cockpit to the cabin, to bay.

The energy of the people hits me straight away. I've never seen or felt such a fervor onboard the Academy. We've had guests from time to time, as well as Agents coming back after a difficult mission, but all in all our team is pretty subdued. We'd had to operate in secret for so long that I guess it taught us all the value of restraint.

This is like a sports match. An arena concert. Nobody even seems to bat an eye when Savon emerges behind us. The cheers echo in the large expanse of the docking bay as we move down a narrow corridor created by the crowd.

As I look out among them, I notice some of the teachers' faces. Mrs. Dembo, head of Year Ten. Mr. Kennewick and Mr. Sorensen—teachers I would have had for my next two years of training. I'm not sure they could teach me anything I haven't learned already, as a result of everything that's happened.

Avery and I walk down the length of the docking bay, following Alkine. The crowd parts to let us through, but that doesn't stop hands from reaching out to attempt awkward high-fives. It's a blur of faces as I'm led out the wide door and into the familiar corridor at the bottom level of the ship.

Everything's as I left it. The stale smell of the recycled air is comforting, as is the sheen from the lights overhead.

We take the elevator up to the top levels. Skandar's long since been transported away. I wish I could do the same—find a place where I can be alone with my thoughts. But I know that even if we find an hour or two to unwind, I'm at the center of this war. It won't be long before I have to join the battle again.

The elevator lets us off on Level Five, home to meeting rooms, classrooms, and Alkine's office.

He stops, then turns and hands me a com-pad. "Give me a few moments. I want to brief my men before we talk strategy. Grab something to eat if you want. I'll be in touch when we're ready." He glances over my shoulder at Savon before heading down the hallway.

I let my shoulders loosen and exhale—a long sigh of relief. The panic that I felt in Alkine's ship has faded, replaced with a weird familiarity. The Academy. With all its old worries that seem so small now. At least I know what to expect here. And better than that, I know the kind of firepower the ship's capable of in a fight. I saw it firsthand in Seattle a few months ago. Alkine can order maneuvers on a scale that I couldn't compete with on my own. Will he really be able to help us?

"Shower," Avery says. "I need a shower before I'm good to do anything."

I nod. We all do. We need a second to get our bearings, to refuel and reorient ourselves to this battle. Because it's going to get worse before it gets better. That much I don't even have to question.

31

Cassius had never felt such freedom before. Even piloting a government cruiser came with its own restrictions. In contrast, the Ridium board underneath him functioned as an extension of his own body. It took but a thought to control it.

Even so, he was forced to look away often during their Ridium-fueled trip cross-country. If it wasn't the Chosen Cities in the background, exposed and burning, it was the numerous Fringe Towns they passed through.

The Fringes weren't a nice place at the best of times. But now, it was clear that many towns had been the unlucky settings of attacks from the Authority. The smell of smoke and blood became a constant reminder as skeletal buildings passed by. Three times, they'd narrowly avoided crashing right into the middle of a conflict. Whether it was simply an uprising of sorts or a battle against the invaders, Cassius didn't know.

All he knew for sure was that they kept going forward.

He didn't have much of a plan, but he knew that they were heading west. And west, more likely than not, was where he'd find Fisher.

Their sleek craft moved at a remarkable speed—fifty

times faster than any land transport he'd ever known, including the Unified Party's Chute system. Even better than that, his effortless control of the Ridium didn't leave him feeling any more fatigued than when they'd left the site of his submergence. Once he got it going in the right direction, the craft moved on its own, pushed along by some impossible inertia, as if nothing—even the particle-filled air—would get in its way.

They stopped once at an old storehouse to ravage through some food, but barely spoke. The entire situation was too hard to comprehend. Words didn't quite do it justice.

Soon, night came. Even though he could have kept their transport going, they decided to stop outside a Fringe Town, a place called Saint Francis—though several of the letters were missing from the city's sign. It was too small to be inhabited, but that didn't mean that there wouldn't be a Fringer or two around.

They found an old farmhouse on the outskirts of town, with a bed and a couch downstairs. Both had seen better shape. They decided to take turns keeping watch. Cassius elected to go first, partly because he wasn't particularly tired and partly because he wanted some time alone.

He sat on the wraparound front porch of the old farmhouse, his back against the outside wall. He'd allowed the Ridium to slip from his head, forming what looked like a combat bodysuit around the rest of him. From far away, people would probably mistake it for something as simple as a black shirt and trousers. In the darkness, there wasn't even much of a reflection off the material.

A Shifter.

He concentrated on the Ridium clinging to his chest. With but a thought, he could pull a strand of it into the air, thicker and longer until a trunk of blackness oozed from his chest. He flattened it into a shieldlike circle in front of him, then all at once snapped it back against his body to look like a suit once more.

He thought back to Theo—Matigo's son—and remembered how the boy had seemingly been driven crazy by the substance. For a panicked second, he wondered if the same could happen to him. But the kid had always been wrong in the head, and Cassius didn't feel like he was losing a grip on anything. In fact, it was the opposite. Everything seemed clearer, like the world had gone from flat to round right before his eyes.

"Cassius."

He heard Madame's voice behind him, soft in the silence of the night air.

He didn't turn to look at her. "You're supposed to be sleeping."

"Wishful thinking." She moved beside him. "What's on your mind?"

He chuckled. Like she cared about anything that was troubling him. She'd never cared, only pretended to so that she could use him.

"This is a marvelous substance," she continued, her

hand reaching out to touch his arm before stopping inches away. "I remember when you first came to me, with that box made of Ridium. I labored over it for some time, trying to discern where it had come from. Imagine my surprise when I realized that it was not from Earth."

He shook his head. "You could have done so much more."

She paused for a moment in silence before continuing. "I've failed you, Cassius. I know you think me too prideful to make such an admission, but it's true. I'm understanding that more and more. Each time I see you in action, I see my own shortcomings."

"Is this supposed to make me feel better?"

"No," she said. "We're past that now, aren't we? No one feels good about anything anymore. We simply carry on."

Cassius continued to look out into the night. Part of him wanted to flip the Ridium up over his eyes, just to get away from her, but he didn't.

"I'm not an apologetic person," Madame continued. "You know that, I'm sure. I wouldn't have been able to get where I am today defending myself at every turn. But it doesn't matter anymore. What use is power if there's no one to wield it over? The Unified Party is in ruin. It may never be rebuilt. We've seen tragedy before, but nothing on this scale."

Cassius's brows rose. "If you've come here looking for someone to make you feel better, you can save your breath."

"No," she replied. "I'm not that naïve. I've come to apologize, Cassius, for all I've done to you. For your entire life. For the façade I put up when you were younger, for the secrets I kept, and for using and abusing you these past few months. I was drunk on my own ambition. I couldn't see clearly." She paused. "I hope you appreciate how difficult this is for me to say."

He shook his head, chuckling. "It's always about you."

Madame sighed. "There was a time, before Pearls started falling. Before the Scarlet Bombings. I was young. The government was already fragmented. The country was like a jigsaw puzzle, so close to falling into fragments. Many of us didn't want to see that happen. People like myself. People like Jeremiah Alkine.

"I was idealistic." She scoffed. "Such a long time ago. I thought I could serve my people. Little did I know that serving anyone was not in my nature. Battle lines were already drawn deep when I arrived at the White House. Had our country been spared the initial attack from Haven—had we been forced to work together without the luxury of Pearls— that idealism I felt might have been enough to sew up the fractures. But idealism is the first thing to go when confronted with the horrors of war." She paused. "Stark realism, and a need to survive. That's what I am now. That need quickly turned to desperation. Desperation turned to cold, calculated apathy. That's what I was when you came into my life, Cassius. I'd changed, and it wasn't something even you could undo."

He shook his head. "That's a nice story, but I don't buy it."

Her head bowed. She sighed. "Fine. I'm trying, Cassius. I don't want this to end without some sort of understanding between the two of us."

He closed his eyes, concentrating on the pulse of the Ridium against his body. It trembled along his skin, spiking upward and out, looping and arching in varying directions like he was some kind of moving art installation. When he opened his eyes again, the substance had settled. "I think it's too late for that."

Madame nodded. "I see. Well, I can tell you this much. That old adage they say is correct. Absolute power corrupts absolutely. Take it from someone who experienced it first-hand. Be careful what you do, Cassius. The road to forgiveness is long, and doesn't always end in the manner you'd hope it would."

With that, she moved back into the house, leaving him alone with his thoughts. A gust of wind brushed past him. He hardly noticed. Within seconds, he forgot about her and returned to his post. Waiting.

32

I stand in the doorway to my dorm room, hair still wet from the shower, wearing a fresh set of Academy clothing.

As I stare into the room, I notice how small and dirty it is. Nothing's been tampered with since I last left it. The bed is unmade, blankets sculpted in hollow peaks. The blinds to the window are drawn, though lines of sunlight poke through, especially in the bent places.

That's where I head first, to open them and let some light in.

Savon enters the room after me. I watch his good eye appraise the place. I can't tell from his expression what he's thinking. Not that it really matters.

"This is it," I say, somewhat embarrassed. "This is where I grew up. Well, for the last few years at least. I used to have a room down on the ... " I trail off. He doesn't care about these kind of details. Why would he?

My father takes a seat at the edge of my bed, finding the one spot where the blankets actually lie flat.

"Jesse," he starts, "your brother is getting closer."

I drop the wand connected to the blinds. "Cassius? How do you know?"

"I sense it," he says. "Ever since we left the ground, I've had this feeling, like a homing signal in my gut. I don't know what happened, but he's coming to us. This is good news."

"I hope you're right." I push a pile of clothes into the corner with my foot. "Listen, I've been wanting to talk to you about something. I've been having these dreams. They started a few days ago, but back on the Surface, after I passed out, I saw the visions again."

"Visions?"

"Fire," I say. "I'm in the middle of it. Before, Cassius had always controlled it. But this last time, he wasn't even there until the end. And then ... then he came running at me. *Right* at me. And he sorta disappeared. The fire turned green, like a Pearl, and that was it."

Savon nods, though he doesn't look at me. "I wouldn't put too much stock in dreams, Jesse. You've been under a lot of stress lately. We all have. Your subconscious is likely to play tricks on you."

"See, normally that's what I'd say." I cross my arms. "But the past few months, these kind of dreams always lead to something. They're not normal."

"Sit." He motions to his side, waiting for me to join him. "Before long, we'll be joined in battle. There won't be time to talk ... only to fight. I want you to know, Jesse ... you and Cassius both." He pauses.

"I haven't been around to watch you grow up. Trust me when I say there's nothing I would have rather done than follow you to Earth immediately. But it wasn't to be.

Still, I have a great deal of respect for you and what you've been through. I know it wasn't easy, what your mother and I asked of you, but our hands were forced. We needed to get you to safety, and we needed a way to ensure our allies would be able to fight against the Authority."

I nod. "I understand."

"All the sacrifices we made," he continues. "All the doubt you harbored, will be for nothing if we let Matigo win. You and Cassius, you mean the world to me. So promise me this."

"Anything," I say.

"When the battle is upon us"—he turns to me—"look out for each other. It is vital that neither one of you falls. Absolutely vital."

"Yeah," I reply. "I get it. Neither one of us wants to fail."

"No," he says. "You must stay close. The Key and the—"

"Catalyst," I finish.

"Yes," he says. "Stay close to me."

I rub the back of my shoulder, trying to work out a twisted muscle. "Of course."

He nods. "Together, you're stronger than anything. Alone, you're a scared child. And scared children don't win wars."

I grit my teeth. "So that's why we're waiting for Cassius."

"Yes," he replies. "That's why."

"And if he doesn't come?"

Savon stands. "He will."

I nod, taking a deep breath as my gaze falls to the floor. "What's the first thing we're going to do, after the war?"

"I don't understand."

"It's a stupid question," I continue. "I know. I just... I can't help thinking about what happens after the Authority is gone. We have... we have a whole life together. How's it going to be?"

Savon rests his chin in his hands. "I... I suppose we'll remain on Earth. Find your mother, if that's what fate has in store."

"There's so much I can show you," I say. "There's... this whole world is new to you, right?"

He nods.

"Cassius and I... we can both show you what it's like to be on Earth."

"I'd like that."

I bite my lip, shoulders slumping. "Me too. That would be... that would be pretty flaunt, huh?" I glance around the room as I try to think of what to say to him next. "There's nothing special in here, I guess. You want to see where I used to train?"

"Of course," he says. "Show me your ship. It's best to know your surroundings in case of an emergency, right?"

"Yeah." I stand and head for the door. "Yeah, of course."

As we walk into the hallway, the image of our family won't leave my mind. What will we all look like together? How can we possibly live a normal life after all that's happened?

Then I remember. Cassius doesn't even know that Savon's alive. We've been out of contact for so long. I can't imagine what his reaction will be when he finds us, but I can't wait to see it. Having him here will make everything seem real.

Just as I close the door, I hear a beep from the com-pad Alkine gave me before leaving. He's ready for us.

I look up to my father. "Guess we'll have to take a rain check on that grand tour. We've got a meeting with Alkine."

"So be it."

"This way." I motion. "The elevators are the fastest. You don't want to be late when Captain Alkine calls. Trust me."

Savon follows me. "I'm not worried about your captain, Jesse. I've survived years under the Authority's rule. I doubt whether anything could intimidate me."

I laugh. "Okay, then. Well, he still scares the crap out of me. So let's hustle."

33

Cassius took a seat at the edge of the porch, fighting the lure of sleep. He had only thirty minutes more before Eva arrived to take over lookout, and he wanted to make the most of it.

He opened a slot in the Ridium suit to get to his pocket. There were still four senso-cubes in there. He knew it wasn't very safe to go off into a memory when he was supposed to be keeping watch over the house, but he told himself that they would be quick. And more than that, they would be important. The first two had already shown him so much. More than anything, he craved to learn what had happened to his parents. The Authority had captured them. Had they escaped? He was desperate to find out.

With that thought, he delved into the first cube. It turned out to be a disappointment, sharing no more than an extended look at a street corner, most likely a sliver of one of Haven's vast cities. While initially fascinating, given the strange, free-flowing architecture and the crowds of interestingly dressed civilians, it didn't offer any answers. Cassius could barely even make out individual conversations. The city was so bustling and noisy.

The next two cubes offered looks at similar scenes—shots of buildings and the interiors of hallways. Whispered conversations too quiet and fast to pick up, even though they'd been translated to English for his brain.

The fourth and final cube, though, held a different story.

At first, he wasn't sure if it had worked, for the surroundings he found himself in were as dark as the one he'd left on the front porch of the farmhouse.

But soon, he felt trapped. He stood in the corner of a tight room. No windows, no doors that he could see. There were, however, two large objects in the center of the room. Cassius couldn't make out details, but they seemed to be a pair of tables.

Then, out of nowhere, a voice rumbled through the room.

"This is not a request. A request you can shirk. This is a *demand*."

Cassius plastered himself against the wall. He looked down and noticed that he wasn't wearing the Ridium suit any longer. He felt more vulnerable in normal clothing.

He recognized the voice immediately from another saved memory he'd witnessed. The characteristic boom, the impossible harshness of it. It was Matigo, leader of the Authority. But Matigo wasn't in the room now. His voice came from speakers, or some similar kind of technology.

"I'm aware that you cannot speak any longer," the voice

continued. "That is fine. I don't need your words. I already have your voices. What I crave now are your thoughts."

Cassius continued to look around the room, convinced that there was someone else in there with him. The longer his eyes had to adjust to his surroundings, the more he could see—bottles full of strange liquids lining dusty counters on one wall, sharp tools hanging on another. It was like being stuck in some mad scientist's underground laboratory.

"Pearls," Matigo said. "I understand their significance now. Soon, the Authority will have its own armada, twice as strong as your Resistance." His voice paused, then cut through the silence once more. "It's not Pearl energy that I'm interested in, it's Pearlbreakers. The Key and the Catalyst. You've found a weapon against my Ridium, haven't you? A weapon that needs to be destroyed before it becomes a threat to my people."

Cassius swallowed, listening carefully while trying to work up the courage to venture deeper into the darkness. He knew that nothing in the room could hurt him or even touch him, but he was scared of what he could find if he moved closer to the tables. More than that, he was scared of how helpless he would feel. There was nothing he could do here but watch. And listen.

He took a step forward as Matigo spoke again. "Even now I am pulling the secrets from your brains. Things you've forgotten you've stored, things you haven't even told each other... not that it will matter once I'm done."

He laughed—a dry, hollow sound.

Cassius took another step. The walls vibrated with Matigo's voice.

"Rest with the knowledge that I'll find and kill your children just as easily as I've captured you. You won't be around to see it happen, so you'll have to trust me. Sending them to Earth was a mistake."

Another step.

Cassius reached out, making sure that he wouldn't bump into anything in the darkness. As the pair of tables grew closer, he could make out more details. Etchings wound around the sides of the slabs. They'd been carved from some sort of stone, cool to the touch when he ran his fingers across the surface.

Before he had a chance to peer closer, the ceiling lit up. Red.

He bounded backward, shocked by the sudden change in the room. He had to shield his eyes as a powerful crimson glow emanated from somewhere far beyond the ceiling.

It illuminated the bodies on the stone tables.

Cassius forced himself to look down.

He recognized the two of them at once, though he'd only seen one photo back in Seattle when Madame's Ridium-constructed box had opened and revealed the image of his parents.

Savon and Adaylla. They were unmistakable, even with the lower half of their faces obscured by heavy clamps and their legs and arms harnessed to the slabs.

They lay on their backs, like human sacrifices to some

powerful scarlet god above them. Even though Cassius could see very little skin outside their stained white clothing, he could tell that they were injured. Bruised, beaten up. His father had a black eye, his mother a large scar across her forehead. They both wore large, constricting vests of metal, which weighed their midsections down against the stone. Cassius recognized this particular device as the same one he'd seen in the forest—the weapon the Authority woman had used on the man called Jorbun. The one that had ultimately killed him.

His first instinct was to rush forward, to wrap his fingers around the restraints and try to pull them off, but he knew that it would do no good. This was all in the past. He couldn't help them. He couldn't even talk to them.

Matigo's assured, frustratingly elusive voice came again. "Your allies think you've gone into hiding. That's the message we've fed to your networks. They won't know the truth until well after you're gone."

Cassius watched his father glance over at his mother, a subtle expression in his eyes that—even though neither could talk—could only mean goodbye.

"It's a brave battle you've waged," Matigo continued. "You have nothing to be ashamed of. You were simply not up to the challenge."

Cassius backed away, looking straight up at the glowing red, trying to see past it. Maybe there was an added dimension, the kind he'd seen with the suit of Ridium across his face.

If there was, he couldn't break through it. The brightness forced his eyes away as Matigo delivered his final words.

"I have what I need," he said. "It's been an honor. Say goodbye to all of this."

"No," Cassius replied, not even trying to keep his emotions at bay any longer. "No."

The devices around his parents activated and suddenly the room was filled with a sickly smell as their bodies decomposed right in front of him, reduced to a pile of flesh, bones, and soaking blood that spilled over the sides of the tables.

Cassius reached out a hand as if to pull them back into life. "No."

With that, the memory dismantled around him, fading into blackness before it was replaced by the horizon of the Fringe Town in front of him. He stood on the porch, bolt upright, and looked out into the night.

His breath was a tangle in his throat. His shoulders heaved. He wasn't sure how long he stood there before Madame's voice interrupted his panic.

"Cassius."

He turned to see her standing in the doorway again, hair messy. Her face was free of glasses—scuffed up and tired. She looked older, somehow.

He stood for a moment, staring at her, saying nothing.

"You shouted," she whispered, glancing over his shoulder at the darkness beyond.

He swallowed. "My parents are … my parents are dead."

She met his eyes. Her jaw tightened, like she didn't know what to say. Instead, she held out her arms. He staggered forward, allowing her to embrace him.

"There, there." She patted his back like she used to do when he was little. He could argue with her again, run away into the night, but it was easier to simply give in and let her hold him.

After a while, Cassius pushed away and wiped his eyes. "Thank you."

"They would have been very proud of you, Cassius. As proud as I am."

"Please don't talk about yourself."

She nodded, a soft chuckle betraying her frown. "I'm sorry. Force of habit. But you've got to understand this. You're more than a soldier." She stepped away, resting her back against the wall. "There's no debating your skill level. There never was. But beyond that … there's something else inside of you. The kind of bravery that people like me can only dream of possessing. The ability to risk your life—not for yourself, but for everybody else.

"I don't know where it came from," she continued. "Certainly not from me and my teachings. You're incredibly special. Your parents must have been incredibly special as well."

He glanced up at her, searching for a hint of duplicity or insincerity. For once, it wasn't there.

He looked away. "That's nice of you to say, but it's a lie."

"Oh?"

"I'm a soldier, like you said. That's what I was trained to be and that's how I ended up. I fight. It's all I know how to do. And when that doesn't work, I kill. There's nothing brave about that."

She sighed, appraising him for a moment before speaking. "We'll see."

Silence fell between them, so quiet that Cassius could hear insects chirping in the distance. Encased inside his Ridium suit, he knew that all he would have to do is turn and focus and he'd be able to work out their exact location. He could probably conjure a fly-swatter from the dark stuff and snuff them out before they even knew what hit them.

He swallowed. "I accept your apology, but that doesn't mean things are going to be easy between the two of us."

"I never asked for that."

"Good." He wiped the bottoms of his eyes. "You fight by my side, with no motive or exception. That'll go a long way in proving that you mean what you say."

"Of course," she replied. "I can't think of anything that—"

Her expression froze. She laid a hand on his shoulder, pulling him forward again. Her voice was a whisper as she gently prodded him around to face the scenery beyond their farmhouse. "Do you see that? We need to get inside."

He squinted. At first he didn't notice them, his mind still clouded by Madame's words and the memory he'd just witnessed. But as more and more appeared from the darkness, they became impossible to ignore.

Red dots. Pairs of red dots.

The eyes of the enemy, as the Drifters had called them.

The dots surrounded the farmhouse, the closest as near as the dried-up tree in the front yard, the farthest half a block away, across the street hiding in the faraway brush.

Cassius counted twenty-four dots in total, which meant twelve soldiers—easily more than they'd ever faced before.

Instantly, he ordered the Ridium suit to cascade up over his head, covering his entire body. As before, the world transformed. Through the Ridium, he perceived outlines of their bodies. He noticed every subtle movement. The darkness no longer seemed a hindrance to him.

There were more than twelve. And worse yet, they were ready to attack.

34

My fingers drum against the tabletop. I feel hopelessly out of place, but I don't let that get to me.

Captain Alkine stands in front of a window so big that it stretches across the entire wall of the curved meeting room, offering a panoramic view of the Pacific Ocean outside. Eight of his closest advisors sit on either side of the equally impressive tabletop, while Savon, Avery, and I take the far end. It's Skyship Academy's largest situation room—a place I had never been granted access to before this whole fiasco.

Alkine paces, head bowed as he speaks. "What do we know? That's the first order of business, and that's why you're so valuable, Jesse."

I glance at my father. There's so much to tell, and I don't know where to begin. But even knowing all I do about the Authority and Haven, I still can't offer much in the way of concrete battle plans.

Savon responds before I can say anything. "We're awaiting his brother, Cassius Stevenson."

Alkine's brows rise. "Cassius? The same kid who nearly got us all killed?"

"My father thinks—"

"I don't *think*," Savon interrupts. "I *know*. My two sons, together, can bring the end of this invasion."

Alkine stops. "How, exactly?"

"I designed Pearl transport. The effects on their physiology run deep. The Authority won't be able to—"

"And what is the Authority meaning to do, exactly?" Alkine leans his hands on the edge of the table. "Besides destroy our civilization, that is."

I look over to him. There's a crackle in the air between Alkine and my father. They're likely the two strongest men I've met. I know neither quite trusts the other. That schism can't be allowed to grow into anything more.

"Look," I start. "I know we haven't seen eye to eye very often, especially lately. But Savon says Cassius is on his way, and I trust him. I've been having these visions and ... and he's already saved my life more than once. Hear him out. There's more that Cassius and I can do than you know about. There's a reason we were chosen for this."

Alkine sighs, glancing at each of his advisors before speaking. "Point me in the right direction. That's all I ask. I want to help, not to get in the way. But I need something to do. As far as we know, we're the only operational Skyship in the country. That's got to count for something."

I nod, waiting for my father to speak. He doesn't. Instead, he closes his eyes. His entire face tenses for a moment before relaxing again.

Then I feel it.

The familiar tug of Pearls pulls on my chest. The hairs on my arms stand on end. I look past Alkine, at the ocean beyond the glass. In seconds I see a pair of green orbs shooting down at a diagonal, headed toward me.

Alkine catches my distracted expression. "Fisher?"

I grit my teeth. Normally, I'd welcome the arrival of Pearls, but not when I'm onboard a ship like this. I don't want to do any more damage to the Academy than I already have.

"Move away from the window," I say. Just in case.

I stand and bring my arms out in front of me, as if readying to conduct an orchestra. I watch the Pearls' descent carefully, but more than that I feel them in my gut. I can't let them get too close before breaking them.

Raising both hands at once, I wait until they're in full sight and clench my fists.

Each and every advisor at the table careens backward, instinctively reacting to the dual explosions outside. For a second, the once-calm panorama beyond the window is a sea of dense green energy. Whatever hits the ship itself works its way into the circuitry, giving our engines a nice boost. The rest shoots into the sky in all directions.

It takes a moment before I see the Drifters freed from the falling Pearls. I expect them to pinwheel off in varying directions, shock-addled by the new world they find themselves in, but instead they continue on in their exact paths toward the meeting room, pointed like daggers descending on the window.

I step back. "What?"

I bring both arms forward, hoping that maybe I can manipulate the energy around them—force them in a different direction. Even if they hit the window, they can't be strong enough to break through the thick layer of fiberglass. They aren't Pearls anymore.

I'm wrong.

Both Drifters easily bore their way through the window, assisted by their fields of green energy. Before I can react, the glass shatters in two oversized bullet holes, letting loose an instant vacuum in the room. Anything not nailed down flies out of the openings. Advisors bolt to the far end, nearest to the inner wall.

I don't move. Instead, I watch the Drifters come at my father, so fast and intent that there's no way I'm stopping them.

He backs away, but not before they collide with his body, setting forth an explosion of green that sends everyone but me tumbling off their feet.

The energy courses into my body, making me stronger.

My father lurches downward, but remains standing. Barely. The Drifters pulse backward in the air, then come at him again. Punching. Kicking. Biting. Anything they can do to keep him from getting the opportunity to fight back.

They're crazy. Rabid. I have to do something.

Once I'm able to overcome the shock of it, I stumble forward, fighting the pull from the air as it whips past me. I focus in on the closest Drifter—reach out my hand in clawed desperation—and grab hold of the energy. With as much strength as I can muster, I pull my arm sideways across my chest and watch as the Drifter follows the same arc, yanked back through the air until he smashes into the window.

He struggles, arms and legs flailing like a giant insect, but I keep him flattened against the glass. And when I let go, the suction from the nearest hole instantly pulls him out.

Savon still fights against the second Drifter—hand-to-hand combat that moves so fast it almost becomes a blur. I latch onto the Drifter's energy and try to slow him down, pull his arms behind his back so that my father can strike a decisive blow.

It doesn't take much. The poor Drifter doesn't stand a chance against our combined power. Once I've got him frozen, my father hits him with a powerful punch to the jaw. I gently lower the now-unconscious Drifter to the ground.

Free from the threat of attack, I realize that Savon and I are the only two left in the room. Everyone else retreated out the door to the corridors beyond during the fight. It's a good thing, too, as the chamber's becoming more and more depressurized as the openings in the window continue to spread.

I try to meet my father's eye, but he turns away, heading for the door.

I step forward, unsure of what to say or do. I've never seen friendly Drifters act like that before. Not only had they been strong enough to breach the room, but the kamikaze-like intention in their movements was uncharacteristic for a newly freed Drifter, and more than a little unsettling.

Plus, they'd gone straight for my father, like they'd been programmed by the Authority or something.

"We've gotta get out of here," I shout to him. "Before the—"

"I need to talk to you, Jesse," he interrupts. "Alone."

With that, he pulls on the door handle and disappears into the hallway. I take a deep breath and follow, hairs still on end, heart beating double time.

35

Cassius pushed Madame back toward the doorway of the farmhouse. "Get back inside."

"I'm not leaving you here alone." She stood her ground.

Cassius stole another glance into the darkness. He wasn't sure if the foot soldiers' intent was to sneak up. If so, they were failing. If not, their movement seemed unusually slow. The longer they took, the less convinced he became that they meant to attack at all.

Ignoring Madame, he took the two steps down from the porch and stood in the front walkway, waiting.

The soldiers continued their approach. Cassius could see their every move—darkness or no darkness. They formed a semi-circle in front of him, eyes glowing crimson in rapt attention. It was as if they were analyzing him. Like they weren't sure exactly who they were looking at.

Cassius stood his ground, taking deep breaths to keep himself calm. *Don't let them think that you're afraid of them.*

He balled his fists at his side. The Ridium quivered against his skin, ready to obey any command he gave it.

Instead of attack, the nearest soldier opened his mouth to speak.

Cassius knew that his words were another language. Part of his brain couldn't understand them at all. Yet somehow the Ridium translated. Somewhere deep inside his mind, the meaning became clear.

"Soldier," the Drifter started, "what is your number?"

Cassius hesitated, unsure of what exactly the guy was asking. Then he remembered what Fisher had said about the Drifters—that they all had numbers attached to their names, that it had something to do with social standing on Haven.

He decided to play along. Taking a quick stock of the brigade before him, he didn't notice any obvious weapons. That didn't mean that they couldn't be concealing something, but they clearly didn't know who they were dealing with. Lying would be a reasonable option.

"Two thousand seventy-eight," he answered. He wasn't sure if his reply came out in English or the new Haven language, but the soldiers seemed to understand.

"A middling number," the man replied. "And what are you doing in this territory? There is nothing here of note."

Cassius gritted his teeth. "I could ask you the same."

The alien chuckled. "Careful. You have not yet asked my number. You should not be so confident that you outrank me. I'm the one asking the questions here."

Cassius smiled. He'd dealt with soldiers like this before. He'd grown up with them his whole life in the Lodge. There was no use trying to be funny or casual. This guy put his stock in the chain of command. Rules and regulations. Nothing more, nothing less.

The Drifter kept his feet planted, eyes fixed on Cassius. "You should come with us, soldier. It's not wise to be out here alone, waiting for instructions that will never come. The people who live in these places... they are the most rudimentary and aggressive of all the humans we've come across. This is their territory and they know it well. You are at a disadvantage, here by yourself. It doesn't matter how strong your suit is."

Cassius raised his shoulders, refusing to move any closer to the battalion. "Where are you going?"

"Our final attack begins soon," the Drifter replied. "While our non-Shifting allies continue their disruption of this civilization, we must be in position, ready to answer the call when it is given. It's lucky for you that we were passing through this area and felt the presence of your suit. Even luckier that I am not King Matigo himself. He surely wouldn't be thrilled with a soldier of his own training shirking the responsibilities that were so honorably given to him."

Cassius wanted desperately to glance back at the house and see if Madame was still standing behind him, but he knew that if he showed the slightest amount of concern, his cover would be blown.

Too late.

The soldier's next question trapped him.

"Are you aware that there are humans inside that building behind you?"

Cassius shook his head immediately, instantly regretting it. A "no" too early could be just as much an admission as a "yes."

"Hmm." The lead soldier turned to glance at the battalion to his right, then to his left. He didn't need to say a word. The black-clad soldiers sprang into action immediately, bounding toward the farmhouse. Cassius wanted to shout out, to warn Madame and Eva. But there wasn't time. The Authority moved as one unit, swift and unforgiving. His only option was to fight back.

But what use was he—a kid who'd just discovered the power to shift Ridium—against a battalion of trained soldiers, presumably Shifting for years now?

Luckily, Cassius had never been one for fair fights.

He let loose with all he had, all at once. The Ridium exploded around him, transforming into dozens of tentacles, all reaching out in different directions. Coils surged at each of the oncoming soldiers, forcing them to defend themselves.

And they did, with little trouble.

As impressive as his initial assault had been, the Authority soldiers cut through his attacks in moments. Some sculpted their Ridium into sharp, knifelike blades. Once sliced, the tentacles from Cassius's suit dribbled into mush, rolling across the ground to reform with the rest of him.

Others responded with vast Ridium shields. What looked like black umbrellas formed over their torsos, easily pushing back his meager creations.

He'd given himself away. As soon as the soldiers realized that they had a battle on their hands, they moved all their attention from going after Madame and Eva to attacking Cassius head-on.

He went from the offensive to defensive in a matter of seconds, conjuring tendrils to push back against them. But he was only one against a small army. No matter how fast he moved, they had more firepower.

One of their Ridium coils wrapped around his leg, just below the knee. Before he could pull away, he was yanked upside down, into the air. He flew backward, away from the house. His arms flailed as the ground came up at him. Just before hitting, he managed to form a cushion of Ridium in front of his body. He bounced before landing on his back.

Tendrils whipped at his body, covering ankles, toes. They were gonna pull him apart, piece by piece. Is that what these people did to traitors?

"Wait!" He heard the lead soldier's voice call from somewhere past his feet. "Keep your hold tight, but don't kill him. I want to ask a few questions first."

Cassius squirmed on the ground, held down by dozens of oily black coils. He kept from Shifting his own suit, knowing that they would only force him to the ground again. He needed a moment to refuel. If this guy wanted to talk, Cassius would take it as an opportunity to regain his bearings.

The lead soldier's eyes, red as lasers, came into view overhead. Everything else was black. "Tell me, number two thousand seventy-eight … if that really is your number … who do you serve in this war?"

Cassius remained silent. He let his limbs fall still, refusing to struggle against the coils. He knew that he should try to keep up the lie as long as possible and give the guy the answer he wanted, but he couldn't bring himself to do it.

"Silence, from you, will mean a limb torn from your body," the soldier continued. "Shall we start with an arm?"

Cassius gritted his teeth, unmoving.

The soldier continued. "I'd like to think that your outburst was blind panic and nothing more. But you are harboring humans in that building, and that violates Authority rule directly. You've no doubt heard what King Matigo does to traitors. If he were here now—"

"I'm sorry," Cassius interrupted. "I've … I've lost my way." He took a breath, trying to decide what to say next. All the while, he began to concentrate on the energy inside of him. He'd gotten lazy, too focused on his new shifting powers when he could be attacking using his preferred method. "When my Pearl landed … something was … faulty. I was confused … about the mission. I wasn't even sure who or what I was. I ran across these two—"

"Enough." The soldier leaned forward. "I don't know whether I should laugh or simply bash your head in. If you think I would believe—"

A hailstorm of bullets interrupted him. The foot soldier stumbled forward, nearly collapsing onto Cassius's body.

Instead, he staggered to the right, lurching through the night like someone had just stabbed him in the gut.

The tendrils holding Cassius down slithered away immediately as the other Drifters fell to the ground.

Cassius scooted back and sat up, peering across the distance to the house's wraparound porch. Through the mask of Ridium, he could see two figures clearly. Madame and Eva stood side by side, each brandishing what looked like an old-fashioned rifle. They fired into the darkness. He knew that meant they could just as easily hit him as they could the bad guys. But this was Madame. No risk, no glory.

Cassius also knew that no simple bullet could take these guys down. Once they realized where the attack was coming from, the Ridium would deflect the shots with ease. Luckily, the girls had taken the soldiers by surprise. They'd bought Cassius time.

He felt his chest begin to boil—heartburn to the hundredth degree. Even so, this time felt different. The Ridium suit acted as a sort of cushion between the fire and his body, dulling the usual warmth.

He wondered if he could somehow use both powers in conjunction. Ridium plus fire—would it result in anything different? In the past, it had been difficult to focus the flames. If the Ridium acted as a cushion, maybe he could use it to more accurately channel the torrents. The problem was: how to do it?

His suit didn't give him a chance.

Without a thought, the blackness exploded around his

body in all directions—a multi-pronged, multi-tentacled monster. A succession of Ridium-formed hoses whipped through the air like branches in a hurricane.

Each found their mark quickly, wrapping around the stunned bodies of the Authority soldiers.

Before they could react, Cassius felt fire course from his body—hot and concentrated and brimming over. Instantly, flames scorched the dozen whips around him, setting forth a dramatic frenzy of inferno.

He could barely control it. Bands of fire ripped through the atmosphere, each extra appendage carrying with it enough flames to level a building.

The heat burned straight through the soldiers' suits. Ridium hissed—an otherworldly sound as Cassius tore it open. The soldiers tried to counter, but nothing was under their control any longer. They flailed and writhed on the ground as Cassius's flaming tendrils ate away at them.

After a certain point, Cassius didn't even realize what he was doing anymore. He couldn't stop the fire from generating inside him, nor the Ridium from coiling along the ground like an army of oily snakes.

He felt his fingers squeeze together, forced shut by the suit. The black coils wrapped around the soldiers once more, burrowing right through their bodies. It cut them into pieces right before his eyes—cauterizing flesh less than a second after it had melted through.

It happened too quickly for screaming. Still, the sight

was enough. Cassius stumbled back, unwilling to look at what he'd done.

Madame and Eva ceased fire. All at once, the flames died, as if silenced by a single, forceful gust of wind. Cassius watched as the Ridium recoiled to his skin, settling against him in absolute silence. A massacre of soldiers lay before him, unrecognizable in their current state. The night fell still.

"Cassius!" Madame ran toward him, but she wasn't fast enough to catch his body before he sank to the ground.

He didn't feel the least bit winded, but the suit's sudden power surge had taken its toll.

His skin tingled, like a thousand bugs crawled over him.

"What did you do?" Eva's voice rang out somewhere above him. "What the hell did you just do?"

He closed his eyes, feeling a renewed closeness to the suit that both reassured and terrified him. It had protected him, but not before completely taking over his body. Is that what he wanted? Maybe it would take a monster to win this war, he reasoned. And for now, that monster appeared to be on his side, protecting him. But he knew so little about Ridium. What would happen if it shifted alliances?

"Cassius?!?" Madame's concerned voice cut through the silence once more.

She'd always taught him to live under the old adage: keep your enemies close.

But this could be cutting it too close.

36

I stagger down the corridor, still off-balance from the chaos in the meeting room.

Most of the advisors have scattered, but Alkine is waiting for us.

Savon pushes past him without a word. I'm not so lucky.

"Jesse." He grabs my shoulder, not letting me pass. "You wanna tell me what just happened in there?"

I pull away. "I need to see if my father's all right."

"First, you need to tell me what you know." He grabs my arm.

I glare at him. "I know nothing, okay? Now let me free. You've gotta get the pressure stabilized in there, anyway."

"Already on it," he responds. "Look, even I know that's not the way Drifters act. They're supposed to be on our side."

"Maybe the Authority's controlling them," I reply. "I don't know. But I've gotta follow Savon. He needs to talk to me."

Alkine loosens his grip. "Anything he has to say can be said in front of me."

"He doesn't trust you." I yank free, rubbing my arm. "If you're really serious about working together on this, you'll let me talk to him before any more of your meetings."

Alkine closes his eyes for a brief moment, muttering under his breath. "Fine. But stay on this level. I might need you."

I nod. "Go secure the room. I won't be long."

Without waiting for a response, I run after my father, catching up with him just as he turns a corner into another corridor.

"Savon," I start. "Wait. I don't know what just happened, but I—"

Savon stops, looking over his shoulder before finding the nearest door and pushing it open. "In here." He steps through.

I move in after him, taking in the surroundings as I let the door shut behind me. We stand in one of the Academy's many classrooms. In fact, this particular one belongs to Mrs. Higgins, Head of Year Seven. It's been since last fall that I took a class in here, but the familiarity—the ordinariness—of it puts me at ease immediately. There was a time where these types of rooms gave me more stress than I could handle. They were arenas for guaranteed failure. Now, the Academy's trials and tests seem like child's play. I'd kill to have that back.

I watch Savon stride to the far end of the room and stop under a display of inspirational posters, the kind that litter the walls of every classroom onboard.

I take a deep breath. "Do you have any idea what just happened in there? I tried to stop them from coming, but they were too strong."

"Your brother's close," he replies, back turned to me.

"You're not worried? We were just attacked by our own kind!"

"You were not attacked. Those Drifters had a very clear agenda. An unfortunate move, I'd say."

"I don't know—"

"Cassius is close," he interrupts. "But he needs a push. Something extra to show him exactly where we are. I need him onboard." He pauses. "A distress signal should do nicely."

I take a step closer. "Are you okay? Did they hurt you?"

He laughs. I'm struck instantly by what an odd response it is to the question. Maybe he's in shock. Maybe he really is hurt. "You're so thoughtful."

"What's going on?"

He shakes his head, then turns to look at me. "It wasn't meant to play out like this, but then again, I couldn't have planned it better." He glances around the room. "An enclosed area, thousands of feet in the air over an ocean. A floating prison."

"Father…"

He laughs again, interrupting me. "In another time, your naiveté might be charming. But you're blind, boy. Absolutely blind. There's a reason I want you and Cassius together." He takes a step forward. "But it isn't to save the world."

"What are you talking about?" I feel the words catch in my throat.

"Jesse Fisher." He smiles. "Your Earth name. Born to Savon and Adaylla, leaders of Haven's Resistance." He continues to approach. Slow, deliberate steps. "Your parents are dead, boy."

I shake my head. "No. You're—"

"Too trusting," he says. "You let hope cloud your judgment."

"You're my father." The words come out barely audible. "You said—"

"I *killed* your father." He stops. "And your mother. Wretched piles of matter, that's all they are. I watched them melt."

"No." I stumble back.

He smiles. "Say my name. I know you know it."

I shake my head.

"Say it!"

I stop, frozen in place by fear. "M-Ma-Matigo?"

With that one word, everything crumbles inside of me. All hope in a future where I know my family. All hope in allies that can win this war and stop the Authority. I feel completely empty, like all the breath has been sucked out of me at once. I can barely stand.

"Yes," he replies. "Very good. You don't know what a burden it was for me, posing for so long. Biding my time." He pauses. "There were soldiers who would've happily carried this out on my behalf, but it had to be me. I needed to become your father to understand you. I needed to be close. Gain your trust. Watch that hope surge inside of you, only to fizzle."

He laughs. "It's the greatest victory of all. And that's before I've killed you."

I swallow, barely able to get a word out. "Stop."

"No." He approaches. "Never. I am Matigo. I do not stop, even for a moment. You see, I need to kill you and your brother at the same time. That's how it must be done. I have a window of an hour, maybe two, before the powers of one slain brother transfer to the other. I can't allow either of you to become the Key *and* the Catalyst. Cassius must join us. You must die together."

Then I watch the dark patch over his left eye begin to dribble down his face. At first, I'm not sure what's happening, but then it becomes obvious. I should have seen it before.

Ridium. The patch is made of Ridium.

It oozes down the side of his neck, curling around his shoulders like a serpent as he speaks. "I often wondered about you, boy. Never once did I picture such a pathetic, quivering mass."

I turn to run. Before I can, the Ridium whips out from his shoulder, forming a claw and clutching me around the neck. The oily blackness throws me into the wall, pinning me against a bulletin board.

Matigo moves nearly as fast, pulled forward by the force of the Ridium. The last of it drips from his eye, revealing a deep hole, burning crimson. The red energy pulls me in, even as the Ridium constricts around my neck. His mouth juts into a horrifying frown before speaking again.

"This should get his attention. Now how do I wound you badly enough without killing you? Maybe start by cutting off some limbs? Your friend's already lost a hand today. Maybe you'd like to join him?"

He laughs, gleeful in the part he's played. Unrepentant and proud of how fully he appealed to my insecurities.

"Come dawn," he continues, "everything will be gone for your people. Your world will be remade. The great Flood is coming, and there won't be anywhere to hide. A part of me wishes you could watch the destruction, but like your parents, you're too dangerous to live."

I kick at him, but it's no use. The Ridium pulls tighter, so tight that I can barely breathe. Seconds more and I'll black out—won't be able to fight at all.

I open my mouth to call for help, but can't make a sound above a whisper. Matigo lifts me higher, brings my feet off the ground.

The room starts to blur as details disappear. Darkness forms around the edges of my vision. Unconsciousness beckons. After that, death.

I have only one chance. The Academy's airborne. There's no way they would have made it all the way across the Pacific at this altitude on solar alone.

I need a Pearl.

I close my eyes, trying to forget the pain as my neck buckles. I ignore my own shallow breathing, though it's the only thing keeping me alive at the moment.

Instead, I feel for Pearl energy. I search the entire ship, throwing a desperate plea to the farthest corners of each level. There's got to be a Pearl onboard. Alkine wouldn't let the ship travel without backup.

Something snaps. A bone? A jolt of pain runs down my spine. It's all I can do not to scream.

Then I find it. Two levels down. Dr. Hemming's lab.

With everything I've got, I call it forward, knowing that it might already be too late.

I feel the world drift away. I'm halfway dead—I know it without any question. Matigo's laughter echoes through the empty room.

I can't tell how far away the Pearl is. I only know that it's coming. But I haven't got time. Nobody's coming to help me and my lungs are starved for air. I clench my fist, acting more on instinct than anything else.

An explosion tears through the room. The Ridium whips away from my neck as the wall behind me crumbles. I fall backward into the corridor beyond the classroom, unable to deflect the oncoming rubble from the collapsed wall. I open my eyes to see a burst of green filling the air, just as a large piece of fiberglass pins my leg to the ground. These walls are strong. They shouldn't explode so easily.

A large sheet of wall tumbles down on me. I protect my face, but not enough to avoid the rubble. A second more and I can't see anything. Matigo could be anywhere. He could be readying for another attack. I've used the only Pearl I could find.

I'm completely defenseless.

37

Cassius forced himself to his feet and stared at his hands, breathing heavy. He pushed the Ridium away from his head, though it didn't retreat easily. He didn't want his face covered with it. He needed to see clearly, without its influence.

He turned to Madame and Eva. They had already stepped down from the porch and stood before him, guns at their sides.

"That was intense, Cassius," Madame said, spinning to take in the sight of the bodies strewn around them.

His hands fell to his thighs. "I didn't do it. The suit took control. For a few seconds there … it was guiding my moves."

A gust of wind sent a rustle through the dark, dead brush around them. Eva raised her gun, but there was nothing to shoot. "Long enough to save us," she said. "There are worse ways this night could end."

Madame moved closer, though Cassius could tell that she still felt uneasy around the Ridium. "You were talking with them, before they attacked. I didn't catch a word of it. It wasn't English, Cassius."

"The words were from Haven." He paused. "But I could understand them. The Ridium translated." He kept his eyes on the darkness, never too sure when they could be snuck up on again. "It's like what I saw in the memory from the senso-cube. The Authority's going to flood the country with Ridium... snuff everyone out in one move. It's going to happen soon."

Eva clutched tighter to her gun. "Can we stop it?"

"Not unless we kill every Shifter on the planet," he replied. "But it's not realistic. They're surrounding us, stationing themselves in every corner of the country. It would take a miracle to get to them all in time." He looked down. "Even with this... this suit, I'm not enough."

"But you know you can kill them," Madame said. "The way it used your power. The fire, combined with the Shifting... you're stronger than they are."

"Maybe," he said. "But that wasn't me. That came from somewhere else."

"Not from what I was seeing," she countered.

"I don't even know if I can do it again," he continued. "And even if I can, I'm only one person. One against hundreds. Maybe thousands."

"So we need a way of reaching them," Eva said.

"First we have to locate them."

Madame grabbed his shoulder. "Ridium attracts Ridium. I heard you say that once."

"That's how they found us here," he responded. "That's how Matigo's Herald first came to Earth in the red Pearl."

She nodded. "If they can do it, so can you. You can trace them, if you focus."

"Hasn't happened yet," he said. "It's not like … I mean, this stuff is unpredictable. Sometimes I feel like I can control it, and other times it feels like it's controlling me. I didn't even know I was a Shifter until a few hours ago. These guys have years of practice."

Madame smiled. "That's never stopped you in the past."

He considered it. Back at the Lodge, he'd been known for his fearlessness. Even as a young child in training exercises, he'd take on Pearlhounds twice his age without a thought. But that was a different time and certainly a different place. There may have been stakes back then, but they were controlled. They were totally different.

Eva lowered her gun to her side, finally relaxing a bit. "Just look at that … that *vehicle* you created. You got us across the Fringes in record time just by conjuring up some Ridium. And back when you were submerged in the stuff. You *flew*. You disappeared into the sky. That's even crazier than the stuff I've seen Jesse do."

He reached up and cradled his head in his hands. "It's all a blur. It was like instinct, at first. When I think about it—"

"Well, it's not as if we can *help* you control it." Madame crossed her arms.

"I just—"

A loud reverberation in his head interrupted him. It came on suddenly, so strong that he was forced to his knees.

The sound echoed through his eardrums, pounding away at his brain to the point that he could hardly see straight. Madame and Eva moved down to comfort him, but he couldn't hear anything they were saying.

Without warning, the Ridium slipped over his head again, muffling the sounds from inside his ears. His eyes shut.

The blur of an image filled his consciousness. There were shadows, one much larger than the other. Then, an explosion—an activation of some great force. He heard a voice calling his name, though it was much too muddled and quiet to identify. What he felt for sure was an overwhelming sense of dread, a feeling that something terrible had just been unleashed on the world—worse than anything they'd faced so far. And if he didn't do something about it soon, everything would be over.

A second flash gave him a location.

Off the west coast. Somewhere in the sky.

The Ridium ripped from his head, taking the blaring sound with it. He stood, so quickly that he was nearly knocked over again.

Madame stared at him, eyes wide. "What is it?"

"Something bad," he replied. "We need to be there."

"Where?"

He ignored her. It was the instinct thing again, taking over. He held out an arm and allowed the Ridium to drip into the ground beneath him. In seconds, it had flowed into a solid disc, encompassing all three of them. Eva and

Madame looked at him nervously, wiggling their feet so as not to get stuck in the goop.

He watched as the edges of the disc rose into the air, forming walls around them.

Eva spun, laying a hand on the growing black wall curving over her head. "Cassius. I don't like this!"

"It's okay," he said. "Think of it as a shuttle."

She placed her second hand on the closing wall. "A shuttle with no windows. How are we supposed to breathe?"

"It'll be fast," he whispered, watching as the last of the Ridium filled in overhead, trapping them inside a perfect sphere, like a smaller version of the vessel Theo had conjured weeks before. It closed without him even thinking about it, encasing them in an unbreakable prison.

"Cassius!" Madame bumped into his chest as the space grew tighter. All light extinguished, creating a vortex of pure blackness. It was worse than closing your eyes. Pure blindness.

He couldn't establish any sense of distance or perspective, which made it impossible to tell when the sphere began to rocket into the sky.

But it did. They shot as a cannonball from the Surface, moving as fast as any Pearl. Their feet remained fixed in place. They stood utterly still, even as they were catapulted into what was sure to be certain danger.

38

"Fisher!"

I hear the voices of the Agents, disconnected. I don't know how close they are.

"Are you all right? Where are you?"

Then I hear the screams. They've noticed Matigo.

All I can see are ankles through a break in the rubble strewn on top of me. My own ankle throbs. My left arm's pinned to the ground, along with most of my torso. My legs feel like they've been cut open. For all I know, they could be.

Gunshots. The clank, clank, clank of combat boots on metal. Then the sounds of bodies slammed into walls. The sickening slurp of flesh being sliced open.

My eyes begin to flutter closed. I could go out any moment, but it's not gonna be that easy.

Black coils squiggle through the chunks of wall keeping me prisoner. Then, in a blurred succession, the rubble's lifted from my body, piece by piece. It happens so fast. It's like a tornado working in reverse.

Matigo's face comes into view. He smiles—a sickening

grin that lets me know that he's already won. At least he thinks so.

I watch a slab of Ridium form into a razor-sharp scythe over his shoulders, a guillotine ready to slice my head from my body.

The blade drops. I try to pull myself away, but the coils push down on my chest, keeping me in place with the force of a dozen boulders.

A blast comes from somewhere down the hall. Bullets fly overhead, followed by a small missile. It connects with Matigo's torso, breaking his concentration and throwing him onto the ground behind me. It won't be enough to kill him, but it saved my life.

A hand reaches down to grab mine and pull me from the rubble. I struggle to my feet—something's definitely wrong with my left leg—and fall right into an Agent's grip. Without a word, he pushes me down the hall, into the arms of another.

They continue to pass me along, from Agent to Agent, until they've built a wall between Matigo and me. It's not going to do them much good. I remember how powerful Theo had been against Cassius and me, and he was just a small boy. Matigo— powers or no powers—is easily twice my size.

An Agent pushes ahead of me, obscuring my vision of what's happening in the center of the hallway. I feel some-one grip my shoulder and turn to see Alkine's face staring at mine.

"Head to a lower level," he says.

"But—"

"You've taken care of yourself for long enough now," he continues. "Let someone else fight the fight."

I want to scream warnings at him, tell him that there's no way a bunch of humans are going to defeat a Shifter like Matigo, but there's not enough time.

A burst of Ridium cascades through the corridor, spearing some Agents, missing others. It flows down the hallway like the arms of an enormous octopus, twisting and looping to find me.

"Duck." Alkine pulls me to the floor just in time for a second missile to shoot over our heads. I watch it angle up at the ceiling before meeting the ground several meters away.

An intense explosion rattles the corridor, blowing loose rubble from the ceiling. Everyone's knocked backward by the force. Fire precautions trigger, blanketing the hallway in flame retardant foam up to our waists. We're fighting in a tight, deadly bubble bath.

"Go!" Alkine shouts, but he's too late.

A grotesque hand of Ridium comes at him from out of nowhere, grabbing him by the head and tossing him in the air. He follows the path of the missile until he lands somewhere in the foam. I've got no protection.

There's nothing to do but run. Nowhere to go but the sky around us.

I turn and book it down the corridor, out of the fray.

Matigo hasn't seen me yet, but he's too fast. I could sprint like this and still be eclipsed by him in a second. Just like in countless training programs onboard the Academy, hiding is my greatest asset.

Matigo doesn't know the layout of the ship beyond what I've already shown him. That won't stop him from crashing through every wall and ceiling he has to, but I have so few advantages against him. I have to take anything I can get.

I find the nearest stairwell and tumble down, holding onto the railing to keep myself from tripping. I need Pearls. They're the only thing that's been any good against him. But I know the Academy has few onboard—partly because the ship's been on the run for months, partly because I made such a stink about collecting them for energy in the first place.

Anything we do will have to be far away. Storage is on the ship's lower levels. I hadn't sensed any extra energy back in the classroom, but Matigo had me pinned. In my panic, I might have missed something.

I round another staircase. The ship seems empty. Barren, almost. This time of night, most people would be in their rooms, though they've no doubt heard the explosions from the missiles upstairs. I want to tell everyone on board to get on a shuttle and get the hell off before Matigo finds them. It's me he wants, but that doesn't mean that anyone else is safe.

With every step I descend, I feel an increase of Pearl

energy. There may be one or two left in storage. I can use them against Matigo, but then what? I have to find a way to either destroy him or get him off the ship.

Docking bays. They're the only part of the Academy exposed to the sky. If I can lure Matigo down there and hit him with a double attack of Pearl blasts, maybe it will be enough to knock him off the ship. He said his power to fly had faded. Of course, that could have been another lie.

My father. He was pretending to be my father.

I knock the thought out of my head. I'll have plenty of time for emotion when this is over. At this point, it's a luxury I can't touch.

Two more flights of stairs and I'm at docking bay level. Everything's silent. No blasts or explosions. It's unsettling. I may have put some distance between myself and the fight, but all that really means is that I'm in the dark again. The Agents might have lost and I wouldn't even know it.

Then, the blast I've been waiting for. It comes from above me. Right above me.

I crane my neck and stare at the ceiling, terrified that it'll all come down in pieces large enough to bury me once again.

A voice from the far end of the corridor pulls me out from that terror.

"Jesse!"

I recognize it immediately, though my mind can't process that it could be true. Until I spin around and see her, I'm convinced that I'd imagined it.

Eva stands at the entrance to the docking bay, weapon at her side.

To the right of her is Madame, but she's not the one I stare at.

Between them, encased in a black suit of Ridium, is Cassius.

39

Cassius had never seen his brother so panicked before. The look in Fisher's eyes was one of hope lost. Impending doom, and then some.

Fisher ran at them full speed. There wasn't time for reunions or small talk. When he spoke, it was more like the words had been put in his mouth, like he was channeling some ancient warning. Too much information to get out in one sitting.

"Matigo!" he started. This was the word that caught Cassius immediately, and made it difficult to listen to anything else. "The ship..." Fisher continued. "He's on his way down... Ridium!"

It wasn't much of a sentence, but Cassius understood the meaning of it plainly. It matched the overwhelming intensity he'd felt just minutes earlier, when the Ridium had taken control back on the Surface. It was the same muddled message that had forced him up to Skyship Academy. He hadn't known the ship was back in American territory. But like a compass, something onboard drew him in. His spherical Ridium transport had landed in the ship's docking bay only moments ago. Finding Fisher so quickly had to mean they were in the right place.

Eva stepped up to grab Fisher's arm and give him a gentle hug. "Slow down, Jesse. I can't understand what you're saying."

Fisher pushed away from her, nervously pacing—his entire body amped up. "Matigo," he said in a panicked whisper. "He's onboard the ship. I thought ... He's trying to kill me. He'll be here any second."

Cassius nodded. The Ridium quivered against his skin, eager to Shift into something more useful to him. Fisher seemed to not notice it, too consumed with what had happened before.

Fisher pushed past them, motioning wildly toward the bay. "I have an idea," he said. "There are Pearls down here. Pearls seem to hurt him. I figure if I can knock him off—"

An explosion rattled the ceiling. Cassius turned to watch a trunk of Ridium slice through metal on the far side of the hallway, feet from where Fisher had been standing seconds ago. The thick band of black widened to pull open a massive hole in the ceiling. Screeching metal echoed through the ship as the Ridium parted, revealing a bulky figure standing before them.

Cassius felt his own suit slide up over his head, leaving a hole for his face. He couldn't help but gasp when he laid eyes on Matigo.

His father. Matigo looked just like his father. The same man he'd watched melt in that dark room on Haven stood before him now, eyes shining red with rage. Somehow, Matigo had killed Savon and taken his place. Just as that female Authority soldier had stolen the voice of the Resistance fighter in the forest, Matigo had stolen a body. He'd transformed himself to look like Savon, down to every last detail. And from the look in Fisher's eyes, he'd done enough to fool everyone.

But Cassius could see it clearly. There was a fury inside of him. It spilled from his features, uncontained. This man was nothing like his father. This wasn't even a man. This was a presence—something more deadly and unforgivable than anything he had ever seen.

In that moment, Cassius couldn't conjure anything but rage. His battle training left him, replaced with a hatred beyond bridling.

"You killed him!" His voice echoed along the hallway.

Matigo stood still for a moment, allowing the Ridium to coil around him. Then he started to laugh. His smile spread until it became distorted, like that of a snake or crocodile. Cassius recognized the laugh from other memories—so strong that it nearly shook the ship.

"I have both of you," Matigo said after composing himself. "In one place. Right on time."

Fisher stepped back until he bumped into Cassius's shoulder. "He's gonna kill—"

"Shh."

"It's true." Matigo approached, shoulders up. Confident. "I killed your parents, though it took longer than I'd hoped to find them. They were a tricky pair, evasive and foresee-ing. Luckily, it seems as though these particular traits didn't trickle down to their offspring." His smile widened again.

Cassius's suit sprang into action, ballooning around him to reveal dozens of jagged arms. Some were daggerlike, flat and sharp. Others narrowed into a point like an ice-pick. Many were simply hoses—channels for fire waiting to strike.

Matigo's smile weakened. "It's not possible. A Shifter?"

Cassius took a step forward. "That's right."

"I take it back, then." Matigo chuckled to himself. "It seems as if your parents had one more trick left in their arsenal. I've aligned myself with the wrong son."

"Yeah?" Cassius took another step. "Well, we killed *yours*."

Matigo laughed. "Theo? Theo was waste. A part of my plans, yes, but I was never close to him. He was always des-tined to die. Just like yourselves." The Ridium at his sides crawled up his legs, forming a layer over his body. "This is cute. Your boasts are appreciated, but at the end of it, you're only a boy. I've been Shifting Ridium for decades now—longer than you've been alive. You're not even close to my equal."

The last of the Ridium covered Cassius's face. "Tell that to the battalion of your soldiers down in the Fringes."

"Enough."

A thick blast of Ridium came from Matigo's chest. It blasted down the hallway, too fast and thick to deflect.

"Duck!" Cassius shouted to the others, though he didn't have time to heed his own warning. The Ridium smashed into him full force, driving him down the hallway. If it hadn't been for the shielding from his suit, the blow would have killed him instantly. As it was, he had to use every ounce of strength to break free from it. Unconsciousness threatened to take over, but he set his brain to pull out fire—allowed the hoses to channel heat.

He succeeded in creating small fissures in Matigo's surge of Ridium, enough that he could drop under the full blast and hit the ground, heaving on his back.

The Ridium continued to flow overhead, a sideways twister.

Then, all at once, it froze. For a split second, it was statuesque in its stillness. But it didn't last.

The Ridium began to drip, a trickle at first before multiplying into a waterfall. It sloshed against the ground, a tidal wave ready to swallow him up. Cassius couldn't move.

40

"Move!"

I crouch on the ground, watching the Ridium surge past overhead.

As soon as it's safe, I stand and make a break for the door. I can't worry about Cassius right now. If I go after him, Matigo will kill us both. The only advantage of his attack is that he's concentrating solely on Cassius. The Ridium flow is so large that it blocks his view of anything else.

Eva and Madame follow me. We round the corner into the docking bay, leaving the chaos of the hallway behind. Earlier, this place had been filled with people. It had been a celebration. Now, it's completely empty, cut off from the rest of the Academy by Matigo and the Ridium. Even if someone wanted to come in and help me, there'd be no way for them to get here without the threat of attack.

Eva pants beside me. "Please tell me you have an idea."

"Yeah," I say. "You and Madame? Grab a shuttle and get the hell out of here."

"No way!"

"It's not *you* he wants." I frantically glance around the bay. "If you leave, you'll be safe. He won't follow."

Madame frowns, stealing a look back at the entrance to the bay. It's silent, except for the soft crashing of Ridium against walls as Matigo fills the corridor outside. "He's going to flood the entire country," she says. "If we leave now, we'll only be dead tomorrow." She takes a deep breath. "We fight."

"Okay." I cough. "You really wanna help? Find some weapons. You'll hold him off if you need to. Bullets won't kill him—not with the Ridium protecting his body—but they might slow him down. Try to drive him toward the edge of the bay, if you can."

Eva nods. "Storage cabinets across from the refueling tanks. But what are you gonna do?"

"Pearls," I say. "It's all I've got."

I watch the two of them dart away, Eva showing Madame where to find the blasters. I run in the opposite direction, pinning myself in a nook between two outcroppings of wall. I need to be as invisible as I can, at least until I can find a Pearl.

As soon as I get there, I crouch on my knees, as if in prayer. I close my eyes and try to focus, but it's impossible. My whole body's in an unstoppable panic. Worse, I can't stop thinking about Cassius. I don't know what's up with him suddenly being able to Shift, but even with that—even as good a fighter as he is—he's no match for Matigo. Not by himself.

"Please please please please please." I mutter the words under my breath.

I lock on to the first Pearl I can find. It's not too far away, so I yank it forward with the pull of my mind.

Mistake.

The ship lurches. The lights in the bay flicker off before resuming full power. An unsettling rumble spreads along the ground as the emergency thrusters power on. I must have taken one from the generator. We'll be able to run on half power using whatever energy's left inside, but unless there's another Pearl hanging around here somewhere, I just doomed the Academy to a crash landing.

I can't think of the consequences now.

"Please please please."

I feel the energy stream closer, so near I can reach out and touch it.

When I open my eyes, it hovers before me, a green glow spotlighting my face. I grab hold and pull it close to my chest. The energy calms me for a moment, at least until the question pops into my mind.

I've got the Pearl. *One* Pearl. Against Matigo.

What's the best way to use it?

41

Cassius pulled himself to his feet, even though every last nerve ending was screaming in protest for him to give up. *It's not worth it,* his body told him. *You'll never win.*

But he had to try.

Slick tendrils of ooze came up at him from the churning river of Ridium underfoot. They grabbed onto his arms, legs—anything they could find—and attempted to pull him back down. It took all the concentration he could muster to defend against them, keep his footing. One wrong move and he would be swallowed. Suffocated.

All the while, Matigo approached. He took slow, deliberate footsteps, collecting errant Ridium as he went. Cassius felt his own suit begin to pull from his body. Matigo was slowly taking it over, like a magnet yanking harder than Cassius could match. If he didn't have Ridium, he was finished.

With one last gasp, he conjured a whip, extended from his right arm. It cracked through the air, long enough to wrap around Matigo's neck. Without wasting a moment, Cassius conjured fire. He allowed it to stream down the length of the coil until it met with Matigo's skin.

"Aargh!" Matigo staggered backward, visibly surprised

by the effectiveness of the attack. It fractured his concentration just long enough for Cassius to Shift a stiltlike device of his own, which launched him up through the air, making a wide arch over Matigo's head. He softened the fall by sculpting a Ridium slide. He landed on his feet, free from the sludge of darkness on the opposite side of Matigo.

Matigo laughed. "Fire? Of course. You're lucky. Two powers are better than one, even undeveloped as they are."

Cassius responded by thrusting his hand out in front of him and conjuring a torrent of fire. It engulfed Matigo entirely, blazing for a short moment before the Ridium around him dulled it to a sizzle. He'd irritated him, maybe, but that was about the extent of it. And if that was all he could do, he was in trouble.

Matigo attacked again, sending forth a flurry of Ridium daggers. They whizzed through the air toward Cassius, easily deflected. But they gave Matigo enough time to charge forward.

Cassius flattened against the wall, narrowly avoiding him. With the moment he had left, he sprinted toward the docking bay. It was no use fighting in closed quarters like this. There wasn't enough room to do anything besides defend against attack after attack. He'd become exhausted eventually.

A dark tendril chased after him. He brushed it away as he careened into the bay.

An open mouth of sky stretched before him, seventy-five yards away. Fisher's idea repeated in his head—throw

Matigo out into open air. Even if it didn't get rid of him for good, it would at least get the monster off the ship.

But he'd need to injure him somehow first. Otherwise, Cassius was sure that Matigo would just construct a vessel of Ridium and come right back. After all, he'd done the same just minutes ago. And if Cassius could do it, the King of Shifters certainly wouldn't have a problem.

Frantically, he scanned the room for weapons. He wasn't as familiar with Skyships as he was the Surface. The last time he'd been in this bay was to capture Fisher. He hadn't had time to look around then.

Fisher.

Madame and Eva, too.

Had they run into the bay as well? Or had they escaped somewhere else? As far as he could tell, the vast space was empty. Other than a few shuttles parked on the edges, it stretched before him—a wide, flat chamber. Nothing to fight with, nowhere to hide.

He spun to see Matigo, framed by the doorway. Before he could do or say anything, a tendril whipped at him, grabbing his waist in a tight, unbreakable squeeze.

He fought against it, but even his own Ridium couldn't pry him free. He noticed his suit streaming away from him in pieces, slipping from his skin to join Matigo's supply. Matigo had taken it over as easily as lifting a finger. He'd taken charge of anything Cassius might have to use against him.

He fought, kicking and squirming, as Matigo pulled him through the air. They met in the middle of the bay,

Cassius cocooned from the neck down like a fly in Matigo's web. Matigo held him tight, inches in front of his face. He turned so that Cassius could see the stars. It helped to have anything to focus on besides Matigo's horrific features.

"You didn't really think that I was showing you all I had?" he whispered in Cassius's ear. "I wanted to test you first. I wouldn't mind a bit more, but you're a liability that has to be dealt with quickly."

Cassius tried to summon fire again, but all he could manage was a few sparks from his fingers, which pointed straight at the ground, arms pinned to his sides. They had all the effect of a sparkler.

"First *you*," Matigo continued, "then your brother."

"No."

Matigo chuckled. "Oh, *yes*."

A second voice came from near the edge of the bay. "The boy said no. I suggest you listen."

Cassius looked up to see Madame's silhouette, standing before the backdrop of stars beyond the docking bay's mouth. She held an enormous blaster, the top half of it curving up to rest against her shoulder.

"Cassius." She flipped a switch on the side of the weapon. "To your left, please."

She pulled a series of triggers and the blaster opened up, revealing three holsters. A missile erupted from each, coming straight at them in a hypnotic pinwheel motion.

Cassius understood immediately, and drew on all his remaining energy to throw his weight to the left. Matigo staggered only a step, but it was enough to tilt him in just the right direction. Right into the detonation zone.

The missiles made contact all at once, sending a multi-pronged blast through Matigo's entire body. Cassius was flung to the side. He landed on his stomach, several yards away.

Matigo stumbled back, his body obscured by continued explosions as the missiles detonated in waves, attacking him like a hornet's nest.

Cassius raised his chin to watch Madame reload the blaster. She flipped the controls on the side once more.

Then a massive tendril of black shot from the nexus of the explosions, headed straight at her.

"Watch out!" Cassius could barely summon the words.

He watched in horror as the band of black collided with Madame's chest, sending the blaster toppling over her shoulder, onto the ground. It continued to push forward on her, so fast and strong that she didn't have a hope of escape.

Cassius attempted to stand, but found himself toppling over again. A hand of Ridium whipped from the explosion and pinned him down again.

He watched as Madame was pushed from the docking bay, into open sky. She didn't even have time to scream.

"No!" The word fractured as he shouted it. She was gone.

Matigo dragged Cassius by the ankle, back into the fray. He flipped around on his back, trying to get control of some of the Ridium—Shift it into something useful. But try as he might, he couldn't fight the mental block working against him. Even after the explosions, Matigo still had a better hold on the stuff.

Then, just as he was about to be dragged right back into Matigo's waiting arms, Fisher jumped out from somewhere behind them. He had a Pearl, and Matigo didn't even notice.

A bright-green explosion rattled the bay, directly behind Matigo's back. The energy collided with the ground, looping up into a succession of what looked like green fists. Fisher channeled it, pummeling Matigo with each new blast of energy.

The Ridium around Cassius's ankles flew away, rejoining with Matigo's body.

Fisher continued to attack, punching at the air a safe distance behind Matigo. With each thrust, a new blast of Pearl energy swept up and forced him closer to the edge of the bay. Matigo struggled against it, but Madame's missiles had weakened him. He was no match.

Three more punches and Matigo fell out the mouth of the bay, taking the Ridium with him.

Freefall. Done.

For now.

Fisher rushed to Cassius's side, grabbing his shoulders. "Are you okay?"

He shook his head, finding it hard to breathe. "She's gone." He stared up at his brother, panic in his eyes.

"You're gonna be okay."

"No," he responded, pleading. "No, she's gone." His body sank to the ground. All fight left him. "Madame's dead."

42

Cassius is broken. Beyond whatever physical damage is done, I can sense it in his eyes. I've never seen him like this. Helpless. Lost.

If he can't stand up to Marigo, what chance do I have?

I swallow, unsure of what to do next. The last of the Pearl energy dissipates, working its way into the circuitry of the ship. It'll keep us aloft for awhile longer, not that that's the problem I'm worried about.

"Here." I bend down to help Cassius up. He winces as I pull him to his feet. We stand in silence for a few moments. I watch his breathing slowly return to normal. There are no tears—no shouts or screams. I think this is beyond that kind of thing. When he finally does speak, it's with an insignificant sort of tone. Almost disinterested.

"Ankle's twisted," he mutters, then pulls away from me, limping to the mouth of the bay.

I walk behind him. "Cassius! Don't get too close...it's dangerous."

Eva's voice comes from behind me. "It's okay, Jesse."

I turn to see her standing in the corner of the docking bay, a pistol in each arm. Neither weapon is big enough to do much damage. She must have known that the entire time. I'm sure she watched the whole thing, cursing herself for not getting to the big-ticket weapons first.

"Give him a moment," she continues. "It might be the only one he gets."

I nod, then turn to watch Cassius stop several yards from the open sky, arms against his sides, shoulders slumped.

A battalion of Agents storm through the entrance and enter the bay, stopping as they notice the emptiness around them. They form a semi-circle in front of me, weapons at the ready, eyes darting around the room.

"You're too late," I say. "He's gone."

An Agent in the front lowers his weapon. "Killed?"

I shake my head.

Eva runs up beside me and grabs my arm. "I should've been faster. I hesitated. I ... it wasn't all her fight."

"I didn't even see her," I whisper. "Not until it happened. The Pearl blast—"

"Hurt him," she says, finishing my sentence. "Jesse, you're the one who can stop him."

"I know, but I need more energy. I need all the Pearls I can get."

She swallows, then envelops me in a hug so sudden that it takes me by surprise. I have to remind myself that we haven't seen each other since the bunker—that we lost contact shortly after. She probably thought I was dead. I certainly wasn't sure if *she* was alive.

She pulls back, expression grim. "How are you going to do it?"

"With help from my friends," I answer. "Beyond that, we've gotta change tactics."

One of the Agents approaches us, expression grim. "If I may, kid... uh... sir. This probably isn't the safest place right now. If we can head up to the Bridge—"

"Is Alkine okay?" I glance up at him.

The guy nods. "Infirmary. He's pulled through worse."

I nod. "We'll head up to the Bridge, but here's what's gonna have to happen."

I expect the guy to interrupt, or laugh in my face, but he stays still, listening intently. It's a far cry from how Agents usually treat me.

"We're bringing the Academy inland," I say. "East. Cut the onboard power by... by... " I look at Eva for assistance.

"By forty-two percent," she says. "Anything we don't need goes. Dorm rooms, class rooms, extra temp control—all down. Put everything into the thrusters." She turns to me. "Jesse, what are you thinking?"

"I want to be central," I respond. "Matigo knows we're onboard. It'd be stupid to go into hiding. We'll bring him back here, but I want to have an army when he shows up."

The Agent nods. "I'll radio second-in-command."

Footsteps sound behind me. I turn to see Cassius walking toward us, face hardened again after that brief moment of vulnerability. "Whatever you're thinking, we'll need to move fast."

"Are you okay?" The words fade even as I'm saying them. Of course he's not, and no matter how many times I ask, it's not going to change.

"When I was submerged in the Ridium," he says, "when I became a Shifter, the world changed. I can see things that weren't there before. Feel things that are invisible to you. That's how I knew to be up here when Matigo attacked. That's how I know what's happening right now, below us on the Surface." He pauses, looking at the ground for a moment before meeting my eyes once more. "It's starting."

"What?"

"The Flood," he replies. "The Shifters are gathering. Matigo's about to give the order. By this time tomorrow, we won't have a world to fight for. I need to be on the Surface."

"I agree."

"My fire hurt him," he continues. "Even if it was just for a second, it took him by surprise. My fire … your Pearls … "

"I know what you're thinking." I flash back to the words Matigo said just before he attacked. He'd been boastful—obviously thought we'd both be dead by now. But I remember exactly what he'd told me.

The Key and the Catalyst together.

He was scared of that. I don't know why, and I don't know exactly what Cassius and I are capable of, but there's only one way to find out for sure. And with the world hanging in the balance, now's as good a time as any for a leap of faith.

43

My controlled, eye-on-the-target veneer cracks as soon as I see Avery.

It's many minutes—maybe even an hour—since our confrontation with Matigo. She emerges at the bottom of the stairs as I trudge my way through the corridor, entire body shaking. She runs at me, arms outstretched. I let her pull me close, tears staining my face.

"Oh my god," she says. "Are you okay?"

"No," I respond.

And it's the truth. I couldn't be less okay. Not only is my greatest enemy loose, with more power than I ever dreamed of, but my parents—and all the hope they held—are well and truly gone.

"I'm such an idiot," I whisper into her shoulder.

"No, Jesse."

"Yes," I continue. "I'll believe anything anyone says. Isn't that how it's always been? I believed you when you were really working with Madame. I believed Alkine when he said he wanted to help with Pearls. And now…now…I'm so stupid…"

Avery pushes me away, holding onto my shoulders,

looking straight into my eyes. "Jesse, he fooled everyone. There was no way you could've known."

I shake my head, my voice catching in my throat. "I'm never gonna see my parents."

Avery sighs, biting her lip. There's nothing she can say to change things, and she knows it. "No," she says finally. "But you can defeat the son of a bitch who killed them."

I close my eyes. I have no choice now. After what we just witnessed, I'm not sure that Cassius and I have a chance against Matigo. But I have to try. I have to do it for my parents. They died for what they believed in. I can't let that be in vain.

"Madame's dead." The words spill out of my mouth without my realizing it. I can tell instantly that they catch Avery off guard. Her lips part. Brows furrow in confusion. It's like she can't even believe that Madame was capable of dying. Or maybe she just isn't sure how she should feel.

"He killed her," I continue, "back in the docking bay."

She swallows, her face once again regaining composure. "How's Cassius?"

"Not great," I respond. "He'll meet us in the Bridge soon. I think he needs some time. I wish we had more."

She nods. "Jesse, no matter what happens, you've gotta know that you're not fighting this fight alone. You have friends—so many people who care about you—and we're not going to let Matigo win."

"Thanks," I say, though it's completely hollow. She can reassure me as much as she wants, but somehow I know that this is going to come down to me and Cassius, just like it always has.

———

Fire.

I'm back in the fire.

I recognize it instantly as a dream, the continuation of the one I'd had before. I don't know where I found the time or space to doze off, but sometime after talking with Avery, sleep must have gotten the better of me.

The flames ripple around me, as if pushed by a vortex of wind. I spin, trying to get a good look at the entire perimeter, searching for a way out.

The fire's solid, so thick that I can't see anything beyond it. For all I know, it might stretch on forever.

"Cassius?" I shout his name, remembering what happened at the end of the last dream. "Are you there?"

No response.

Balling my fists, I take a step forward. The flames quiver but remain as a curved wall, blocking my way. Last time, I'd been able to touch the fire without anything happening. Maybe this time I can walk through it…see what's on the other side.

I continue forward, not the least bit nervous or apprehensive. The flames continue to dance, crackling with a heat I can't feel.

Suddenly, a voice stops me in my tracks.

I turn to see Cassius, standing behind me, head bowed.

I swallow. "What are you—?"

He pushes his hand out in front of him, silencing me. His head rises, eyes lit by more fire.

"Cassius?"

He opens his mouth to speak, but instead of words coming out, a thick torrent of flames snakes from between his teeth, winding up in loops to meet with the rest.

Then he begins to disappear again.

"No." I stumble forward, annoyed that he's leaving me once more. Why was he in this dream at all if he's just going to disappear every time?

As the fire continues to leave his mouth, his body disintegrates until there's little more than ashes left behind. I watch his face crumble, the last to disappear.

I freeze in the center of the fire ring, breathing heavy. "What are you trying to tell me?"

The flames quiver, as if in response. Before I can do or say anything, the ring begins to spin. It's slow at first, but soon speeds to a rate so alarming that I can feel the gusts being thrown off.

I stay completely still, watching in horror as the fire constricts. The ground disappears beneath it, eaten up. Soon, I'm left with hardly any room to stand. The flames push in at me from all angles. Suffocation.

I open my mouth to scream. It's a mistake.

As soon as the opening's there, the fire funnels into a

thick tendril of orange—the same sort that I'd seen come from Cassius.

Before I know it, the flames plunge down my esophagus, taking residence in my gut. My arms instinctively fling out to my sides. My head's pushed back. I feel my eyes widen as I stare up at a bed of stars, finally revealed behind the extensive blaze. They're the only comfort I have as the fire continues to snake its way into my body, more and more. Faster and faster.

When it's finally over, I collapse into the dirt, darkness all around me. The stars pulse above with an added brightness.

I pull in my arms, clutching my stomach. It doesn't feel hot, or particularly uncomfortable. But I feel full. Bursting.

I sit on my knees for minutes, maybe longer. It's hard to get a sense of time with nothing but the stars to guide me.

But the stillness doesn't last. Soon I feel it rising in my gut. A million stars bursting inside of me. I reach down and push on my skin, willing the pain to go away.

Tears lash their way across my insides—fissures so deep that I have no hope of stopping them.

I crane my neck, look up into space, and scream. There's no one around to hear me. Nothing responds.

The fire works its way up my throat, sizzling muscle and organs on its way. I close my eyes and try to go someplace new. Somewhere with no pain.

It isn't to be.

Seconds later, I explode.

Ashes. That's all I am now.

44

Dawn.

The sensations in the dream stick with me, even hours after I've woken. I feel the heat inside my body, as if it never left. I replay the visions in my head. The stars. Cassius. The ring of fire. Each time I think about it, I feel like I'm going to throw up.

Better not to think about it, then.

We stand in the Bridge at the very top of the Academy. The sunrise beams through the 360-degree view behind us.

We're all here: me, Cassius, Eva, Avery... even Alkine, along with dozens of Agents and pilots and technicians and who knows what else. The rest of the Academy waits on the lower levels. I wonder how much they know. I wonder if they're aware that they could be mere hours away from total destruction.

"Colorado," someone calls from behind me. They've been doing this with each state we pass.

Alkine stands beside me, arms behind his back, leg in a cast. "This good?"

"No," I respond softly. "Wait until Kansas. Kansas will be better."

Cassius and my plan is twofold. The fact that we have a plan at all seems to impress everyone around me. It's definitely not my normal way of functioning, but this isn't a normal situation.

One: If Matigo's tracking us, I want to make it hard for him. Every moment we're apart is a moment I'm building up my strength. I'm gonna need it all. Cassius too. I can feel it in my gut. The connection with Pearls around the world grows the more I concentrate on them. What I'll need to attempt here, I've never attempted before.

Two: I want to cast a wide arc—pull from every corner of the country. I can't do that on the coast. I need a reach, a breadth of land big enough to compile an army. We'll see how that works. Right now, it's theory. The most Pearls I've ever broken at once was back in Portland. They were in one room. One *huge* room, yes, but one room all the same. This will be different. This, if necessary, will be nuclear in force. This I might not recover from.

Cassius closes his eyes beside me, then begins to speak as if he's channeling words from another universe. "Everything's in place," he says. "The Shifters are pulling Ridium from the ground. The first places to be hit will be the coasts, and it'll make its way inward. And quickly."

"We're broadcasting to anyone who can hear us," Alkine says. "Telling everyone left behind in a Chosen City to find all functioning ships and get into the sky."

Eva cringes. "What about the Fringers?"

"Out of luck," I mutter. "As usual."

It's not meant to be insensitive, but sadly it's the truth. I picture entire towns covered in the thick black stuff. If what Cassius said is true, it will move too fast for them to run away. If they were to climb on top of buildings, arms and coils of Ridium would likely tear them down. Nobody will have seen anything like it.

Cassius opens his eyes. "Warning the Chosens is a start, but they won't all make it. The Shifters'll stretch the Ridium into the air—grab hold of tailfins and wings and pull ships back down again."

"Oh man."

I turn, drawn by the familiar voice behind me.

Skandar stands in the center of the room, arms crossed, shaking his head.

I gawk at him, like I'm staring at a ghost. He's dressed in an Academy suit, hair combed back and face clean from the Fringe dirt that covered it the last time I saw him. I notice a slight shine coming from where his left hand used to be. It takes me a moment to realize that the doctors onboard have replaced it with an artificial one. Strips of metal, yet to be covered with skin grafts, catch the reflection of the lights overhead.

"Skandar!" Eva bolts toward him, catching him off guard with a tight embrace.

He grins. "Relax. Everything's all right."

Avery and I approach him, marveling at his new limb.

"Pretty flaunt, huh?" He maneuvers the fingers, clenching them into a fist and then back out again. "It's gonna take some getting used to, I think, but it's a lot stronger than my old one."

"I'm so glad you're all right," I say.

He smiles. "Wouldn't be if it hadn't been for you guys. Thanks for taking care of me out there. But I feel like I've been asleep for days. Some of the docs caught me up on what's been happening." He meets my eyes. "How are you holding up, mate?"

I shrug. It's not worth rehashing my feelings one more time. I have to be the strong one, like Cassius, and keep my focus.

Skandar nods in understanding, then cranes his neck to look at Alkine behind us. "Permission to rejoin the team, Captain?"

"It's good to see you on your feet again, Harris." Alkine gives a slight nod. "Permission granted, of course."

"Look Fisher," Skandar starts, "those bastards took my hand. I've got a score to settle. Just point me in the right direction. We're not going down without a fight."

"Kansas!" The call comes from behind us, loud and confident. I look over to Alkine. He mutters something under his breath—a prayer, perhaps—and meets my eyes, waiting for orders.

Alkine, waiting for orders from *me*.

I shake my head, looking at Avery. "What about you? Are you ready to fight?"

She frowns. "Coming from you, that's an unexpected question."

"It's our last stand," I continue. "Right in the middle of the country, flattest state we've got."

Alkine nods. "I'll see how many temp-regulator suits I can pull out of storage, get as many men ready to go as I can."

Eva grabs onto Skandar's arm, dragging him forward. "What can we do?"

I stare at them for a moment, not used to so many people looking to me for instructions. Giving Eva orders is so twisted that it almost makes me laugh. She's been my protector for years, even when I didn't know it. Grade A. Trained beyond her years. I can't help but wonder how differently this all would have turned out if she'd been the one given my powers.

But I can't think like that. There's no benefit in playing the what-if game, and certainly no advantage to getting down on myself. Instead, I have to take strength from people like Eva—follow her lead and hope that I can be half the soldier she is.

"Go with Alkine," I say. "Get suited up. And … and be safe, okay?"

Skandar squeezes my shoulder. "Be safe, man."

"We'll be down there looking out for you," Eva adds.

I offer a faint smile. "As always, right?"

They leave, following Alkine toward the center of the Bridge. The space around me is a sea of motion—Agents running around, specialists slowing the Skyship to a halt over the barren Fringe landscape. For a moment, I'm not sure what to do with myself. Pause, I guess. Let my strength come all the way back.

Cassius moves closer. His eyes shut for a moment before he speaks. "It's happening now. I can feel it. All along the coastline ... they're pulling Ridium from the ground."

"How long—?"

"Tidal waves," he continues. "That's what it'll be. We better pray that there are enough ships ... that people heard the warning and got into the air, high enough off the ground to be out of reach."

I nod. "When we're down there ... I'm going to try to target the energy—hit as many of the Shifters as I can. I don't know if I'll be able to do it from this far away, but I have to try."

Cassius clasps his hands in front of him. "Matigo falls, so does the Authority."

"That's what we've gotta keep telling ourselves."

His eyes meet mine again. "Promise me one thing, Fisher."

"Yeah?"

"We fight until the end. One of us goes down, the other keeps fighting. Until we've won, or we're both dead."

I nod. "It's the way our parents would have wanted it."

"It's what they would have *expected*." He turns to move away.

"Cassius?"

He stops. "Yeah?"

"Whatever happens, I'm glad I ran into you on that Fringe rooftop."

His brows rise. "You know, I was trying to kill you, then."

"I know." I shrug. "But I think under the circumstances, you're forgiven."

A hint of a smile crosses his lips. He pats my arm. "You're a good soldier, Fisher."

"Thanks. I've learned from the best."

He laughs. I can't tell if it's genuine or self-deprecating. "C'mon, they're gonna want us down in the docking bay. You ready for this?"

My teeth chatter. Shoulders shake. I'll never be ready for this. But I know what good soldiers say. I know what Cassius would say. So I lie.

"Yeah," I reply. "Bring it on."

45

Cassius kicked at the dirt, watching it fly away in a cloud. The Fringe heat didn't bother him. He hardly noticed it, especially beyond the frenzy of challenging emotions battling within him.

The Academy had ferried them down in shuttles—every last soul onboard that was willing and able to fight. Some had stayed on the ship itself, ready to use any extra firepower available to them, but there was little doubt that this would be primarily a ground war. It had been so up to this point. No reason for that to change now.

Now that they were on the Surface, the Academy's battalions formed a massive circle, several football fields in diameter each way. It functioned as a protective ring around Cassius and Fisher, thick with layers of Agents and troops. Fringers had come calling, too, from neighboring towns. The shadow of the Skyship, tempered with the fear of invasion, attracted them like a magnet. They were easily convinced to join the battle, once they knew what was at stake.

But humans alone weren't going to win this war. If Fisher did his job right, their small army would soon be joined by Drifters—the more, the better.

Cassius looked over his shoulder. Fisher sat cross-legged, a hundred yards away. His back was turned to Cassius, his head bowed. It was hard to concentrate in the center of the circle, sitting in the Fringes waiting for an attack, but it had to be done. Concentration was key. Only then did Fisher have any chance of connecting with the Drifters around the country.

Cassius had his own challenges. He turned back, scanning the horizon beyond the outer rim of soldiers. He'd heard that Kansas was the flattest state in the country. It sure looked like it. The landscape, brown and unremarkable, seemed to stretch on as far as he could see. In some ways, this was good. While it offered limited to no protection, it also guaranteed that the enemy wouldn't be able to sneak up on them.

Captain Alkine's people had been warned about the Ridium underfoot—the way the Shifters could pull it up in blades or weapons. Never stay in one place for too long. That was the best advice he could offer. Beyond that, he needed to do what he could to preemptively clear the battlefield of the substance.

Concentration, again.

But before he could think about making it hard for the Authority, he needed his own protection.

Closing his eyes, he focused on the ground. He couldn't see the Ridium yet, but he could sense it, churning under the dirt like oil waiting to be dredged up. He brought his fists down to his sides, then spread his fingers apart, lifting them in the air like they had string tied to the ends and he was controlling a puppet. It was an altogether different strain on his body than conjuring fire had been. There was no heat—only the force of the ground working against him.

When he opened his eyes, he watched several snakes of black begin to work their way out from the ground. They coiled around his ankles, melting into an ooze. The liquid climbed up his legs, covering every piece of him, then moved toward his chest. Once it had slipped down the entire length of his arms, he allowed it to trickle over his face.

For a split second, he couldn't see at all. But that was over with quickly, as the world came into focus once more. Though he didn't have time to spare, he couldn't help but marvel at the sights around him. It was like before. Everything seemed more detailed—fuller. He looked up at the sky and could see longer and better than he'd ever thought possible.

Beyond that, he could feel.

It was as if he stood in the middle of an enormous pool, waves approaching from every angle. They were far away now, but getting closer every moment. He could pinpoint every last Shifter … feel their strain as they pulled massive amounts of Ridium from the ground and forced them onward. He wondered if this was how it felt to Fisher, being able to sense the Drifters.

He remembered what one particular Drifter had once told him. *Ridium seeks Ridium.* It was as simple as that.

That's how he was able to sense Fisher being attacked by the stuff back at the Academy, and that's how he could sense the beginning of the Flood now. He was plugged in, more than ever before. And he needed to use that.

But as much as he could make out from this distance, one particular force stood out more strongly than any other. He couldn't get a picture in his head, but it was larger and meaner than the rest.

Matigo, of course.

Having sparred with him directly, Cassius could locate Matigo with ease. As they'd all suspected, he was on his way. Moving fast.

And when he arrived, every piece of Ridium would be a weapon to him.

Cassius couldn't stop Matigo from coming. He couldn't keep him from gathering Ridium, but he could make it difficult for him.

Crouching low, he grabbed hold of as many deposits as he could manage. With a great heave, he plucked them from the ground. Several dozen balls launched into the air, like they'd been propelled by underground cannons.

He watched them soar in wide arcs away from the crowd, only to land several miles away. Satisfied with the effect, he pulled the same maneuver again. Several dozen more spheres of blackness shot away at dizzying speeds.

He repeated.

Repeated.

Within minutes, he'd dredged up the entire area. The

only Ridium left was the collection that made up his suit, and there was no way he was letting that go. He'd made the mistake last time. Matigo had been too strong.

This time, he'd be ready.

46

I ignore the crowd around me—totally tune out every sound and movement beyond Pearls. Alkine could be barking commands my way and I wouldn't even know.

But that's not likely. Before sitting down and closing my eyes, I took one last 360-degree view of the circle of troops. I'm not sure this many Shippers have been off of Skyship Academy since it was first launched. They stand waiting—a protective force for Cassius and me.

It's some comfort, and it's definitely nice not to be alone out here. But I'm responsible for bringing the real firepower.

I've had little luck with Drifters so far. Break a Pearl and they come flying out, zipping away from me faster than I can explain myself. And even when I slow one down enough to talk to them, no single Drifter has been able to give me a full story.

Still, with experience comes knowledge. The longer I've had to use my powers, the stronger my connection to Pearl energy has become.

I start to feel them now. Even if I can't connect to every single one, I can sense their location. There are thousands of green Pearls around the world, ready to be broken. They'll *need* to be, but not quite yet. First, I'm after Drifters. Particularly those that can still fly.

I broadcast myself to them now. I've never really tried it before, but if I can control Pearl energy after it's broken, there's no reason I can't nudge a few Drifters our way as well.

Truly, I have no idea if it's working or not. I don't risk opening my eyes to check if any have landed, for fear of breaking my concentration. Instead, I push my thoughts forward. It's like calling a friend to your side, except I can't use my voice. It's deeper than telepathy. This is more gut than mind.

I give it five minutes, max. After that, it's time to go after Pearls. I managed to hurt Matigo back at the Academy, even if it was only temporary. To deal a blow capable of killing him, I'm going to need more energy than I've ever handled before. After what happened back in the reactor chamber in Portland, I don't know how I'm going to be able to control it all without passing out. I'm no use to anyone unconscious or dead, so I have to be careful.

I begin pulling from all around us, homing in on Pearls that have fallen and ones yet to land. The moment I sense one, I latch on and nudge it in my direction. I notice my shoulders jolting up and down. My face twitches with each Pearl I grab. The more I find, the easier it gets to control them.

I open my eyes and watch them stream at me, looping in the air like someone's outside tossing them into our circle. Instead of catching them, I let them land beside me, providing another protective barrier around my body. They lie in dormant piles until I need them. I hear the whispers, but even that doesn't fracture my concentration.

As this is happening, I notice the emergence of the Drifters for the first time. They descend upon us like angels, joining ranks with the Academy soldiers and Fringers. They heard my call.

Within minutes, the halo around Cassius and me pulses with its own share of Pearl energy. For every ten humans, there's a Drifter. Their green glow adds a buzzing, radiant presence to our battalion.

I pause for a short moment to admire it. For the first time, I allow unrestrained confidence to course through me. We have an army. It's what all of the Drifters had told me to do, time and time again. I gathered an army. We can win this.

As I continue to pull more Pearls near me, I notice the surrounding Drifters move. One on the right side of the circle holds his hand aloft, pointing straight to the stars. Another joins, mimicking the movement. Then a third. A fourth. Soon, every single Drifter is pointing at the sky.

I watch as energy pours from their fingertips, widening in a large net as it leaves their bodies. One Drifter's glow intersects with another's, melding together into a flat plane of green that stretches into the heavens. It takes me a moment to realize what's happening.

They're making a shield.

Like the Bio-Nets that used to surround Chosen Cities, the Pearl energy grows until it forms a dome overhead, encompassing all of us inside. The sky's dulled to a soft green. I feel it emanate in every direction, even as I continue to pull Pearls from outside.

The Drifters drop their hands. The shield remains in place. I'm not sure how long it's going to last, but the very presence of it gives me hope. Can Matigo break through this?

I'll soon find out.

The sky darkens. It's so obvious, I can see it even beyond the green.

My stomach lurches. For a moment, I can't even breathe.

An army approaches from all angles. They seem to have come from nowhere—simply materialized in the air. I hadn't sensed their arrival. There's no warning. No cannons or battle cry or even firepower. Not yet.

I spin to take them in. Hundreds, all at once, making barely a sound as they approach our shield. The darkness is the only thing I can see. They swoop in like locusts—a black plague ready to demolish everything around them.

Some are on foot, others fly. They descend quickly. I stand and look past the glowing dome. This is it.

The Authority.

47

Cassius's throat tightened. He peered above him, admiring the solid green shield overhead. But it wasn't long before his eyes focused on what was outside. At first, they looked like a swarm of insects, or a flock of birds circling for prey. But as they neared, he could make out their humanoid shapes—black body armor encasing them from head to toe.

Much of the blackness wasn't Ridium. That he could tell, even from a distance. Most of the Authority's Shifters were otherwise occupied, creating the flood that barreled through the country. These were foot soldiers—some wearing jet packs, others on the ground. Even if they couldn't Shift, it didn't mean they were any less dangerous, particularly to the Shippers in the outer circle. Not everyone possessed the powers that Cassius enjoyed.

He watched the army beat against the shield of energy, letting loose a volley of firepower. Bursts of red collided with the field, sending crackles across its surface, like sheet lightning. Several detonations went off, weakening the shield. Cassius wasn't sure which was stronger—red or green Pearl energy—but he wasn't about to rely on what they had at their disposal.

He felt the Ridium quiver along his body, and imagined all the things he could do with it. Fire had hurt Matigo last time. That was Cassius's secret weapon, but there had to be a better way to channel it.

The Authority soldiers continued to fight against the energy dome, rupturing more and more cracks the longer they were at it. In a few minutes, they'd be through—if *that* long. Cassius hoped that the exertion would weaken them some, use up their firepower before the battle really began.

Alkine's troops held still, ready to deliver an opening volley as soon as the Authority moved in.

It wasn't long.

The dome shattered, seemingly all at once. Authority bullets and fragments of Pearl energy streamed in a maelstrom around him. The circle of soldiers erupted with firepower. Drifters flew into the air. Others landed. None approached Cassius.

He looked over his shoulder. Fisher, too, had been spared.

That could mean only one thing.

Before he could think about it, a figure swooped down, landing so hard that his feet created a pair of small craters in the earth.

Matigo stood between Cassius and Fisher, arms out to his sides, ready to attack. Cassius watched Fisher turn to face him. He focused on his brother's terrified eyes for just a moment—could've sworn they glowed a faint green—before turning all his attention to Matigo.

Fisher attacked first, breaking a Pearl and funneling the energy in a sideways tornado right at Matigo's chest. Matigo jumped sideways and avoided most of it, but at least it kept him on the defensive.

Cassius raised a fist, but Matigo struck too quickly, sculpting a pair of Ridium scythes from his shoulders. The blades twirled in a blurred whirlwind, forcing both boys back. Fisher summoned another Pearl, just as Matigo leapt from the ground toward Cassius.

Cassius tried to dodge, but Matigo collided with him, grabbing his shoulders and pushing him into the ground.

His breath escaped him, leaving behind a reverberating thud in his chest. It took all the strength he could muster to summon a shield of Ridium overhead, moments before Matigo tried to squash him with a weapon of his own.

They clobbered each other for several rounds, neither getting past each other's suit, until a blast of Pearl energy sent Matigo into the air. He twisted awkwardly, pummeled by the stuff, before flying to the ground.

Fisher sprinted to help Cassius up. "We have to work together."

Cassius ran the back of his hand over his lips, leaving a dark smear of blood on his skin. "He's too—"

Before he could finish, Matigo whipped around and sent a battering ram of streaming Ridium right at Fisher's chest.

Cassius watched his brother be carried away, forced

through the air until he toppled onto the ground at the far side of the circle.

The Ridium yo-yoed back. Matigo jumped forward, charging at Cassius.

Fire. He had to explode with all that he could manage. He clenched his fist, felt his chest tighten. This couldn't be small.

A pair of black tentacles surged from Matigo's midsection, so fast that Cassius barely saw them. Before he knew it, they'd wrapped around his waist, pulling him closer.

Same thing as before, Cassius told himself. He could fight against it. He could pry himself free.

But he didn't expect what happened next.

With a powerful surge, Matigo left the ground, rocketing straight into the air. He took Cassius with him, holding on so tightly that the wind couldn't even pull him away.

They barreled past the remnants of the energy shield and soared into the stratosphere. All the while, Cassius fought to free himself. He manipulated his Ridium in a blind panic, barely controlling it. As they flew closer and closer to the stars, it took all the concentration he could muster to simply keep the dark shell affixed to his body. Without it, he knew that the rapidly depleting oxygen would make it impossible to breathe. That, or the air pressure would crush him. The Ridium was the only thing keeping him alive.

He couldn't conjure fire at such heights. Choices of attack were severely limited. He had no way of fighting back. Matigo could steer him in any direction he wanted.

The sky began to darken. Soon, it would be black. The only thing that made the impossible journey less horrifying was the fact that Cassius had made it before, when he'd first been submerged in the Ridium.

But this was different. Last time, he'd been in control. He'd enjoyed the power of flight, if only for a few moments. The substance could grant this ability, but he wasn't sure how. He'd formed the bubble to get to the Academy, but that had been when he was back on the ground. Panic clouded all of his instincts.

Matigo's face was covered. He existed as a dark, humanoid blob in front of Cassius—a weight dragging him up to the stars, breaking gravity.

The last of the blue sky faded. Cassius sensed an otherworldly iciness around him, though he couldn't feel it directly through the insulation of his suit. Stars pulled into sight. Planets, far in the distance.

Matigo's coils eased their grip around Cassius's body. He felt himself tip backward. The darkness of Matigo's silhouette disappeared, replaced by an infinite amount of celestial landmarks.

Though he couldn't see every movement, he knew that Matigo had drifted apart from him now. He would fall back to Earth to finish the job he had started with Fisher. He'd separated the two of them. He'd made working together impossible.

Cassius's arms spread. His legs fell, supported by nothing. He began to float—lifeless, unable to move.

In orbit.

48

I arch my head to the sky, craning my neck to see if I can make out any details. They're gone. Both of them. They might not be coming back.

I move to a sitting position. My body feels like it's been crushed under the weight of an entire meteor. I cough, which is incredibly painful. Broken ribs, maybe. Matigo's attack hit me with seismic force. Worse, I hadn't been expecting it.

As soon as my gaze moves back to the scene in front of me, I notice a pair of Drifters—no, *three* of them—shoot into the sky. At first, it looks like they're retreating from battle. Going to find reinforcements, maybe.

Then, as I watch them disappear into the stratosphere, I realize where they're headed.

They're going to help Cassius.

Thank god.

No sooner do they disappear when a dark figure drops into the center of the circle.

Matigo doesn't even take a moment to breathe or recharge. He hits the ground with the force of a Skyship and steps forward. Blackness pools from his face to reveal his features.

He may have fooled me before, posing as my father, but there's no mistaking him now. His twisted, hideous expression makes a mockery of my dad's character. His grinning mouth opens wide, like a lizard's, ready to boast a victory that's all but guaranteed.

"One down," he says, and leaves it at that.

I can't respond. Even if I could form words, it would only kill time that I desperately need. Instead, I spread apart my arms and call forth Pearls, one from each side of me.

I send them forward at a blistering pace. Matigo doesn't have a chance to defend himself before I break them.

Twin explosions detonate on either side of him. Before the energy can drift into the battle around us, I curl my fingers and force it right at his body, hitting him with hundreds of jagged jolts of Pearl energy.

He staggers back. Steam comes off his shoulders. It hurts, I can tell, but it doesn't kill him. Why doesn't it kill him?

I keep the Pearls coming—two more, exploded and funneled toward him with the same desperate ferocity.

He sends forth a coil of Ridium, trying to hit back. It doesn't reach me.

I could keep this up, Pearl after Pearl, but after the initial blast, the explosions don't seem to be doing as much damage. It's keeping him at bay, but I need something that will destroy him. Forever.

Several soldiers swoop in on either side of us, trying to take me out while I'm distracted. It won't happen.

I guide streams of energy toward them. An afterthought, almost, and they're blasted away, lying unconscious in the dirt. This is a battle between Matigo and me. It's always been, even if I wasn't aware of it.

Come back, Cassius.

It's all I can think, even as I'm fighting for my life. I shouldn't let it distract me, but I can't help it. I wait for the Drifters to come down, bringing my brother with them.

Nothing.

Matigo continues to throw everything at me. I keep him off-balance, lobbing great waves of Pearl energy at him. Every few moments, one of his attacks breaks through, forcing me to shift from offense to defense. The more times I have to do that, the closer he approaches.

The sounds of battle rage all around us. Our once-strong circle of protection has broken into a vast crowd of chaos—Drifter fighting Drifter, human fighting soldier. There's no clear way to tell which side is winning, if such a thing even exists in a battle like this.

I try to block it out as easily as I did before, to avoid the thought of my friends being slain around me. I see bodies fall out of the corner of my eye, but I can't put faces to them. For all I know, they could be Avery. Eva. Skandar.

No. I can't think like that.

Matigo hits me with a cannonball of Ridium. It flies from his hand like a dark Pearl and connects with my right shoulder, sending me staggering back into the dirt. I steady myself, but not before a second attack blasts into my chest.

This one's too much. I fall backward, hitting the ground with a painful thud.

In seconds, he's on me, crouched above my body like a snake ready to bite. His hate-filled face is all I can see now, staring down with a mix of pride and pity.

He leans closer. "Say goodbye to your planet."

I venture one last glance at the sky, hoping to see Cassius. It's empty.

Matigo raises his arm in the air. I watch Ridium begin to spike around his fist, creating a jagged, skull-crushing weapon. I've got seconds before he brings it down on me.

I pull the energy from around my body, grabbing anything that I can shoot at him. There isn't much left. I need more Pearls, but they're too far away. If I had a minute, I could locate them and bring them closer, but Matigo won't give me such a luxury. It's kill or be killed.

The spike continues to form above me. Apparently, he's not content with murdering me in the quickest, simplest way. He wants to make it terrifying. He wants to create unbearable fear before he does it.

It's working.

I gather energy, forming a protective shield over my body much like the dome the Drifters concocted at the start of the battle. It won't protect me forever, but it might buy me a minute while he tries to break through. The problem is, it takes unbelievable concentration to keep it strong. I can't defend myself *and* find new Pearls. It's a losing battle.

His fist comes down on the energy just as it's finished forming. I watch the shield give way slightly. The Ridium pounds inches from my face. A couple more hits and I'll be done for.

Cassius. I whisper the word in my head. *Come back. I need you.*

The images of my dreams come back to me. Cassius disappearing, the fire working its way inside of me. Then I think of Matigo's words—how desperate he'd been to have Cassius and me together so that he could kill us both at the same time. He's horrified by what we can do.

Which begs the question: what *can* we do?

I wish more than anything that I could find out. But Cassius is gone. I might as well fold up and join him. I'm not strong enough on my own.

I wince as Matigo attacks again, breaking the shield faster than I can rebuild it.

Cassius's fire. It's been the one reoccurring element in all of my dreams.

Then it occurs to me. All these months, every time Cassius and I fought—together or against each other—he never turned his flame on me. And when it got close, when he saved me from the Authority foot soldier in the Nevada bunker, the fire didn't do any damage to my body. It's a reaction to my own energy, just like my parents' recording told me. And if the fire's a reaction, that means my body must be able to understand it. To channel it.

Maybe that's why Matigo's scared of the two of us, side by side. Maybe that's how we'll defeat him.

The realization lifts my spirits briefly, but it's not enough. Had I imagined this possibility twenty-four hours ago, I wouldn't be in my current situation. As it stands, a half-baked theory isn't going to do me much good at all.

Cassius is gone. There's no sign of him coming back. And I've got all of ten seconds to figure out how I'm going to live through this.

49

This was how it would be now.

Cassius let himself succumb to the thought for a moment as he drifted through space, on the very edge of Earth's orbit. He needed a moment to panic, to release all the emotion he was feeling, before calming himself once more and thinking rationally.

He'd studied space. He knew of inertia—how an object would keep floating in one direction unless some force pushed it elsewhere. No amount of flailing around would turn his fortune. He was a small fish in the middle of an ocean. Everything around him looked the same. Stars on three sides. The blue glow of the Earth emanated over his shoulder, though he couldn't see it directly.

Still, the blue surprised him. The planet seemed nothing but brown when standing on the Surface. From space, he imagined, Earth's problems looked much less significant in the grand scheme of things.

The Ridium over his face kept him breathing, though he knew he'd run out of air eventually—sooner rather than later. Anything he did, he'd need to do fast.

Fire. It always came down to fire. He thought that if

he could conjure a torrent big and strong enough, the sheer force from it might propel him downward, back into Earth's gravitational pull. But what would happen when Earth started pulling? Cassius didn't like the idea of becoming a human comet.

Sure, the Ridium suit protected him to a degree—even kept him alive at the edge of space—but would it be able to survive burn-up as he fell to Earth? More pointedly, would Cassius be able to will it to happen? His concentration had fractured. His willpower was shot.

He began to stoke the flames inside of him. They came slowly—a tinge of heartburn at first, lowering into his gut.

As he worked, he started to think of life back on Earth. He didn't mean to, but his thoughts strayed to his childhood, to all those years before he considered Pearls anything beyond an incredibly lucky energy source.

He tried to push the memories away. This wasn't the appropriate time to get caught up in nostalgia—emotional or otherwise. But up in space, with the stars his only audience, he couldn't will his mind to focus on anything else.

It started with Madame. From there, the floodgates opened.

He remembered her, younger than she'd been when she died—less fragile and worried. He remembered following her around on weekends, watching how she dealt with people. Interactions had always been thinly veiled power struggles. She hadn't ever admitted defeat back then. She was always able to frame a setback as a victory.

She'd saved him.

That was it. No matter what struggles they'd been through, no matter what betrayals she'd pulled, in the end she'd saved him. Standing there, at the edge of the Academy's docking bay, was the least selfish Cassius had ever seen her. Thinking back on his life, he couldn't remember a single time she'd sacrificed anything for the benefit of somebody else. She'd asked for more than her fair share of favors from others, but she'd always been top of the pack. Served. Never serving.

Still, it had always been in her eyes. That was what had kept Cassius coming back, time after time. It didn't matter how she'd treated him. He'd found that connection as a small boy and never let go. Ally to adversary and back again—that connection had never frayed, not completely.

Now, what was there to do? Who was there to matter to him?

He couldn't bring himself to care about Haven the way he'd cared for Madame. He knew it was selfish, and maybe she'd instilled some sense of that in him, but everything— from the Drifters to his real parents to the stars in front of him now—felt so distant.

Fisher.

He was it.

He was the thing worth fighting for. Since the rooftop early in the spring. Cassius would have killed him then, had he had the chance. He would have gladly watched his brother fall from the building and taken the Pearl as his prize for service to his government. Selfish. Again.

But even then, though he hadn't understood it fully, he'd felt that same connection. It was like, even though they were so diametrically opposed to each other, Cassius could *understand* him. Fisher was everything that he was not. The good and the bad. The flip side. In a way, they were both half a person, only whole when they worked together.

He was surprised to find tears streaming down his cheeks. The thoughts, the stars, the silence... it all came together for him at that moment. A purging of sorts. A rebirth? He wasn't sure, but something had changed. Something big.

The fire continued to build inside him, strengthened by the emotion funneling through his body. If someone like Madame could sacrifice, Cassius could do more than that. He was stronger than he'd made himself out to be. Strong physically, yes, but there was more to it than that. And he and Fisher? Together, they were stronger than anything. He knew that now. Understood it.

He stretched his arms above his face, tucking his knees into his stomach. He made himself as small as possible, rationalizing that if he limited the surface area he was creating, the fall wouldn't be as damaging. It was a gamble, no matter what he did.

The fire began to stream through his system, up to his shoulders and down his arms. He remembered the first time he'd exploded—so sudden and uncontrollable. It seemed as if it had happened ages ago. He had to remind himself that it hadn't even been a year.

The heat teetered on the edge of his fingertips, ready for release.

Just before he closed his eyes and triggered the energy, two pairs of hands wrapped themselves gently around his shoulders. He glanced in both directions to see a pair of Drifters—one on either side. Their green Pearl glow lit up the darkness around him. Their grip was soft, but firm. He knew instantly that they were only there to help him.

The fire retreated inside of him, stored for later. He fell limp in their arms—let them carry him downward, back into Earth's gravity.

They were like heavenly creatures, the pair of them. Ascension, but in reverse. He shut his eyes and relaxed as they took him back to Earth.

This was the beginning of the end. That's all his mind would allow him to think. He was heading back to end things. No excuses. No distractions. Only fire.

He was the Catalyst, after all. It was time to set things in motion.

50

My shield of Pearl energy breaks. I roll sideways. It's stalling, at best.

Matigo's pulverizing fist of Ridium hits the ground so hard that it leaves a visible mark indented into the earth, a reminder that all it will take is one good swing and I'll be done for.

While he's off-balance, I fire back with a jolt of energy. It knocks him to the side, freeing up time for me to get to my feet again. But I can already see his next attack coming. Violent whips form from between his shoulder blades, ready to wrap around my stomach and pull me apart.

Then, I sense it.

Something comes down on us from the sky—a concentrated amount of Pearl energy, already broken.

I glance above me. A pair of Drifters descend to the ground, carrying a dark figure with them. I recognize it instantly as Cassius. He's alive. They saved him.

I allow a glimmer of hope to rise in my gut. For a while there I thought for sure that I'd lost him, that I'd have to find some way to do this on my own.

The Drifters carefully set him down several yards from

us. I can tell right away that he's ready to blow. His hands tense at his sides, shaking with added energy. The blackness around his face peels to reveal an expression of gritted teeth and sunken, defiant eyes. He looks almost feral, standing with his back slightly hunched over, breathing heavy.

Matigo turns, freezing for a moment as he tries to work out what to do next. Attack us both, or pick one off first? He thought he'd finished Cassius. I can tell from the look in his eyes that he expected this to be over. It's the first time I've seen him the least bit shocked. I savor the moment, even if it's just for an instant.

I lock eyes with Cassius. He raises an arm, ready to attack Matigo before he can make any move to defend himself.

"No!" I reach out a hand, though I'm not nearly close enough to stop him physically. "Cassius, don't!"

Sparks begin to ignite along his fingertips. His eyes narrow, flashing me an incredulous look.

I motion toward my chest. "Me, Cassius! Straight at me!"

Matigo stomps on the ground, lifting a swell of Ridium that streams toward us at staggering speed.

Cassius pulls back, confusion in his eyes.

"Trust me," I continue. "This is how it's meant to be! This is what we are. Hit me with the fire... everything you've got!"

He hesitates for a moment. It's nearly long enough for the Ridium to slam into me.

But then, with a deep heave, he lets loose.

A torrent of fire, stronger and more concentrated than I've ever seen before, barrels toward me. My first instinct is to dodge it—to flinch and run—but that's what the old Jesse Fisher would do. I can't go back to that. I don't have the luxury of hiding.

I swallow. Wait for it.

Everything freezes. It's as if the world has stopped for a moment in anticipation of what's going to happen next. I mutter a prayer under my breath.

The fire hits me square in the chest. I expect pain. I expect to be burnt faster than I can put out the flames, to feel my body searing away from me.

Instead, I feel a surge against my skin, like standing on a beach as a huge tidal wave rushes over me. It's not hot— not even warm, really. It defies such an easy description as temperature.

It's just like my dreams.

My body absorbs the fire. I step back, finding it hard to stand straight against it. I lock my knees and establish a foothold on the ground. The flames are so bright and so close that I can't see much around me. I don't know what Matigo's doing. He could be attacking, but if he is I don't feel it.

As the fire continues to funnel into my body, I start to feel bigger. It's not like I'm growing physically, but something inside of me is expanding. I'm not even sure it's something I knew was there in the first place.

This is for my parents. This is for Mr. Wilson and Agent

Morse and August Bergmann and Madame. For everyone the Authority has touched, both on Haven and on Earth.

My eyes close. Suddenly, I can sense everything around me. It's like the world used to be folded up into a ball and suddenly it's unfolded, revealing everything inside and around it. My body becomes a shell. I'm much bigger than it.

Without realizing it, I start drawing Pearls from everywhere. They speed at me from every corner of Earth, from the skies and stars and oceans. My consciousness zooms out until I can see the entire world, all at once. Our little circle in the middle of the Fringes seems ridiculously small. Matigo, in comparison, is an insect.

I watch an army of green Pearls collect at the edge of our atmosphere, bunching together in a soup of trembling orbs. They come at us, pulled by invisible strings bringing them to our exact coordinates.

My mind snaps back. My consciousness is inside my body once more. My eyes open.

I see Cassius through the fire. He keeps it coming—one steady, uninterrupted stream of flames. It's like he's not even doing it anymore. Something's been set in motion between the two of us. A cycle.

The Pearls pull closer—hundreds of them, maybe thousands. Every last remaining bit of energy works its way into my corner, supporting me in my next move.

Then I notice something. My eyes meet Cassius's and, for the first time since we've met, I see a blankness in them, like he's checked out of his own body. I can tell that it's different from what's happening to me.

I glance farther down his silhouette, which is barely visible through the oncoming fire. The closer I get to the ground, the more it fades. His head and shoulders are clear, but his legs... they're disappearing.

My concentration fractures. "Cassius!"

I look back at his face. His expression is nearly unrecognizable. His mouth hangs open, empty. I watch his pupils begin to disperse into the whites of his eyes until they're gone for good.

"Cassius, no!"

But it's too late. He can't hear me.

A few seconds more and there isn't anything left of him. I watch his body disintegrate, pulled forward by the fire in bits and pieces until he's nothing but energy. Nothing but fire.

Without him, the stream trickles down. The last of it hits my body with a powerful force, knocking me back. I've got no time to process what's happening before my eyes fly shut again.

The network of Pearls fills my consciousness once more. My hands lift and bring them toward me. I tilt my head into the air and open my eyes to watch them circle down on us—a twisting, DNA strand of green. Everything stops around me. Fighting is useless in a time like this. No one resists the urge to look into the sky. The energy's so bright, it's practically blinding.

Cassius, where are you?

My body does the work for me. My vision increases again, looping and climbing until I can take in the entire country. I see the Flood of Ridium pulsing from the coasts of America. I get a read on every last Shifter. I mark their coordinates—a list of points so incredibly long that under any other circumstance, I'd have no way of remembering them all.

Cassius. He's helping me do this.

Somehow, even if I can't see him, I sense this to be true. I'm not alone. I'll never be alone again.

I lock onto every member of the Authority, like a missile targeting its prey. My hand twists above my head, fingers tensing. Matigo is nearby, but I sense he's no longer a threat. This maelstrom of Pearls above me—it's otherworldly. Unprecedented.

The hairs on my arms pull into the air, threatening to leave my body completely. My skin buzzes with such a rumbling energy that I'm convinced I'm going to disintegrate just like Cassius did.

A thousand Drifter voices speak to me. Whispers from the Pearls above join together until the words don't even sound like words. It's a wave, coming down at me. Feeding me.

Three.

I start the countdown.

Two.

This is for Cassius, wherever he is. This is it, the true

meaning of the Key and Catalyst. We're stronger together. We always have been.

One.

My hands fly back. I collide my back with the Earth. A hurricane of wind cycles around my body. The world blurs into a sea of incongruent colors.

The explosion is deafening.

51

It started with one Pearl—a blast that triggered a chain reaction. Seven hundred eighty-two of them broke in such quick succession that, to the naked eye, they might as well have exploded all at once.

A nuclear-strength force ripped through the sky just above the battle, sending forth a thunder strike so loud and powerful that it knocked everything off its feet for miles around.

The energy released from the explosion streamed in all directions before corralling together in a horizontal disc of emerald green, which proceeded to blanket the sky as far as the eye could see. Each portion of it had been carefully controlled, driven to its specific place with the focus and power of one individual.

The energy wave spread farther and faster, breaking apart into jolts of jagged rain. Free to pursue its victims, the rain strengthened into thousands of mighty lightning bolts, erupting not from clouds but from the depths of the sky itself.

The Authority had nowhere to run. The targets of the

bolts had already been established, and there was no breaking the link.

The Pearl lightning issued from the heavens with unparalleled force, striking down upon Shifters and foot soldiers alike. All at once it came, direct and precise and from every corner of the sky. And all at once it was gone, so fleeting that those lucky enough to avoid it would hardly have noticed at all.

Matigo was saved for last. The attack on his army came as a surprise. They didn't have time to feel anything as the bolts shut down their bodies from the inside out. Matigo's destruction would be longer.

A vast whirlpool of green circled above the battlefield, threatening to ingest everything into its churning mass. It spun faster and faster before funneling down and sweeping him off the ground. No amount of Ridium could help him fight against it. The attack came from all angles. It was unrelenting.

His body pulled apart, devoured by energy that sucked him in every direction.

Then, with one final sonic boom, the floating whirlpool surged outward and rained down on the Surface.

A green mist hung in the air, not unlike the vapor that crawled through the abandoned streets of Seattle when the Resistance sent its two champions to Earth twelve years ago.

52

I don't realize I'm sleeping until I open my eyes. I don't remember falling unconscious. The last thing I can recall is looking into the sky and watching it disappear, swallowed up by green—more Pearl energy than I'd ever seen in my life.

I wake slowly, like I'm coming into the world for the first time in months. My body feels like it's been punched in every possible spot. I sense the ground, rocky and uneven beneath me. I'm outside. The Fringes, likely. Yet the telltale heat of the Fringes is gone, replaced by a mild humidity, pushed around by a slight breeze that throws hair into my face. I brush it aside.

The first thing I see is the sky, empty except for a fine mist. It's a turquoise-type color, altogether different from normal Fringe atmosphere—almost like it's been raining, except that's impossible. It hardly ever rains in the Fringes, and certainly not enough to wash out the sky like this.

I sit up. That's when I realize that I'm not alone.

A wide swath of people stand before me in a half circle, staring in to watch me pull myself out of sleep. There are hundreds of them, stretching back farther than I can see clearly. Most I don't recognize, though the faint green glow around their bodies is overly familiar.

Drifters. How many did I free when the Pearls exploded? Are they all here now?

As my eyes adjust to take them all in, several figures in the front rush forward. I hadn't noticed them specifically until now.

I stand, though it's a wobbly start, just as my friends come at me.

Avery, Skandar, and Eva fight to hug me first. They hit me with gale force, nearly knocking my fragile body to the ground. There are no words exchanged between us. I'm just happy to see them alive. I'm sure the feeling is mutual.

Alkine's next, followed by what seems like a parade of Agents, faculty, and teachers from Skyship Academy. Avery and the others part to let them through. I don't know everybody, but they greet me like I'm their long-lost brother. Hugs, handshakes, words that I barely hear. It becomes a blur. I'm not sure where I am, or how long it's been since Matigo was ripped apart in front of me.

I begin to feel weak. Dehydrated and dizzy. A pair of hands grab me from behind and supports me. I turn to see Avery's face—smiling, but visibly concerned all the while.

I cough. A shiver runs up my spine. Everything comes flooding back to me. Ridium. The Fire.

"Cassius," I manage through coughs. "Is he okay? What happened?"

Avery moves carefully around so that she can meet

my eyes while still supporting me. She looks at me for a moment without speaking, then pulls me close, into her shoulder so I can't see her eyes. "He's gone, Jesse."

I grab onto her back, nails digging into her skin. "No, no."

"He disappeared," she whispers. "When the fire hit you ... he's gone."

I push away from her, staggering to the center of a circle surrounded by friends. Before I can say anything in response, I feel it.

Something's changed.

"Cassius?" I look around me, from face to face, into the sky. I don't know why I'm like this, how I can think that he's still here, but I feel him. His familiar presence drifts around me like the mist in the air. I reach out a hand to grab a fist of the stuff. It evaporates as soon as it touches my fingers.

I turn to face Avery again. "He's here."

"Jesse." She reaches out to comfort me. "I ... I don't know—"

"No," I interrupt, moving back. "He's here. I can feel him. I ... "

I don't know what it is, but every last bit of fear leaves me. I feel like I could do anything. Bring it at me and I'll take it on.

It's an unusual sensation—a completeness, a sense of myself that I've never had before. I hadn't even noticed. Fifteen years and I'd never realized that something was missing. I'd been a piece of something bigger. Half of a whole.

Pearl energy nears as a Drifter pushes through the wall of people before me. They let him pass without objection. I don't recognize him, but I sense what he's going to say before his mouth opens. It's in English, though at this point I'm not sure it matters.

He points at me, eyes meeting mine with a focused intimacy.

"The Key," he starts, keeping his finger completely still, aimed right at my chest. "And the Catalyst."

At that moment, I know exactly what's happened. There isn't a shred of doubt in my mind, though it's almost impossible to fathom.

Cassius hadn't disappeared in battle. He, like all of us— like every creature on this or any other planet—is energy. He became the fire that streamed inside of me. He's here now, a part of me. We're not brothers. We never were. I am him and he is me. Light and dark. Strong and weak. Brave and fearful. Slacker and student.

We'd been running around all our lives, neither of us complete without the other. Two sides of a coin. Matigo knew he had to kill us both. Get rid of one and the other becomes stronger. We're strong, now. *I'm* strong.

But it never could have happened if Cassius hadn't had the guts to take that leap of faith. He could've stopped the fire from coming—cut it off before it took him with it. Could I have done the same?

I don't know. But now ... *now* I can do anything. He's here. With me. I'm more than I've ever been before.

I turn back to Avery, smiling. I can tell from her expression that she doesn't understand. It doesn't matter. No one will understand completely. I just hope Cassius—whatever part of me that he is now—knows what he's done.

The Resistance has won, but it's bigger than that. The world is new. The world is good. And I'm ready to make it even better.

53

A week later.

It's a different country down there.

With the Tribunal killed in the sinking of Skyship Atlas and the Unified Party dismantled by the Authority, there's a vacuum of power in America.

Skyship Academy, in a bizarre twist of fortune, is the largest operational Skyship in the world, not that that won't change once human resilience kicks in.

But we're not just human anymore. More than a thousand Drifters have joined our ranks on planet Earth. Without the glow from Pearls around them, they pass easily amongst the rest of us. In a perfect world, there would be more. Pearls wouldn't have been destroyed so freely for so many years. As it stands, they're welcome refugees. In several decades, I suspect their legacy will dim. As they interbreed with the rest of us, the memory of Haven will become less of a reality and more of a fable.

But their presence now, combined with the fact that we're king of the skies in a war-torn nation, has every set of eyes on us. Alkine's been in meetings all week with those that are left of the ruling elite from the Skyship Community and the Unified Party. The way that things are playing out, I'm not sure either of those government labels will have much meaning in the New World.

Pearls are gone. I exploded every last one of them back in Kansas. There are no more Drifters coming, and no more energy we can suck from the skies. Skyship Academy floats solely on our backup sources—a mix of solar and biomass. I'm not sure how long we'll be able to stay aloft this way without Pearls, but the very working existence of our ship is symbolic to everyone on the Surface. We'll keep it going as long as we can.

The Surface.

The massive Pearl explosion in the Fringes was enough to fundamentally alter the atmosphere, kind of the same way the Scarlet Bombings changed it so long ago. The green mist has faded from the skies since then, but the Fringes are starting to stabilize. You can't really tell by standing outside. It still feels as hot as it always was. But our scientists have been taking readings. There's something new in the air. The winds of change, if you wanna get all poetic about it. Maybe in a few years we won't need things like Bio-Nets or Skyships anymore. It's too early to tell.

I leave that to Alkine and the others, for now. What was left of the Ridium summoned by Matigo's Shifters has repositioned itself underground. I'm fairly confident that I could Shift it like Cassius could, but I'm not sure I want to bring up the idea to anyone but myself. After hearing how Haven fell apart, I don't think Ridium—like Pearls—is the answer to anything. There are no easy answers. All they do is get you in trouble. To make things fall into place and stay there, you have to work at it.

Cassius is teaching me that.

I feel him inside my consciousness now, as I stand at the edge of Lookout Park, protected by the enormous dome overhead. Behind me stretches Skyship Academy's main tower. I know Alkine's up there now, probably pacing. I'll leave him to it. My worries are over, at least for the time being.

In front of me lies our makeshift monument—a giant semicircle of found objects, flowers, and notes, erected as a tribute to those who lost their lives in the final battle against Matigo.

I had been so focused on my own struggle that I hadn't noticed the chaos around me. Before I managed to defeat the Authority, the battle had not been going in our favor. There were numerous casualties. Some Fringe, some Skyship. All significant.

In the hours since, friends and loved ones have dredged up items from the dorm rooms of the fallen. Stuffed animals, photos, books, clothing—anything that serves as a reminder. A few students gather together several yards from me, their heads bowed in silence.

I clutch Cassius's communicator in my hands, the same one I'd used to talk to him back when we'd been separated. Before Matigo. Before Theo, even. In the few short months that I knew him, this old, clunky communicator was our closest link. In some ways, I knew him better as a voice on the other end than as an actual person.

I run my fingers over the speaker at the bottom of the device, then crouch and set it amongst the rest of the objects.

He's not really gone. I just don't need the communicator anymore. And he deserves some physical reminder, if only so that others onboard will recall him as a hero, rather than the Unified Party Pearlhound that hijacked a Skyship transport and broke into the Academy.

It should feel strange, sharing my consciousness like this. Instead, it feels completely natural. Before the battle with Matigo, I'd second guess myself with every step. Now, the world seems simpler. Everything that used to be an obstacle is now a challenge. Slight difference, but an important one.

A hand touches my shoulder. I turn quickly, on alert.

"Whoa, there." Avery pulls away.

"Oh." I meet her eyes. "Sorry. I didn't hear you behind me."

She smiles. "I've always been good at sneaking around." Her gaze falls on the communicator. "Is that what I think it is?"

I nod. "It didn't seem right... having this monument set up without anything for Cassius. I mean, it's not like he's gone—"

"Yeah," she interrupts. "You're gonna have to explain that one to me again."

"I'm just figuring it out myself." I point to my chest. "But he's in here. We're together."

Her lips purse. "A little strange, Fisher."

"It should be," I reply. "But somehow it's not."

I grab her shoulder and pull her close.

"Wow." She lays a hand on my chest. "Aren't you aggressive?"

"Sorry."

She chuckles. "I didn't say it was a bad thing, did I?"

"It's a new beginning. Everything's changed, Avery." I pause. "I never believed in destinies or anything. For so long, I thought that if I just knew my parents…found where I fit…that everything would turn out okay."

"I'm sorry," she interrupts. "I know how badly you wanted to see them."

"It's okay. I'm not sure it was about them at all. This needed to happen. This was all part of the plan. I can see it now. Everything feels right."

She pulls away, looking down at the memorial. "I can't believe it's all over. The Authority, gone. Madame, gone. What are we gonna do with ourselves, Fisher?"

"I can think of a few things."

Her brows rise. "That was such a Cassius thing to say."

I shrug.

"Well, I'm glad you're happy." She smiles. "You deserve it, after all you've been through."

"And you're okay." I squeeze her arm. "Thank god you're okay."

She laughs. "Are you kidding? It takes more than an alien invasion to take me down. You of all people should know that, Fisher!"

54

This is it.

I head down the Level Five corridor on my way to the training facility, fingers balled at my sides.

There are marks all over the walls here—scratches and pulverized craters of metal where Matigo first attacked after revealing himself. I'm sure Alkine will order them fixed once everything else has settled down. For now, they're a reminder of what I've overcome—what I've *survived*.

During my first training year at the Academy, I'd have never imagined living through so much. I'd have fainted at the first sight of trouble—tripped and gotten myself killed. It seems a lifetime ago.

I stop outside the doors to the training room, hesitating for just a moment before pressing the button and watching them spread open in front of me.

The last time I played a round of Bunker Ball, I ended up unconscious. Eva of all people had to help me up from the ground—*save* me, practically.

I can't help but chuckle at the thought of it. No wonder she considered me a wimp back then. I had no self-confidence, no drive to do anything but avoid challenges.

The very thought of something outside of my comfort zone made me queasy. I laughed it off, deflected every bit of doubt by telling myself that it was the world that was fighting me, not the other way around.

Cassius would have never done that. *I'm* not going to do that now.

I step through the door onto the Bunker Ball field. It's laid out the same way it was the last time I played the game, before I knew anything about my powers or destiny.

The metal floor gives way to sand. I stand in the middle of a battlefield of dunes and portions of brick wall, which jut from the floor like teeth. Boulders form plenty of hiding places around me, but I'm not planning on hiding this time.

I never knew what my body was capable of until now. It's like all the potential was there, but I'd placed a block on it. My brain had literally handicapped me. The constant doubt and fear crippled my chances of being what I'd always wanted to be.

I walk up a lengthy dune and meet the others in the center of the field.

Avery, Eva, and Skandar stand there, decked out in full Bunker Ball mode. Straps filled with detonators wrap around them like sashes. It's three against one.

Just the way I like it.

Eva smiles as soon as she sees me. "The field looks smaller, doesn't it, Fisher?"

I nod. She's right. After fighting in the Fringes, there's

really no comparing. Everything, from the sand dunes meant to slow us down, to the detonators with their dull sting upon exploding, seems like a child's game.

Avery's brows rise. "You really think you can take all three of us at once?"

I smile. "I could take on five more, if you're interested."

Skandar laughs. "Whoa, mate. You sure this is you talking?"

I grab a detonator from my belt, taking a step back. "What's all this waiting around, anyway? I'm ready to kick some butt."

Eva crosses her arms. "I'm sure I don't have to remind you not to hesitate."

I toss the detonator in the air and catch it. "The days of hesitation are long gone, Rodriguez."

"That's a challenge if I've ever heard one." She smirks.

Avery takes a deep breath. "Just promise me one thing, Fisher. Now that you're a … a … "

"Warrior?" Eva interrupts.

"Sure," Avery says. "Now that you're a warrior, don't lose that kid I fell in love with in the first place."

I meet her eyes. I've realized these past few days that she's my anchor. She's the true, devoted place that Cassius never had. Maybe that was *his* block.

I nod.

"Okay, then." She laughs. "Let's get this over with. I'm starving."

I watch her sprint away, probably to hide before attacking.

Eva moves to join her. I grab her arm. "Don't hold back," I say. "You too, Skandar. Come at me with all you've got. We ... I mean, *I* ... can take it."

Eva nods, teeth grit. "Thirty seconds and the game begins. You better go find a rock to cower behind."

With that, they're both off. I stand alone for a moment, strategizing. I'm not worried about the clock. Not concerned with when they'll come at me or how fast. I draft numerous attacks in my head. Plan A, Plan B, Plan C, D, E, F ... all the way down the line. I've never thought like this before, never even used this part of my brain. It's liberating.

No matter how they choose to do it, I'll do it better. I know this in my gut. I'm unstoppable.

When I'm ready, I turn, offering my back to them. With ten seconds left, I sprint down the sand dune, jumping on top of the nearest boulder with a full view of the field. I'm unprotected. It's a leap of faith, standing here in the open.

The warning chimes begin to sound. Five seconds. Three.

I take a deep breath and center myself. My arm shakes with anxious energy. I can't wait to let loose. It's like a bridle's been stuck around my body and I'm about to tear it off. It's uncomfortable. I need to move. I need to fight.

The alarm goes off, signaling the start of the game. My fingers tense as I grab a detonator from my belt. It warms with the touch of my skin. The metal feels powerful, gripped tightly in my hand.

I barely have to think. They come at me, all at once.

I attack.

© Emma James

About the Author

When he was a young boy, Nick James's collection of battle-scarred action figures became the characters in epic story-lines with cliffhangers, double crosses, and an unending supply of imaginary explosions. Not much has changed. The toys are gone (most of them), but the love of fast-paced storytelling remains. Working in schools from Washington State to England, Nick has met thousands of diverse students since graduating from Western Washington University and braving the most dangerous job in the world: substitute teaching. Luckily, being dubbed the "rock star teacher" has granted him some immunity. He currently lives and teaches in Bellingham, Washington.